T0329491

STAR TREK –

A PSYCHOANALYSIS

STAR TREK –
A PSYCHOANALYSIS

THOMAS H. PICARD, MD

Algora Publishing
New York

Library of Congress Cataloging-in-Publication Data —

Names: Picard, Thomas H., 1959- author.
Title: Psychoanalysis of Star Trek / Thomas H. Picard.
Description: New York: Algora Publishing, [2018] | Includes index.
Identifiers: LCCN 2018015142 (print) | LCCN 2018028264 (ebook) | ISBN
    9781628943290 (pdf) | ISBN 9781628943276 (soft cover: alk. paper) | ISBN
    9781628943283 (hard cover: alk. paper)
Subjects: LCSH: Star Trek television programs. | Psychoanalysis and
    television.
Classification: LCC PN1992 .8 S74 (ebook) | LCC PN1992 .8 S74 P53 2018
    (print) | DDC 791.45/75—dc23
LC record available at https://lccn.loc.gov/2018015142

Printed in the United States

Acknowledgments

I thank my beautiful wife and partner Betty Picard, whose love and support nourished me as I developed and fleshed out this project. Appreciation also goes to my brother Ron Picard and Deborah Kohler for feedback on the manuscript's style and content.

I am indebted to the professionals at Algora Publishing, who were indispensable in molding this manuscript into a polished work ready for publication. Thanks from me and all first-time authors.

And to the late Gene Roddenberry, who pushed until NBC gave *Star Trek* the green light, thank you.

Table of Contents

INTRODUCTION

I was six years old when the science fiction television series *Lost in Space* debuted in 1965 on CBS. The first season was filmed in black and white, which was fine with me because I watched it on my family's 12-inch black-and-white TV sitting on a flimsy wire stand in our basement. The 1960s in the United States was a tumultuous time, but I was a little young to understand the upheaval. Those years were also the heyday of the National Aeronautics and Space Administration (NASA). Project Gemini had put a two-person crew into low Earth orbit, and the Apollo program would go on to land Neil Armstrong and Buzz Aldrin on the moon in 1969.

Star Trek entered NBC's lineup a year after *Lost in Space*, in 1966. Wow. Now there were two television shows about space travel. How cool. I was certain that humanity's galaxy-wide future was no longer in doubt. 1966 was also the first year that all prime-time network programming appeared in color. It was still several more years before my family bought its first color television, but when it did—holy smoke! Now *Lost in Space*'s *Jupiter 2* and *Star Trek*'s *Enterprise* exploded off of 19 diagonal inches of red/green/yellow space-age pixel perfection.

Kaiser Broadcasting began in Honolulu, Hawaii in 1957 with KHVH, Channel 13. Its first station on the United States mainland went on air in January 1965 as WKBD, UHF Channel 50 out of Detroit. Growing up in Southeast Michigan, I remember when Channel 50 first started broadcasting because it was a UHF station. CBS, NBC, and ABC all had a unique VHF setting on the television knob, stations 2, 4, and 7 in the Detroit area. For channels 14 to 83, one turned the main dial to UHF then twiddled a second dial to find the station's signal. VHF and UHF used different antennae. We did not have the rooftop version, which was superior. The indoor rabbit ears picked up VHF; the UHF antenna was a loop of wire that protruded off the back of the television set. Turning to Channel 50 was a challenge for a five-year-old kid; both the UHF knob and antenna were touchy.

Kaiser bought the syndication rights for *Star Trek* after the show finished its three-year network run in 1969. For years afterward, Channel 50 scheduled *Star Trek* reruns at eight PM Monday through Friday. There were 79 original episodes, which meant that each one repeated about three times per year. Like other fans, I watched those original adventures over and over again. Captain Kirk, Mr. Spock, and Dr. McCoy became a part of my everyday life. *Lost in Space* reruns were fun too, but as I got older, I left that kid's show behind and became more devoted to *Star Trek*.

My brothers and sisters were also *Trek* fans. It was a game to see who could identify the episode the quickest as the first seconds started to play. My future wife was amazed that we quoted numerous lines from the show in everyday conversation and could speak the dialogue before the characters did while we were watching.

The original *Star Trek* installments ran for 50 minutes and 30 seconds. The United States Federal Communications Commission (FCC) limited ads to no more than eight and a half minutes per hour. Station breaks filled the remaining 60 seconds. The FCC dropped all restraints on the number of commercials in 1982. I recall the debate at the time, with broadcasters insisting that they would never overload programming with advertisements because it would alienate viewers. Even in my idealistic youth, I remember saying to myself, "Yeah, right." As a result, watching *Trek* reruns in the 1980s was bittersweet. Stations cut scenes critical to the story to play more commercials. Is nothing sacred?

In 1987, Patrick Stewart as Captain Jean-Luc Picard walked onto the bridge of the *Enterprise* NCC-1701-B in *Star Trek: The Next Generation*. Picard? That's my last name. Whoa! *TNG* got off to a rough start, but it went on to seven full seasons and has engendered an affection with the public that I find quite interesting. It appeals to people in a different way than the original *Star Trek* and deserves a full discussion at another time. Episodes in season one ran for 45 minutes and 40 seconds, half a minute less by year seven.

I graduated with an MD from Wayne State University School of Medicine in 1985. After a year's internship, my wife and I moved to Topeka, Kansas, where I trained as a psychiatrist from 1986 to 1989. I had never pictured myself living in Kansas, but it was a unique opportunity at the time because I could also enroll in the Topeka Institute for Psychoanalysis. Our daughter Katy was born three months after our move, and our son Adam in 1989.

Watching *TNG* and my psychoanalytic studies led me to reflect on the original *Star Trek* from a new perspective. The themes we discussed in my Saturday morning psychoanalytic seminars were the same I now recognized in the original *Star Trek* series. In fact, it seemed that every topic we covered had at least one *Trek* adventure that applied in some way.

There was one video store in Topeka that had the *Star Trek* episodes available on VHS, and they were not edited to cram in extra commercials. My wife and I made numerous trips across town to rent them one by one. VHS was crude by modern standards, but I could pause and rewind as I took notes. I dictated the first draft of this book on a handheld tape recorder, and my wife typed the text into Word Perfect on our 8088 IBM compatible personal computer. To be at work on time, I rose at 5:00 AM to edit the text and print out drafts on our nine pin dot matrix printer. I then had to tear the pages apart and separate the holed sidebars that the printer used to advance the paper. It was a labor of love.

I secured a literary agent who sold the manuscript to a small publisher, but the book never went to print because the company filed for bankruptcy. My agent lost interest in the project, and I did not have the energy to keep it going. I was disappointed at the time but now feel fortunate that it turned out that way. The book's organization was sound, but the writing was not ready for prime-time.

Two and a half decades later, I am older and wiser. My writing has improved considerably. Streaming media has allowed me to pinpoint moments of interest in an episode with a few clicks of the mouse. Online resources have helped me correct names I had misspelled and include details that I had left out previously.

Star Trek has always looked to the future. With that in mind, I would like to conclude this introduction with a proposal to those in the entertainment industry. One of the reasons for *Trek*'s success was that it appeared when television as a medium was still young, before shows relied exclusively on their in-house writing staff. As a result, it attracted some of the premier science fiction authors of the day, like Harlan Ellison ("The City on the Edge of Forever"), Theodore Sturgeon ("Amok Time"), and Jerome Bixby ("Day of the Dove").

In an age of reality TV, the final frontier remains unexplored. How about involving real-life writers? Why not create a show's format, characters, and act structure and invite the public to submit their best work? The author's profile could run for a few minutes before or after the episode, something like they do on *Penn and Teller: Fool Us.* I am enjoying my semi-retirement, and

I am not looking to be involved—but just in case anyone invites me, I recall the climax of "Mirror, Mirror":

> Kirk, McCoy, Scotty, and Uhura are stranded aboard a barbaric *Enterprise* in a parallel universe. With seconds left to transport back home, Captain Kirk implores the alternate Mr. Spock to lead the Empire down a more benevolent path. Mr. Spock objects that one man cannot summon the future. Kirk responds that one man can change the present; in every revolution, there is one man with a vision.

The bearded Spock's final words are, "Captain Kirk, I shall consider it."

Chapter 1: Live Long and Prosper

"Live long and prosper." Mr. Spock spoke these words for the first time in *Star Trek*'s second season opener "Amok Time." The blessing was ironic. Spock faced prosecution for Kirk's murder; the salutation drove home how profoundly his life had just changed. Live long and prosper? Spock tells Vulcan matriarch T'Pau, "I shall do neither. I've killed my captain—and my friend."

Those four words were prophetic. Over fifty years since it debuted in 1966, *Star Trek* thrives. So far, there are thirteen movies in the *Trek* library. *Discovery* is the sixth series spin-off. *Star Trek* print literature abounds. Recent years have seen a spate of fan-funded web series, the stand-out being *Star Trek Continues*.

Why has *Star Trek* flourished? The question brings to mind a scene from the first-season episode, "The Menagerie, Part One."

Spock pleads guilty to mutiny; he kidnaped his now-disabled former captain Christopher Pike and intended to transport him to Talos IV, a violation of Starfleet General Order VII punishable by death. During the proceedings, Commodore Mendez asks Mr. Spock, "Why? What does it accomplish to go there? I want to know why?"

Mendez objects when Spock responds by engaging the viewscreen, but Captain Kirk intervenes, "By asking why, you've opened the door to any evidence he may wish to present." The answer to Mendez' one-word question is the subject of the rest of that episode and "The Menagerie, Part Two."

An achievement like *Star Trek* begs the same question. Why? What accounts for its success? This book is my answer. I draw on all my lifelong learning in these pages, most heavily from my training in psychoanalysis.

Psychoanalysis is a body of ideas regarding how people develop emotionally and mentally over time, from birth to adulthood. Central to the field is the notion that some thoughts, feelings, and memories originating from our early life are *unconscious*. That is, we are not directly aware of this stuff and its influence even when we are wide awake. Sigmund Freud did not originate the concept of an unconscious mind, but he did write voluminously about why it exists and how it behaves. Freud deserves credit for making "unconscious" a household word. As a way to help people, psychoanalysis strives to bring hidden issues out into the open. The idea is to understand what forces might be operating outside our awareness. Once we are consciously aware of a problem, we can bring our resources to bear on a solution.

The psychoanalytic reason for *Star Trek*'s appeal is that it metaphorically depicts conflicts originating in childhood that persist into our adult years deep in the psyche. Television invites viewers to re-experience these past dilemmas at a safe distance. Vicariously, the audience faces dire threats without ever leaving the security of their living rooms. When the *Enterprise* defeats its adversary, fans feel triumphant over the emotional struggle that the episode depicts. In effect, the drama cleanses and rejuvenates. The ancient Greeks called this emotional purging and renewal "catharsis."

The original *Star Trek* series stands out among television shows because as a body of work it portrays issues from all stages of psychological growth. In essence, *Star Trek* is a complete theory of the human mind. Once in syndication, many people watched the reruns several times over. Viewers not only enjoyed that day's offering but also appreciated the story in the context of *Trek*'s entire catalog. The series as a whole embraces people in their totality.

This book takes an in-depth look at *Star Trek* episodes from a psychoanalytic point of view. Chapters 2 and 3 describe the psychology of newborn infants; the next nine chapters follow growth chronologically through adolescence. The final section discusses the *Star Trek* movies with the original cast, which move in some new directions.

I use a matter-of-fact style in how I present the analytic ideas. However, I am aware that the concepts are debatable and cannot be proven in a rigorous scientific sense. Indeed, I have strong confidence in some assertions, less in others. I have chosen not to qualify each topic with my own level of doubt or uncertainty, as it would make the prose unbearable. My hope is that readers will just take it all in until the end, then think back on questionable ideas in the context of the entire book. Be prepared to feel some discomfort; it is disconcerting to learn that one may be responding to forces beyond one's immediate awareness. The reward is that we can then avoid reacting automatically and discover our true selves.

For many reasons, "The Apple" is an apt place to begin the analysis. The episode uses metaphor and other methods to portray a universal human struggle: gaining independence from our parents.

The Apple

> Kirk, Spock, McCoy, Chekov, Yeoman Martha Landon, and four male security personnel beam down to Gamma Trianguli VI and discover a Garden of Eden. It is a lush and beautiful world; the temperature remains a constant 76°Fahrenheit, even at the poles.

> A flower tracks and targets crewman Hendorf. It shoots poisonous darts into his chest, killing him instantly.

"The Apple" has a strong opening, sometimes called a "teaser" because it plays before the title credits of a show and is meant to engage viewers in the plot quickly, so they do not change the channel.

The writer uses a technique I call "isolation." A character, planet, force, or something else represents just one thing, nothing more. For instance, the alien in "Day of the Dove" feeds on anger. There is nothing more to say or understand about the entity. It does not even have a body. In "The Apple," Gamma Trianguli VI is not meant to portray a genuine planet; it has no variation in topography or weather patterns. It is a version of paradise. That is all that can be said—at first.

The story moves on to use a literary device termed "splitting." There is another side to the alien world which is contrary to paradise. It not only murders people but does it with a flower, a symbol of innocence and beauty. Splitting is used to portray opposites like good and evil or safety and menace.

Metaphorically, Gamma Trianguli VI represents a parent. A planet gives and supports life, something like Mom and Dad. The terms "Mother Earth" and "Mother Nature" capture how our minds link the two subjects. Our bodies consist of elements from Earth molded by our parents' DNA. The land provides us with food; our caretakers feed us from the moment of birth.

The symbolic parent in "The Apple" has two distinctly different personas. It is beautiful, nourishing, and welcoming like the Garden of Eden. It also kills.

> A rock explodes when Spock tosses it aside. Another poisonous flower fires on Captain Kirk, but Mr. Spock pushes him out of the way. The darts injure Spock but not fatally.

Kirk calls off the investigation. They try to beam up to the ship, but a force from the world's surface is making the transporter inoperable. The mysterious energy is also preventing the *Enterprise* from leaving orbit and is pulling it down into the atmosphere. It will burn up in sixteen hours. A lightning bolt seeks out and electrocutes crewman Kaplan. Ensign Mallory steps on the wrong rock and dies in the blast.

The writer raises the stakes. Two more men are dead. Kirk and the others try to walk away, but they can't. The *Enterprise* is now in mortal danger.

The sixteen-hour deadline is a plot device often called "the ticking clock." The idea is to put pressure on the protagonist to resolve a situation within a constrained amount of time or suffer the consequences. One could see the ticking clock as a cheap writer's trick, but I think that would be missing the point. In life, we face restrictions and limits in all kinds of ways.

Kirk and the others discover an unassuming, meek, and childlike man who calls himself Akuta, the Leader of the Feeders of Vaal. He says, "All the world knows about Vaal. He causes the rains to fall and the sun to shine. All good comes from Vaal." Akuta alone speaks to Vaal through antennae he was given in the "dim times."

Akuta leads the landing party to meet Vaal, an altar resembling the head of a reptile. It is the facade for a highly sophisticated underground computer. Kirk asks to speak to Vaal, but Akuta can talk to it only when called.

The group follows Akuta to his village. The People of Vaal are all docile and naïve adults. Kirk asks about children, but Akuta says that "replacements" are not necessary and are forbidden by Vaal. Yeoman Landon asks what happens when a man and woman fall in love. At first, Akuta does not know what she is talking about. Then he says, "Ah yes, the holding, the touching, Vaal has forbidden this."

McCoy discovers that the villagers are free of disease and are not growing old.

Together, Vaal and the planet represent the parent. The master computer controls every individual plant and all the forces of nature, as a person's brain regulates every process of his or her body. Vaal has two very different sides to its character. It has a caring half in that it provides for the people's necessities and protects them from illness and injury. At the same time, it viciously attacks the landing party and the *Enterprise*. It can be both nurturing and lethal.

Vaal's protective and supportive relationship with the villagers is similar to the role of a mother or father with small children. Young boys and girls are heavily dependent on their parents. They need Mom and Dad to protect them from danger, feed them, and provide for other needs. Vaal cares for its people in these ways.

The problem is that the villagers are no longer kids. They are physically mature adults, but they cannot grow emotionally under these circumstances. Vaal has imprisoned them in the role of youngsters; the absence of aging symbolizes this fixation. Vaal demands that the villagers sacrifice their advancement for its survival. They must not think for themselves or make their own decisions. Sex is forbidden. Vaal is a caring but overcontrolling, inflexible, and dangerous parent.

Why aren't the villagers dissatisfied with this peculiar relationship? They appear perfectly content with the status quo. This complacency is not typical or healthy, even for young children. Every parent of preschool kids knows how desperately their little ones want to do things for themselves. This characteristic is utterly absent from the village dwellers. They cheerfully comply with the bizarre arrangement never to mature. Why aren't they discontent, angry, and rebellious?

The native people are an example of isolation as a literary device. They embody one aspect of a whole person isolated from everything else. The villagers personify the side of children that wants to be babied and does not want to grow up. To some degree, all youngsters long to stay dependent on a commanding, authoritative figure. The inhabitants exemplify this side of children and lack any tendency toward disobedience and defiance. Where can we find these lost tendencies?

The *Enterprise* crew depicts the missing qualities. They represent the discontent, insubordinate, and rebellious aspect of children. They are aghast that Vaal treats the villagers like dependent offspring and does not allow them to make their own decisions. Controlling our destiny can be difficult, but it can also be profoundly satisfying. Love, parenthood, and a challenging career are some of the rewards awaiting those who reach maturity. Vaal recognized the landing party as a threat, so it attempted to exterminate them.

The contrast between the villagers and the *Enterprise* crew is a type of splitting. Each group speaks for one side of the mixed feelings we have inside our heads. The adversaries then play out our internal emotional struggles through the action of the episode.

Kirk, Spock, and McCoy argue about the culture. Dr. McCoy finds it offensive. There is no growth, advancement, or self-determination. Mr. Spock points out that the society functions smoothly despite Dr.

McCoy's emotional response to it. He questions whether they should make any intervention. Captain Kirk says that the philosophical debate can wait until they are out of danger.

This segment illustrates a vital way that the original *Star Trek* portrays psychological conflicts. Kirk, Spock, and McCoy each exemplify a different part of the psyche. McCoy represents emotions, Spock epitomizes intellect, and Kirk embodies the ability to synthesize information quickly and take the necessary action. These attributes are all present in real people, but they are isolated and split up among the three main characters for effect. Their arguments parallel the emotional struggles within the minds of viewers.

In "The Apple," we see how the three main characters play their contrasting roles. Mr. Spock looks at the situation seemingly without emotion. He calls it, "A splendid example of reciprocity." This comment raises McCoy's hackles; he complains, "Humanoids living so they can service a hunk of tin!" McCoy finds the culture unacceptable and insists that they do something. He ignores Spock's points that the people appear healthy and happy. Spock, in turn, cannot grasp that the system's efficiency comes at a cost. Captain Kirk listens but focuses on escaping unharmed.

As viewers, we can understand each of these different reactions to Vaal. Like McCoy, we react with aversion to the villagers' subservience. We appreciate Spock's respect for a stable society. Finally, we applaud Kirk's emphasis on getting out in one piece. The trio's deliberations parallel the push and pull of different forces within viewers.

Mr. Chekov and Yeoman Landon kiss tenderly while a male and female villager look on with curiosity. This embrace confuses the native couple, yet they try it for themselves—and they like it. In a flash, lightning threatens the pair.

The native couple begins to discover their sexuality after years of repression, then face immediate execution. Vaal demands total obedience; it crushes the tiniest inkling of self-determination.

Vaal portrays a disturbed mother or father. Healthy parents put their children's needs first and adapt as their youngsters grow. Preschoolers require constant supervision while teenagers need permission to build their own lives. If the people's emotional health concerned Vaal, it would recognize their need for autonomy and growth. It does provide for some of their essentials, but it does so strictly for its own interests. The inhabitants' role is to ensure Vaal's survival and nothing more.

Some parents resemble Vaal by demanding that their youngsters provide for them, instead of the other way around. They expect children to fill some need of theirs, as Vaal compels the villagers to supply its energy. Abusive caretakers use kids as scapegoats or convenient targets for their anger. Overprotective adults may hold on to offspring too tight, for a variety of reasons. Physical abuse is not the only thing that halts healthy development. Caretaking can also stunt a child's emotional growth if it continues past an appropriate age.

> Back in the village, Kirk and Spock continue to reflect. Kirk has made up his mind. He says, "These people aren't living; they're existing. They don't create. They don't produce. They don't even think. They exist to service a machine." Spock fears that they might violate the Federation Prime Directive of non-interference, so Kirk continues, "They're people, not robots. They should have the opportunity of choice. We owe it to them to interfere."

Sometimes viewers learn things before the characters do. The audience has seen how swiftly Vaal threatens retribution when the people get out of line. Although Kirk did not witness it, the scene with the couple kissing has ended the debate. The reciprocity Spock found splendid a few moments ago is enforced with an iron fist. Kirk expands his objective to include liberating the people from their computer master.

In essence, Vaal is an autocratic dictator. He feeds and protects his people better than many despots, but he is still a dictator. The villagers are like citizens of a repressive regime that controls all information, so its population does not know what it is like in the rest of the world. The people in totalitarian countries are often unaware what they are missing because autocrats suppress and manipulate any truth that threatens the status quo. Captain Kirk is on the side of self-rule, autonomy, free-choice, and collective progress when he decides to put an end to Vaal's repressive domination.

The scene also signals to the audience that Kirk is thinking about the *Prime Directive*, even though he has decided to violate it.

The United Federation of Planets' Prime Directive, also known as Starfleet General Order One, prohibits interference with the internal affairs of alien cultures. The principle was introduced in the first-season episode "The Return of the Archons." As a plot device, the Prime Directive helps clarify the thinking of the main characters. If they plan on disregarding the standard, they need to explain why. Elements introduced in one story, however, can also be a burden to those that follow.

The Prime Directive appeared in *Star Trek* in 1966, during the Vietnam conflict. I suspect that it reflected the anxiety of the times, that maybe America does not know what is best for everybody, after all. The doctrine was carried forward into most of the *Star Trek* spin-off series, where it often felt like a hindrance. Perhaps writers should have interfered with the noninterference dogma.

Telepathically, Vaal instructs Akuta that the native men must kill the strangers. Before this, they did not know about murder or even have a word for it; their society was free of violence. Akuta demonstrates what to do. He sets down a coconut-sized fruit to represent the head of one of the visitors, then splits it open with a massive club.

The villagers ambush the landing party. After they club crewman Marple, the rest of the *Enterprise* personnel gain the upper hand. Kirk confines the disarmed people to a hut where they can no longer feed Vaal.

Star Trek fans often talk about the "disposable crew" who beam down with Kirk. Sometimes these characters are called the "red shirts" because they almost always have the crimson uniform worn by security or engineering personnel. "The Apple" kills off four out of the five red shirts in the landing party. The writer spares Yeoman Landon because she is too critical to the plot.

We enjoy poking fun at TV and movie icons like *Star Trek*, but I do not take the disposable crew criticism too seriously. The best *Trek* episodes are plot-driven stories with a point. The Chekov–Landon romance is included to serve a purpose as much as the four deaths. It is ridiculous that the lovebirds are smooching while the *Enterprise* nears its end by burning up in the atmosphere, yet the romantic element is necessary to tempt the village couple. At least Kirk and the others call the lost security men by name. Captain Kirk even comments that Kaplan's father helped him get into the Academy. This personalization fleshes out the crewmen's characters a little bit, so they do not seem like they are just props.

The attack sequence also shows that women on the *Enterprise* can defend themselves as well as men. Landon uses her martial arts talents to defeat two attackers. The director could have had her hide in a hut; the helpless woman stereotype was still prevalent in the 1960s. Cutting Landon's fight scene could have saved some money, as it appears that they hired a stunt double for those few seconds of action. (Stunt doubles were also commonplace for the male characters.) *Star Trek* had a vision of the future in which people of all genders and backgrounds were on equal footing.

Vaal is now vulnerable because it is hungry. Kirk orders Scotty to fire the ship's phasers until Vaal is dead. The native people will now be responsible for their own lives and needs. They will also discover the joys of love and parenthood.

Most of us have not had an overbearing parent like Vaal, but this is not necessary to appreciate "The Apple." At one time, we were all profoundly reliant on our caretakers. That experience is encoded in our minds even if we have no conscious memories of it. A nostalgic longing for the needy period of childhood remains with us throughout life. Growing up has its rewards, but it is also a long and arduous process; it means giving up something safe and comfortable. Dependence on Vaal can sometimes look good when we are facing disappointment, failure, and embarrassment.

As it usually does, *Star Trek* favors growth and development. Kirk and the others liberate the villagers. The former People of Vaal will be free to live their own lives. Kirk says that they will like it. He adds, "You'll learn something about men and women, the way they are supposed to be. Caring for each other. Being happy with each other. Being good to each other. That's what we call 'love.' You'll like that too—a lot."

> Back aboard the *Enterprise*, Spock shares with Kirk and McCoy that he still questions whether they did the right thing on Gamma Trianguli VI. He refers to the Book of Genesis and says that, in a manner of speaking, they gave the People of Vaal the knowledge of good and evil. As a result, they were driven out of paradise. Kirk uses the parallel to poke some fun at Mr. Spock.

The final few minutes of the episode is called the "denouement" or "epilogue." It is used to tie up loose ends, resolve or explain matters, summarize, reflect, let out a deep sigh, or add some humor. The light-hearted seventy-second epilogue in "The Apple" ensures that the audience grasps the allusion of the episode's title and notices the similarities between Gamma Trianguli VI and the Garden of Eden account as found in the Hebrew Bible and Christian Old Testament Book of Genesis.

In the Biblical narrative, Adam and Eve, the first man and woman created by God, are in His paradise where all other creation is vegetation. There is no violence, and the couple feels no shame from their nakedness. God permits them to eat from any of the trees except the tree of knowledge of good and evil. Tempted by a serpent, both Adam and Eve taste the forbidden fruit, commonly referred to as an apple. In response, God clothes their nakedness, for they now feel shame, and banishes them from the Garden of Eden, condemning man to a life of hard labor followed by death and woman to the pain of childbirth and subordination to her husband. By extension, many theologians see Adam and Eve's disobedience to God as the basis or explanation for most human suffering and misery. The Christian doctrine of *original sin* claims that all people, including newborn children, inherit the responsibility and guilt for Adam and Eve's transgression.

In contrast to the Genesis account, the *Star Trek* episode named after the forbidden fruit depicts resisting or disobeying Vaal as the right and proper thing to do. It supports the idea that it is healthy to want more knowledge, to seize control of one's destiny, and to reject a seeming paradise that requires perpetual subjugation and ignorance. The People of Vaal have not sinned; with some help, they have embraced their growth.

The disparity between the Garden of Eden narrative and "The Apple" is striking. What do we make of this? After Spock draws the parallel, the playful tone of the epilogue encourages us not to take the comparison too seriously. Still, the allegory is an invitation to reflect. Sometimes the stories or beliefs of religious groups seem so familiar and correct to those inside the faith that it is hard to imagine what it might be like to encounter the creed for the first time. When the story of paradise is set on a distant planet sometime in the future, it can lead to new insights that might be difficult to achieve otherwise.

CHAPTER 2: PROJECTION

This chapter and the next explore different aspects of an infant's inner experience and how *Star Trek* brings this realm to life. First, we will consider the power of primitive anger and frustration. We will see how babies project their rage outside themselves into another person, object, or entity. Chapter 3 will reflect on moments when newborns feel happy and content.

To comprehend how newborns understand the world, we need to appreciate their physical sensations and needs. Babies' thoughts and emotions are highly dependent on their bodily impressions. The mind-body connection is more profound during infancy than at any other time of life.

Hunger plays a central role in infants' lives. In the womb, the mother supplies nourishment continuously through the umbilical cord. After birth, babies feed every few hours around the clock. Hungriness ensures that sucklings obtain the milk that they need to survive and grow.

Infants feel their appetite intensely throughout their entire body. Starving babies cry at the top of their lungs, their faces flush, and they violently thrash their arms and legs. Their frustrated craving consumes every ounce of energy and involves all parts of their body. During those moments, anguish seems to fill their whole universe. They do not understand that mother's milk or its equivalent is on the way.

Hungry babies feel something akin to rage and have primitive fantasies roughly similar to destruction and retaliation. Infants get angry. They are no different from older children or adults in this regard. When frustrated, newborns become furious and have thoughts of revenge. Their ferocious screaming and thrashing reflect the magnitude of their irritation. Temper consumes their entire mind and body. At these times, they want to destroy, devour, or smash things into a million pieces. Babies do not subdue or control this hostility as they will later in life.

Infants direct their anger primarily toward the mental image they have of their caretakers and things associated with them. At first, the pictures of other people in babies' minds are rudimentary and wildly unrealistic. Infants do not even understand that different parts of their parent's body somehow belong to the same person. For example, they think that an adult's face and hands are separate objects. Sight, sound, smell, and touch all seem unrelated, rather than different aspects of one reality.

Their innate, primal aggression terrifies infants. The destructive fantasies frighten them because newborn people have magic, unrealistic ideas of what their brainwaves can do. An attack on their caretaker inside their head feels very real. They cannot distinguish between their mental life and actual events. To some degree, babies recognize that annihilating Mom and Dad will obliterate the very source of their life and nourishment. They think that their fantasies will physically harm or destroy their parents and thus will threaten their survival.

Infants want to get rid of their anger. Their violent imaginings are so scary that they seek to dispose of them somehow. They rid themselves of this unwanted aggression with a psychological process called "projection." In effect, infants pretend that they do not have any hostile thoughts and attribute their rage to people or objects in their environment. They project terrifying ideas and feelings from their mind into somebody else. They become convinced that it is others who have antagonistic thoughts and intentions, not themselves.

The psychological process of projection parallels the physical act of spitting up food. Both phenomena eject something that is inside of us into the outside world. We disgorge food from our stomach when we regurgitate; projection is like vomiting toxic thoughts and impulses into the environment. The resemblance links the two happenings within our psyche; it shows how intimately mind and body are connected. Later in life, people sometimes throw-up when they are overwhelmed emotionally.

Projection solves one problem but creates another. If infants eject their anger into the environment, the world becomes a dangerous place filled with hatred. Wherever they look, they see their own rage. Menace permeates their view of their parents and everything else in the environment. They have not escaped from their aggression; instead, they think it is coming from somebody or something else besides them. Even their caretakers become venomous attackers. When in distress, babies feel persecuted by the evil, destructive objects that surround them.

Infants will eventually develop a more realistic and less frightening view of the world. When they are physically content, their experience is much different from the picture painted in this chapter. In time, these happy moments will temper the intense anger and frustration.

Projecting hostility outside ourselves is a primitive yet frequent way we deal with aggressive thoughts throughout life. We did this automatically as infants; as adults, we are more prone to paranoia when under stress. Fear can distort our ability to sort out which threats are real and which ones we exaggerate.

Projection is an illusion. We cannot just discard our noxious thoughts and feelings by giving them away to somebody or something outside ourselves. When we feel overwhelmed, however, we sometimes succumb to projection's false promise.

Many *Star Trek* adversaries symbolically represent humanity's projected aggression. Once contact is made with the *Enterprise*, it is as if the opponent says, "Like it or not, you are going to deal with me."

"The Changeling" not only depicts projection but also makes the link to infancy crystal clear.

The Changeling

The *Enterprise* investigates the destruction of the Malurian solar system, which had a population of four billion. An unknown assailant attacks the *Enterprise* with the power of ninety photon torpedos in one burst. Kirk counter-attacks, but the adversary just absorbs the weapon's energy. The repeated hits neutralize the *Enterprise*'s shields; the ship will not survive another blast.

The all-consuming, indiscriminate nature of the violence suggests that the adversary represents the amorphous hostility babies feel when in distress. An infant's hunger can erupt and envelope the entire universe in a flash. Similarly, the attacker appears out of nowhere and outguns the *Enterprise*'s defenses a hundred-fold. The colossal scale of devastation makes whole solar systems look puny.

The absence of any communication between the opponents also alludes to the infant/parent dynamic. The attack is like a baby's scream. It can explode suddenly and demands that the adults respond immediately. As grownups, we are hardwired to react to a baby's crying, just as Kirk and the others are desperate to get the assailant to hold its fire.

The aggressor pauses after a message from Captain Kirk. The bridge crew determines that the enemy ship is only one meter in length.

Spock and Uhura decipher the attacker's response. In a computer-like voice, it says "require communication" and agrees to let Kirk beam it aboard the *Enterprise*.

Once infants have nursed, the fit of rage passes and they seek to engage their parents. Similarly, the toddler-sized spaceship takes a breather and wants to communicate. The source of the attack is no larger than a child because it is a stand-in for a human baby.

In the transporter room, Kirk and the others initially believe that the device is a small ship with little aliens inside, but they quickly realize that it is a machine. It calls itself "Nomad." Kirk recalls that there was a probe launched from Earth in the 2000s by that name.

At first, Kirk and the others assume that there are tiny creatures inside Nomad. This detail supports the idea that, symbolically, infants are the source of its attack. The little devils inside Nomad are human babies.

Nomad also represents humanity's aggression in general. It was fashioned on Earth by *Homo sapiens*; thus, it embodies a part of the human psyche. Its designers then launched it into space, which is a metaphor for the emotional process of projection. We blasted Nomad deep into the celestial void, which symbolizes how we disavow and eject frightening and unacceptable parts of the mind. Inevitably, we cannot escape from the dark side of our nature so easily. As a projection of primitive rage, Nomad returns to haunt the *Enterprise*.

The name "Nomad" also suggests that it is a projection of human anger. It is a play on words; "no mad" summarizes its psychological purpose. By embodying all humanity's violence and hatred, it allows us to deny any hostility of our own. It helps us believe that we are "not mad" or have "no anger." All the rage is in Nomad, and none is in us.

Nomad asks some questions and concludes that Kirk is its creator; it adds, therefore, that the sterilization procedure against the *Enterprise* was unnecessary. It says that Kirk programmed its function to probe for biological infestations, to sterilize that which is not perfect.

Kirk, Spock, and McCoy discover that Nomad has mistaken James Kirk for its real designer, Earth scientist Jackson Roykirk.

Nomad calls Kirk its "creator" in a computer voice mixed with a hint of reverence. The plot development supports the interpretation that Nomad represents a human baby.

Nomad uses the words "sterilize" and "imperfect," both of which have meaning. Its mission to destroy imperfect life forms alludes to the reason why infants become irate. As they see it, Mom and Dad are flawed because they do not satisfy all their wants instantly. Realistically, the most attentive caretaker cannot provide everything a newborn wants whenever the little one wants it. Infants will sometimes have to live with discomfort temporarily. This expectation seems obvious to adults, but babies do not see it this way. All they know is that they are aching and it makes them furious. They wish that their providers were perfect, meaning that they could instantaneously relieve their distress. When this does not happen, they become enraged.

Nomad's intent to "sterilize" imperfect life is a thinly disguised attack on parenthood. Sterilize does not mean kill. It means to make somebody unable to reproduce. Nomad attacks humanity at a very vulnerable point, the ability to have children.

> Nomad hears Lieutenant Uhura singing over the intercom. It follows the sound of her voice to the bridge and asks her, "What is the meaning? What form of communication?" Uhura tells it she was singing, that she felt like music. Nomad continues, "For what purpose is singing? What is music?" It tells her to think about music and scans her with a beam of energy that erases her memories. Mentally, she is an infant again; Nurse Chapel begins to re-educate her. Uhura works her way up to a kindergarten level reader.

Nomad finds Uhura's vocalizing irresistible just as infants are hardwired to respond to their parents' voices. Caretakers talk, coo, and sing to their little ones. This social exchange bonds them together. Nomad travels through the ship to locate Uhura like a child who is drawn instinctively to the sound of adult providers. Like Nomad, infants do not know what the words and intonations mean, but they are engaged and curious.

Babies also fear that they will hurt the very parent they rely on, just as Nomad's scan scrambles Uhura's mind. The energy beam reduces her to the mental equivalent of a nursling. This plot detail is more confirmation that this episode explores issues originating in infancy.

> Mr. Scott rushes to save Uhura from Nomad. The automaton kills him with a bolt of energy. A few moments later, Nomad asks creator Kirk if he would like it to "repair the unit Scott." At Scotty's bedside in sick bay, Nomad brings him back to life.

Mr. Scott's death and resurrection illustrate another aspect of how babies experience the world. To infants, their thoughts and feelings dictate reality, not the natural laws of the universe. They see the world based on their sensations at that moment. When they are angry, the world is a hostile and dangerous place. A few moments later, the world becomes good and giving once again. These two disparate views exist side by side in young children's minds. They have not integrated the contrasting realities into a cohesive whole. Logical contradictions have no meaning to infants. They think that the world changes according to their feelings, which fluctuate from moment to moment.

Nomad's mental state decides Scotty's life and death rather than natural law. When Nomad feels threatened by Scotty, it kills him. When the danger has passed, it brings him back to life. Nomad changes reality depending on how it feels. This fluctuation illustrates how infants' view of the world shifts according to their physical state and emotions.

Spock does the Vulcan mind meld on Nomad. Its mission was to seek out alien life, but a meteor confused its programming and cut it off from Earth. It encountered an alien probe, Tan-Ru, created by another race to obtain sterilized soil samples. The two probes merged. The resulting hybrid believed that its mission was to sterilize imperfect life forms.

Kirk calls Nomad a "changeling." According to an ancient Earth legend, a changeling was a fairy child who was substituted for a human baby. The imposter assumed the identity of the human infant. Kirk adds, "It's space happy. It thinks I'm its mother."

Nomad is a hybrid. All human infants are mixtures in a sense as they are a combination of genes originating from their mothers and fathers. Nomad and Tan-Ru cross paths in uncharted space and unite, just as egg and sperm meet within some mysterious corridor of a mother's body and become one. Children blend the traits of their parents to become new, unique individuals.

A changeling replaces a human child as Nomad symbolizes a newborn infant. Kirk calls himself its mother rather than its father because women are the ones who give birth. Nomad is a deformed, monstrous little baby.

In folklore, the purpose of swapping a fairy child for a human was varied. In this *Trek* episode, the idea of a changeling is a way to deny the natural aggression within an infant by attributing it to a pixie. If we believe that a baby's anger comes from an imposter, we can tell ourselves that real children are unpolluted bundles of joy. Anything cute and adorable is part of the real babe while things dirty or ugly belong to the changeling. We project the aggression of the human psyche into the idea of a doppelgänger.

Nomad's launch into space and cutoff from Earth symbolize reasons why babies get angry. To children, there is nothing more terrifying than being abandoned. Its human parents banished it by blasting it into the unknown. If that were not enough, Nomad felt forsaken when communication with

Earth ended, even though this was not the fault of its designers. Similarly, a child does not understand or care why an adult in their life disappears; it terrifies and angers them regardless of the circumstances. Nomad returns to avenge itself upon humanity.

After Nomad kills several security guards, an angry and frustrated Kirk tells it that he is also a biological unit and he created Nomad in the first place. This confrontation backfires. Nomad examines Kirk's medical records and decides that he is as imperfect as the rest of the humans aboard. In an attempt to kill the crew yet preserve the ship, Nomad turns off the life support systems. Before they run out of heat and air, Kirk accuses Nomad of confusing him with its true creator, Jackson Roykirk. Having made a mistake, Nomad is also imperfect and must destroy itself. They beam Nomad into space where it self-destructs.

As a projection of humanity's aggression, Nomad's fate has implications for how we handle our anger as people. There are both positive and negative messages in Nomad's destruction.

The optimistic part of the ending is that Captain Kirk draws on more advanced mental abilities to gain control over Nomad. He uses language, reason, and an appeal to consistency to convince Nomad to sterilize itself; apparently, it has not learned the art of hypocrisy. The higher nature of humanity prevails over anger and destruction. In healthy development, civilized aptitudes eventually master the caustic side of our personality, as Captain Kirk subdues Nomad.

The unsettling aspect of the finale is that Nomad is projected outside the ship and destroyed. There is no recognition that it embodies the dark side of humanity. Nomad's demise could reinforce the notion that we can eradicate our resentment by attributing it to other people and then attacking or killing them. Slaying such an enemy may bring temporary relief, but our ire will reappear in different forms. We cannot escape our hatred by wiping out others. Kirk or Spock could have made a comment that maybe humanity needs to be more careful when it designs its machines; it might have mitigated the disquieting nature of the episode's wrap-up.

The *Star Trek* team does an excellent job creating a creepy and menacing adversary out of Nomad. The voiceover acting, background mechanical noise, camera shots from just behind Nomad, and other details all come together to deliver a sense of foreboding. In contrast, Nomad's high-pitched silly voice at the end is one element that detracts from the whole.

Spock compliments Kirk on the dazzling display of logic. McCoy says that Uhura is up to college level and should be back on the job within a week. Kirk says, "It's not easy to lose a bright and promising son. It thought I was its mother, didn't it? You saw what it did for Scotty. What a doctor it would have made. My son the doctor. Gets you right there."

The epilogue makes sure Uhura is fit for duty by next week's episode. The light-hearted banter lets off some steam. The scene is one of the countless times that the trio of Kirk, Spock, and McCoy works like a charm.

The tendency to project threatening thoughts and feelings remains with us throughout life. Mostly during times of stress, we may attribute our aggression to somebody else and then feel persecuted by them. After a bad day at the office, we may snap at our spouse just for saying hello. A harried mother may think that her children are deliberately tormenting her, though she realizes this is not true. In these examples, the people involved are upset and frustrated, but they do not feel the anger directly. They project it into somebody else and then feel victimized. These common reactions usually do not develop into major problems. When things calm down, an average person can look at their situation more realistically.

For some people, projection continues to dominate their lives. These individuals are *paranoid*. They view the world as a dangerous, malevolent place filled with people who want to harm or persecute them. People suffering from paranoia have difficulty using reason and reflection to examine their take on things. Frequently, they dispute relevant facts or discount their importance.

When working with people as a psychiatrist, I find that the *cognitive therapy* approach is the most useful when dealing with somebody feeling overly threatened. This way of conceptualizing problems posits that people have *core beliefs* that influence their feelings, thoughts, and behaviors. Therapy involves helping people identify the core belief at play then test whether there is evidence to support the idea. As part of the process, the therapist and patient discuss other explanations for what is frightening the person and examine the evidence for and against the alternate formulation. In this way, therapy helps a person reflect and use language and reason to question and discard some distorted and problematic ways of experiencing the world. Just as Captain Kirk uses rationality and reflection to neutralize Nomad, cognitive therapy can help people tolerate the stresses of life without feeling terrified that they are under attack.

The psychological process of projection also has a collective form, involving groups of like-minded people. The troupe or organization may project its hostile thoughts and intentions into others, then feel threatened from the outside. The first party then wants to destroy the second one, which it considers evil and dangerous. There are countless examples of this dynamic throughout history, often with horrific results. Human sacrifice, racial hatred, war, terrorism, and scorched-earth policies of various sorts all testify to how prominent paranoid thinking remains within humanity. People come to believe that another group causes all society's problems. If members have doubts at first, the gravitational pull to conform will bring them along. Together, there is open or tacit approval that they are justified in tearing down or destroying the other side. This shared form of paranoia is difficult to combat, as the members mutually reinforce the distorted beliefs at the center of their alliance. Dialogue, language, reason, and listening with respect can overcome the divisions between groups, but this is not easy. Often it is an effort just to get two sides talking to one another.

In "The Doomsday Machine," the *Enterprise* faces another adversary of staggering destructive power.

The Doomsday Machine

A garbled distress call comes in from the USS *Constellation*. En route to investigate, the *Enterprise* encounters debris from the destruction of several solar systems. They find the *Constellation* damaged and adrift.

As in "The Changeling," the colossal scale and indiscriminate nature of the devastation hark back to the amorphous rage of infancy. We can expect that the mysterious adversary somehow represents humanity's aggression, as a projection.

Kirk, Scotty, McCoy, and a damage control team beam aboard the *Constellation*. They find the ship's commander Commodore Matthew Decker in a state of shock. The rest of the personnel are gone. An automated weapon of immense size and power attacked the *Constellation*. Decker beamed the crew to a nearby world for safety, only to watch in horror as the mechanism sliced it to pieces and consumed its remains. Decker is overwhelmed with guilt.

Kirk calls the robot weapon a "Doomsday Machine" like Earth's hydrogen bomb. He speculates that it was built as a bluff, too powerful to use because it would result in mutually-assured destruction. It is on course to the most densely populated part of the Federation.

As expected, the Doomsday Machine represents our species' violent nature. Indeed, thermo-nuclear explosives are the most apocalyptic devices ever created. We will discuss the political allegory later in the chapter.

Commodore Decker's struggle is the most noteworthy feature of this episode. He is grieving the loss of his crew and suffering severe survivor's guilt, also known as a traumatic stress disorder. He blames himself for his colleagues' deaths. Why does he feel so tormented? Abandoning their damaged ship was a reasonable action under the circumstances. It was under attack, and a strategic evacuation seemed the only chance of survival. In fact, Decker fulfilled his responsibility by remaining aboard until all others were presumed safe. There is a long-held maritime tradition that the captain would be the last person to escape a sinking ship.

The Doomsday Machine is an allegorical manifestation of Decker's primitive anger and hostility, or humanity's in general. The commodore feels responsible for what the weapon has done, as it symbolically represents humankind's violent instincts. It is as if his rage has taken the external form of the globe-razing automaton, which then carries out his secret, ferocious wishes. Decker's violent fantasies have erupted into a ghastly reality. Guilt, grief, and remorse overwhelm him.

Decker is the captain of a single vessel in this episode, but his title of "commodore" suggests that he has commanded more than one ship at a time at some point in the past. As such, he has risen to a level of distinction above Captain Kirk even if they hold the same rank. We would expect an officer at his level to perform at high standards, but not impossible ones. Decker has concluded that he is unforgivable, a complex mixture of shame, guilt, and a dangerous impulse to punish himself.

> Decker and McCoy beam back to the *Enterprise*. Before Kirk and the others can follow, the Doomsday Machine fires on the *Enterprise* and disables the transporter. The weapon breaks off its pursuit and returns to its previous heading.

> Spock intends to effect repairs and circle back to pick up Captain Kirk, but Decker assumes command as the senior officer on board and launches an attack. The phasers just bounce off the robot's hull. The *Enterprise* loses its energy shield and warp power. Spock insists that Decker veer off. He adds that the commodore's actions are suicidal; Spock will relieve him of duty if he refuses. Decker orders the helm to break off, but by this time the *Enterprise* is caught in a tractor beam. The weapon is pulling them in.

Commodore Decker's behavior seems contradictory. If he feels so guilty about the death of his crew, why is he taking the *Enterprise* to the same fate? Spock is correct to call his decisions suicidal.

Decker is at war with himself. At this point, the *Enterprise* crew are mere pawns in his mental torment. He feels that something unforgivable from inside himself has been unleashed, which has taken the form of the Doomsday Machine. The only way to extinguish his demons is to destroy it. Even so, the attack could not have succeeded. There was no hope of prevailing against the massive weapon, and Decker knew this.

As the name implies, people suffering from "survivor's guilt" are tortured most by the fact that they remain alive while others are dead. Notice that Decker did not scold himself for his actions on the *Constellation*. He didn't condemn himself for his decisions or for beaming his crew down to the planet. He doesn't say that he should have done more. The question that torments him is—why am I still alive?

If he cannot destroy the Doomsday Machine, Decker's exaggerated self-blame demands that he atone by bringing about his death. The need for self-punishment overpowers him and clouds his judgment. Decker's masochistic guilt drives him toward suicide and almost causes the deaths of another four hundred people. Superficially, taking the *Enterprise* into battle would have had the noble purpose of destroying the Doomsday Machine. Underneath, since the campaign could not succeed, its other point is to allow Decker to punish himself for his sins.

Kirk attacks the Doomsday Machine with the crippled *Constellation*, which allows the *Enterprise* to break free. Over ship-to-ship communications, Kirk orders Spock to relieve Decker; the commodore grudgingly stands down.

Decker is to report to sick bay for an evaluation, but he brutally attacks security escort Montgomery and steals a shuttlecraft.

Mr. Decker has lost all perspective. He feels guilty about his crew's demise, but apparently, he is also entitled to beat Montgomery to a pulp. The fight is brutal.

The scenes pitting Kirk and Spock against Decker are some of the most dramatic in the original *Star Trek* series. Some of their power comes from how quickly Decker transforms from sympathetic wounded warrior to suicidal maniac. Many episodes depict forces that take over the ship, but "The Doomsday Machine" is the only one in which an *Enterprise* outsider pulls rank to usurp command. The sequence makes viewers squirm for many reasons, not least of which is that it challenges the notion that the *Enterprise* team is a happy family in control of its destiny. Instead, the starship is part of a pseudo-military hierarchical organization with top leaders who are fallible people.

The actors playing Kirk, Spock, and Decker deserve kudos for their performances. It has become fashionable to accuse William Shatner (Captain Kirk) of over-acting. Partly, this is because nitpicking heroes is often the way we show our love. At times, however, I suspect the criticism contains some envy. Shatner is sometimes so capable that it can leave viewers feeling diminished. If that is the case, I will remind people that television is an artificial world where every second can be reshot and polished. Comparing oneself to video characters and drama should be done with a grain of salt.

Decker pilots the shuttlecraft into the maw of the Doomsday Machine. Kirk tries to talk him out of it, but Decker says that he has been prepared to die ever since he "killed" his crew. The shuttle impact damages the massive weapon slightly.

Notice Decker's words—he "killed" his crew. He does not say, "I got them killed," which would imply responsibility but attribute the act to something else. In Decker's traumatized mind, he quite literally took his people's lives. He believes that he himself is the Doomsday Machine; he talks as if they are the same thing. There is no distinction between him and it. Since he cannot destroy the automaton, he commits suicide to atone for his crimes. Decker and the weapon physically merge into one another as the tormented commander rams himself down its throat.

Kirk rigs the *Constellation* to do the same thing, to enter the weapon's mouth and explode. The transporter engineers beam him back to the *Enterprise* at the last second.

While Kirk awaits extraction, the transporter malfunctions with snaps and bursts of smoke. Viewers know that Kirk will survive and the last-minute technical difficulties are meant to raise the stakes, but so what. The sequence is well done.

The Doomsday Machine is dead.

Kirk says that the record will show that Decker died in the line of duty. He goes on, "Ironic, isn't it? Way back in the twentieth-century the H-bomb was the ultimate weapon, their Doomsday Machine. And we used something like it to destroy another Doomsday Machine. Probably the first time such a weapon has been used for constructive purposes." Mr. Spock wonders if there are any more of those weapons wandering around the universe. Kirk says that he hopes not; he found one "quite sufficient."

The epilogue shows Kirk and Spock walking in front of the viewscreen. The shot contrasts with most scenes showing the front of the bridge from behind the helm. The movement helps viewers' put the TV camera crews and sets out of their minds and immerse themselves in the story.

Though they feel forced, Kirk's words put a positive spin on an otherwise horrific encounter. *Star Trek* is ultimately an optimistic show.

Mr. Spock's concluding comments remind us that humanity cannot rid itself of its innate aggression by projecting it into outside enemies. Mr. Spock wonders if there are any more Doomsday Machines roaming the galaxy. In other words, has the ultimate source of the hostility and destruction been eliminated? Since the real origin of warfare is the human psyche, Spock is right to be uneasy. We cannot come to terms with our inner beast by destroying external threats and enemies; such victories provide temporary relief at best. However, with reflection, patience, openness, restraint, and listening, we will find more partners in the world and fewer persecutors.

The episode is an invitation to reflect on our behavior and policies as a nation. By locating a dilemma far away in time and space, science fiction and other allegorical stories can give us a fresh perspective on the current issues of the day.

On one level, the reality of a weapon that can destroy all human civilization seems insane. This truth is more apparent when one encounters a free-floating menace in space like the Doomsday Machine. In contrast, if one examines the development of the atomic bomb on Earth, each decision along the way might appear sensible. The historical context and step-by-step understanding, however, should not cloud our awareness of the danger we have created.

Humanity has responded to the threat of atomic weapons in a few ways. First, there is a consensus that the number of countries possessing these armaments and the entire world stockpile should be as limited as possible. Second, robust efforts are warranted to keep them out of the hands of non-state actors or terrorist groups. Third, nations possessing these munitions should commit to a no-first-use (NFU) policy; if all countries agree to NFU, there will never be a nuclear war.

Star Trek conveys hope. "The Doomsday Machine" reminds us that all devices, including weapons, are only our instruments. They are lifeless, while people have agency, consciousness, and purpose. We can solve problems. Even difficulties of our own making can be addressed when we think creatively and work together. As a lifelong learner, I am often astounded that the arc of human history is one of progress, in spite of the warfare and other miseries we create for ourselves, not to mention the natural disasters and physical obstacles. There are setbacks, sometimes for centuries, but humanity always seems to get itself back on track and reach new heights.

The next chapter will look at a happier aspect of emotional life during infancy and how *Star Trek* stories capture these moments in metaphor. After all, babies are not always frustrated and angry. There are many hours when they feel satisfied and content.

CHAPTER 3: MAKE IT SO

This chapter will discuss why infants think that they are the center of the universe. Newborn babies believe that they magically create and control the entire world around them. Analysis of "Shore Leave" and "The Menagerie" will illustrate this fantastic but illusory power of infancy.

Let's begin by imagining what nurslings think and feel as they are fed and comforted. How do they understand what is happening when their parents tend to their needs?

Direct observation of babies and working with people later in psychoanalysis both suggest that newborns do not understand that there is a world beyond what they can see, hear, and feel. Their immediate environment is the only reality they care about or comprehend. From a baby's perspective, people instantly appear when they walk into the room and just vanish when they leave. They do not understand that caretakers and things still exist when they are out of sight. Children eventually learn that their parents are still alive and in the world even when they are somewhere else, but they do not understand this at birth.

Picture newborn babies at rest. Suddenly, an aching feeling in their stomach jolts them from sleep. Later in life, they will learn that this sensation is hunger. As newborns, however, they are not sure what the hurting is or why it is there. They only know that it feels terrible, so they begin to cry. Within seconds, Mom or Dad appears and provides the warm milk that relieves their misery. The pain is suddenly and miraculously gone.

How do infants perceive this string of events? They wish for something to relieve their agony, and then that deliverance instantly appears. The whole thing seems astonishing. Infants conclude that their wishes magically construct their parents out of nowhere. They see themselves as the creators of the entire universe around them. This conclusion seems fantastic by adult standards, but it is quite understandable when we put ourselves in infants' shoes—or booties. When Mom and Dad are out of the room, babies think that they do not exist; during the first months of life, they do not understand that their parents are still alive somewhere else in the house. Crying infants wish that a parent would provide for them, and suddenly an adult walks through the door. To babies, their mom or dad has just popped into reality out of thin air. Since the tots were just longing for a caretaker, they conclude that it was their desire or command that conjured the grownup out of nothingness. In the same way, infants believe that they create everything around them. When they turn their head and see a new toy, they feel convinced that they have just caused it to materialize.

This way of understanding the world is aptly called the stage of "infantile omnipotence." Newborns believe that if they wish for something to happen, then it will magically occur. They feel omnipotent, in that they create and control every person and thing that exists.

Babies need caring, responsive parents for the sense of infantile omnipotence to develop. Their caretakers are available twenty-four hours a day, to recognize their children's cues and tend to their essentials. As any parent knows, responding to their newborn baby takes priority over everything else. When Mom and Dad are consistently available, very young children can believe in the magic of their thoughts and wishes.

The experience of infantile omnipotence is what counteracts the terrifying, paranoid moments described in the last chapter. All children feel frustrated and angry at times. Fortunately, when they have caretakers who are sensitive to their cues, they do not stay in this frightening state for very long. Parents soothe their babies' anger and fear by providing what they require. In healthy adult-child relationships, these happy times outweigh any pain and frustration. Youngsters build confidence that the world is a safe place, where they will be fed, nurtured, and protected. They also develop self-assurance that they are not helpless and can communicate their wishes in a way that will be understood. Infantile omnipotence is the foundation of a healthy sense of security and trust.

If infants are abused or frustrated excessively, anger and paranoia may dominate their outlook for many years. A basic sense of trust and happiness may not develop. They may see the world as hostile, depriving, and dangerous. Of course, a person's personality is not fixed at this early age. Later years are also vital, but these first months are critical to getting babies off to a good start. Too much frustration early in life can compromise their later psychological adjustment.

During the first six months after birth, children need to believe in their omnipotence to develop fundamental confidence in their security. Parents instinctively help with this by responding to their newborns as quickly as possible. It is hard-wired in our genetic programming to react to human babies' cries. It would be absurd to argue that two-week-old infants should wait an hour to eat when they are hungry just to toughen them up, or for some other crazy reason. Their bodies need the regular nourishment, while their minds need the repeated experience that their environment will provide for them. Infantile omnipotence and basic trust develop hand-in-hand during those initial months.

Ironically, over the next several years and decades children gradually learn that their place in the universe is not so central after all and that frustration, delay, pain, disappointment, and other stresses are an unavoidable part of life. Bit by bit, they recognize that they are not the prime mover of the cosmos and they do not control other people. Parents have an unspoken understanding of this reality. After the first year of life or so, parents intuitively grasp that they should no longer try to provide everything their youngsters want whenever they want it. Parents begin to say "no," which compels their children to face some frustrating realities. Sometimes kids simply have to wait, and sometimes they cannot have what they want at all. Of course, they throw tantrums. They thought, for good reasons, the world revolved around them. It takes time and growth to surrender that intoxicating sense of omnipotence.

Healthy emotional development requires a reasonable balance between getting what we want and being told "no." Depriving children of food, protection, or love can be emotionally damaging, but indulging their every whim is also detrimental. In both cases, children may continue to think that they are the center of the universe. They feel that the world should grant their every desire. It may seem obvious why coddled children can come across this way to others. They usually get what they want, and so never truly recognize that the world does not revolve around them. It seems confusing that deprived children can feel the same way. If they are used to neglect and privation, why can they appear self-absorbed?

Too much hardship and adversity can prompt children, and adults even, to cling to the illusion of infantile omnipotence well past the first months of life. In effect, their reality is so challenging that they isolate emotionally and comfort themselves by nurturing the idea that the world does, or should, cater to their desires as it did during infancy. They mask emotional pain by imagining that they can have anything they want. This unrealistic fantasy usurps the energy needed for healthy engagement in the world. In the language of psychoanalysis, people can become "fixated" at a developmental stage, meaning they have not developed much beyond it. At other times, people grow but are said to "regress" to an earlier stage when faced with overwhelming stress. Consequently, a fixation at or regression to an illusion of personal omnipotence can result from deprivation and abuse, as well as privilege and indulgence.

Though it is unrealistic, we all dream of getting whatever we want. This desire is understandable since we lived through a period as babies when it seemed that was exactly how things worked. For brief periods, it is fun to pretend that we are that powerful infant who magically controls the entire universe. This fantasy will never lose its appeal.

To see how *Star Trek* portrays the stage of infantile omnipotence, we will first discuss two episodes, "Shore Leave" followed by "The Menagerie." In the next chapter, we will look at Captain Kirk's personality and his relationship to the *Enterprise*.

Shore Leave

> Three months without a break has exhausted the *Enterprise* crew. The landing party discovers a peaceful, Earth-like world, the perfect spot for some rest and recreation. The setting reminds Dr. McCoy of *Alice in Wonderland*. McCoy turns around to see a person-sized white rabbit dressed in a plaid jacket with an umbrella under its arm. The bunny looks at his pocket watch and says, "Oh, my paws and whiskers! I'll be late." It hops away through a hole in the hedges. A pretty young girl follows.

The *Enterprise*'s complement is like a bunch of needy children. The members are tired out and are longing to be soothed and pampered. Like young children who are waiting for an adult to attend to them, the ship's personnel are hungry for a concierge to supply the tender loving care they crave.

The planet has the role of a parent in this episode. It is a beautiful, idyllic place that promises to revitalize the weary crew. Thus, this episode opens with some depleted children and a parent surrogate who can seemingly satisfy their needs.

The appearance of Alice and the rabbit confirms the suspicion that the theme of this episode originates in childhood. Youth is the time of life when we first encounter *Alice in Wonderland*. The overgrown cottontail also sets the lighthearted tone that continues throughout this adventure, despite the dangers that emerge.

Kirk, McCoy, and Yeoman Tonia Barrows examine the rabbit's footprints. Kirk puts all landing parties on standby until the mystery can be solved.

Gunshots ring out; Kirk, McCoy, and Barrows run to investigate. Mr. Sulu is testing an old-style revolver he found in the grass, a make and model that he had coveted for many years. He says, "I know. It's a crazy coincidence." As they leave this scene, an antenna secretly follows Captain Kirk and Dr. McCoy, the first sign of a purpose behind the mystery.

While walking with McCoy, Kirk describes a class bully named Finnegan he knew in the Academy. Within seconds, Finnegan appears out of nowhere and mischievously strikes Kirk in the face, daring him to fight. The scrap barely starts when Barrows screams, having just been accosted by Don Juan. Kirk then meets Ruth, a former sweetheart. They embrace tenderly.

It is apparent at this point that the planet is manufacturing whatever Kirk and the others are thinking about at any one moment. The white rabbit and young girl appeared just as Dr. McCoy remembered *Alice in Wonderland*. The old-style revolver was a dream come true for Mr. Sulu. Kirk was reflecting on Finnegan and Ruth just before they materialized. The landing party's thoughts and memories instantly become real.

The planet is providing for the landing party the same way grownups tend to young children. Just as good parents read their children's cues and deliver what they need, the alien world is scanning the minds of the visitors and bringing their passing fancies to life. To babies, it is beyond comprehension how adults know what to provide. Similarly, it is a mystery to Kirk and the others how the planet is magically bringing their imaginings to life.

It appears as if Kirk, McCoy, Barrows, and Sulu have created these unlikely people and things with the power of their minds. If you think of something and it suddenly appears, it is natural to presume that there exists a cause and effect relationship. With our natural inclination to find patterns in nature, it is easy to understand how newborns conclude that their thoughts create and control everything in the universe. When they want something and then it appears, they instinctively assume that they caused it all to happen. As infants, they have no other life experience to draw upon.

The landing party encounters a tiger, a World War II fighter plane, and a Samurai warrior. When a knight on horseback charges McCoy, the doctor decides to stand his ground. He tells Barrows that hallucinations can't harm them. McCoy dies from a lance thrust to the chest, proving that the inexplicable people and things are dangerously real.

For better or worse, Barrow's character is a female stereotype from another time. She conjures up a princess' gown and needs a strong man to protect her. She sobs when McCoy is killed; in contrast, Kirk and Spock are upset but remain composed. The damsel-in-distress archetype may have gone without comment in the 1960s, but it feels condescending fifty years later.

Kirk shoots the knight with Sulu's revolver since their phasers are not working. He and Spock discover that it is a dummy made of multicellular castings, suggesting that it has been manufactured. The same material makes up the plants and everything else on the planet. When Kirk and Spock look away for a few seconds, McCoy's body and the knight disappear.

Finnegan returns and seduces Captain Kirk into a brawl. They beat each other up, but Kirk comes out on top. Spock asks Kirk if he enjoyed himself. Surprised, the captain realizes that he did. Mr. Spock wonders if the planet is engineering these people and things for the enjoyment of the visitors.

A benevolent, elderly gentleman appears and introduces himself as the caretaker of the planet. He explains that another race built this world for their entertainment and pleasure. It is a high-tech amusement park where anything that pleases can happen. Even McCoy's death is reversible. The doctor returns alive with a beautiful woman on each arm, happier than ever. Captain Kirk approves shore leave for the entire crew. Ruth returns, and he goes off with her.

With the mystery solved, the crew is now free to indulge their wildest dreams. This episode touches people because it takes us back to a time in our lives when this fantasy seemed real. During the stage of infantile omnipotence, it appeared as if somebody anticipated our desires and needs and then provided for them without question. In the adult psyche, there is nostalgia for these early months of life when we believed that we were the source of creation. We long to recapture the sense of unlimited power. This fantasy originates in infancy, but it lives on in our mind throughout life.

The caretaker says some interesting things. "But none of this is permanent. Here you only have to imagine your fondest wishes. Anything that pleases you can be made to happen." The caretaker's people created the world so they could come and "play."

Notice how well this exposition fits with the idea of infantile omnipotence. Nothing is permanent because in a young child's mind the world changes from moment to moment. Imagination creates reality. Wishes will be satisfied. As in "The Changeling," death is reversible because the story echoes an embryonic outlook on the world from early in our lives when the natural laws of the universe did not apply. The entire ship's complement gets to beam down and play without payment of any sort, which reflects the experience of babies; parents feed and nurture their children free of charge. Adults often talk of "playing" as a diversion or respite from serious responsibilities. In contrast, youngsters' play is critical to their growth. It helps them develop physical and cognitive skills, and master new challenges.

Many of society's institutions gratify our latent fantasies of omnipotence. Restaurants cater to our wish to have food appear whenever we want it. When you walk in, you get a menu with a wide variety of possible choices. Just say which one you want, and it will be prepared and brought to you without your lifting a finger. Naming the food magically causes it to arrive. Like the shore leave planet, restaurants read our mind and provide what we want; they feed and care for us. When finished with your meal, you just walk away and leave the mess for somebody else to clean up. However, there is one detail about the experience that differs from childhood. Adults drop a few pieces of paper on the table. We call it "money," but it is just pressed wood pulp. The whole thing is magic, indeed.

Resorts fulfill the same omnipotent longings on a grander scale. A vacation cruise is the ultimate in being pampered. Aboard a luxury liner, one can never grow hungry because there is delicious food available around the clock. There is also entertainment, activities, and other stimulation to keep the vacationer unceasingly pleased, satisfied, and excited. All that is asked of us is one moment at the end when we pay the bill.

The *Star Trek* episode "The Menagerie" also explores the stage of infantile omnipotence; some background information is needed to understand the comments I will make about it. "The Menagerie" is the original *Trek* pilot film wrapped up in new packaging.

The term "television pilot" refers to a standalone episode of a proposed series, used to sell the concept to a network. It is a trial run to see if the show has potential and is worth the investment. If the media corporation likes the sample, it will typically authorize a season's production or a certain number of episodes. Sometimes, the pilot airs as the first installment of the show. In other cases, it is more of a prototype, as elements might change along the way to a full season of episodes.

"The Cage" is the original *Star Trek* pilot film. It featured Captain Christopher Pike in command of the *Enterprise*. Mr. Spock is the only familiar character among the crew, but he had a less significant role and freely showed his emotions. The producers retained Spock in the second pilot and changed his personality to the logical, emotionally unresponsive Vulcan science officer fans know and love. NBC rejected "The Cage" because it was "too cerebral." The reasons for this criticism will become clear as we discuss the episode.

NBC recognized a promising series format and gave *Star Trek* another chance. It approved the production of a follow-up pilot, which starred James Kirk as captain of the *Enterprise*. For the first time in history, a network gave a proposed series concept an additional opportunity to prove itself. NBC accepted the new trial run, "Where No Man Has Gone Before," and *Star Trek* entered the line-up for the Fall 1966 television season. We discuss the second pilot in Chapter 8.

The network wanted to use "The Cage" as part of the series rather than let it go to waste. They presented the episode by enclosing it within another story, "The Menagerie," starring Captain Kirk, Mr. Spock, and the other familiar *Trek* characters. Captain Pike's adventure appears as a remembrance surrounded by the larger narrative.

We will discuss the original episode, followed by the plot created to present it as having happened in the past. The framing story is weak in many ways, but it does correct one of the flaws that prompted NBC officials to reject "The Cage" as the basis for an entire series.

The Cage

The *Enterprise* receives a faint distress call from an Earth ship that crashed eighteen years ago in the Talos star system. Captain Pike refuses to investigate without more substantial evidence that there are survivors. This decision seems odd and insensitive. Something is troubling the commander.

Dr. Boyce, the ship's physician, joins Pike in his quarters. The captain is upset about a recent mission where a few of the crew members lost their lives. Guilt, self-doubt, and resentment fill his mind. He is not happy with the responsibilities of a starship commander and longs for a simpler life. He considers putting in his resignation. Dr. Boyce hears him out but becomes a bit impatient. "A man either lives life as it happens to him and meets it head-on and licks it, or turns his back on it and starts to wither away."

Mr. Spock interrupts to tell Captain Pike that a second message has confirmed that there are survivors on Talos IV. Pike agrees to investigate.

Captain Pike's personality is one reason why NBC rejected this pilot film. He is not very likable. Irritable and melancholy, he torments himself with guilt and self-reproach over their recent mission. He appears unconcerned with the plight of the possible crash victims and does not seem to like his command. Why is Pike so unhappy?

We learn what is troubling the captain during the scene in his cabin. Underneath a competent exterior, he resents his responsibilities. He longs for simpler days when others demanded little of him. Somebody else should make the hard choices and be accountable. Bemoaning the obligations of his rank, he yearns for the life of a youngster.

Self-pity explains why Pike is insensitive to the first distress message. It is difficult for him to render aid when he feels so depleted himself. His callous attitude towards the call for help reflects how he feels the world is treating him, taking him for granted. Woe is me!

Pike is not a happy man and not the type of commander suited for an ongoing television series. His emotional turmoil makes "The Cage" an interesting episode, but it would be difficult to extend his character into other adventures. NBC probably recognized this problem; it rejected the pilot but not the series format.

If Pike feels dissatisfied and bitter, how did he rise to the level of captain? Apparently, he sought the exact opposite of what he says he wants.

Pike's pursuit of starship command is an example of what some have called "counterphobic behavior." He seeks out the very thing that he fears. His dread of responsibility has driven him to come up through the ranks. Pike yearns for an uncomplicated life, but these longings are so frightening and unacceptable that he rejects them. Of course, his accomplishments do not make Pike stop wanting to be young again; it only buries these wishes out of sight.

Captain Pike is a tragic character who longs for something he will never allow himself to have. He is very different from Captain Kirk. Both of them become commanders for unconscious reasons, but Kirk is more likable and inspiring. He is vigorous, self-assured, and loves being in charge. Captain Kirk contributed substantially to *Star Trek*'s success, whereas Captain Pike would have been a liability.

I am not suggesting that Pike or anybody else should walk away from their roles whenever they feel stressed. There are ways to nurture our inner child without throwing off all adult responsibilities. However, we must first accept that this true self is there. We cannot hear its voice if we never let it talk.

Dr. Boyce responds to Pike as a friend and fellow officer. He is concerned and compassionate, but he also conveys the expectation that Pike will pull himself out of his funk. A captain must be ready for action at all times. A doctor of mental health likely would have handled the encounter differently, inviting Pike to say more.

> Captain Pike and the landing party beam down to the fourth planet of the Talos star system where the Earth ship crashed years ago. The survivors are all elderly male scientists, except for a young, beautiful, and mysterious woman named Vina. Dr. Boyce discovers that the survivors are all in perfect health. Vina offers to show Captain Pike the secret of their well-being and guides him away from the group.

> Vina leads Pike into a trap. The alien inhabitants of the planet arrive, drug Pike, and kidnap him underground. The researchers and their camp disappear. It was an illusion used to capture the captain.

> Pike awakens in a cage and confronts his captors. They are small and frail, with large, grotesque heads. The aliens communicate telepathically rather than by speaking and intend to experiment on Pike.

Three elements in this section draw our attention to hidden parts of the mind. First, the Talosians drug Captain Pike; they knock him out. The subsequent action will represent fantasies he keeps away from his awareness when fully awake. Next, his kidnappers take him underground. We often picture unconscious thoughts and wishes as underneath the surface, buried, or deep down somewhere. Thirdly, the Talosians' telepathy directs our attention to the internal workings of the brain, in contrast with the world of reality. The mind-reading, telepathic power of the Talosians puts them in a parental role, as young children typically think their parents know everything.

> Pike finds himself back on Rigel VII, the scene of the crew's recent death struggle. He battles a savage barbarian, but this time Vina is there, and it is up to him to save her. She intrigues him, but he tries not to let this show. Knowing that the scene is an illusion, he wonders aloud why his captors picked Vina again. Why not another woman? He has little time for reflection, as the giant Rigellian attacks. Near exhaustion, Pike defeats his adversary.

After the struggle, the captain and Vina are back in the cage. Pike questions whether she is real or not. She assures him that she is a woman as real and as human as he is. Vina adds that anything in the entire universe can be his, just by thinking about it! She can wear whatever he wishes, be whatever woman he desires. She implores him to pick a dream and let her live it with him, but Pike rebukes her with contempt.

The Talosians are offering Pike the untroubled life he was craving a few hours earlier. He would be free of the command responsibilities that weigh so heavily upon him and could instantaneously have whatever he wanted, including the woman of his dreams. Why doesn't this intoxicating offer tempt the captain?

Pike is, indeed, profoundly enticed but he is afraid to let this show. On an unconscious level, he wishes to be pampered like a child, but these thoughts are so frightening that he forcefully rejects them. When the opportunity appears to live out his secret fantasies, he recoils from it.

Captain Pike deals with his temptation by going to the opposite extreme. He scornfully discards this world of fantasy when he covertly longs for it. He spurns Vina when he would really like to fling himself into her arms. By focusing only on his anger, he attempts to hide his yearning from himself and the world. He uses disdain and contempt to stifle his desire for Vina and his fascination with this world of make-believe.

I am not suggesting that Captain Pike should be happy with the Talosians. Indeed, they tricked him, kidnapped him, and are now holding him against his will. Pike has good reason to be angry. The irritating issue is that he is not honest with himself. His inner torment is on display. Tortured souls are often ill-equipped to prevail in trying circumstances. They are more often the subject of tragedy, not the upbeat, optimistic, happy-ending narratives we associate with *Star Trek*.

Pike convinces Vina to give him some information about the Talosians. Following a nuclear war, they moved underground and developed their mental capacities, letting their physical skills atrophy. Dreams became more important than reality. They hope to find a race who will help them rebuild their planet.

The Talosians punish Vina for revealing too much, while Captain Pike discovers that they cannot read through violent emotions. Anger and hostility block their telepathic abilities. He resolves to keep his mind filled with hate.

Suddenly, Pike finds himself back home on Earth, having a picnic with Vina. In spite of his resolve, he is charmed by the setting and by Vina's affection.

"The Cage" was written by *Star Trek* creator, Gene Roddenberry. He had a vision of the future in which society had overcome racial divisions and other evils that have their roots in human nature. From all appearances, Roddenberry meant to deliver an optimistic message with *Star Trek* and help us understand ourselves a little better. "The Cage" comments on our idiosyncrasies on a variety of levels; it is a complex piece of work.

The following dialogue was cut when the pilot "The Cage" was used as a reminiscence in "The Menagerie." It expresses how Captain Pike had grown as a result of the experience on Talos IV.

Pike pets his horse and sips some coffee while Vina gets lunch ready. He says, "It's funny. Just about twenty-four hours ago I was telling the ship's doctor how much I wanted something not very different from what we have here. Escape from reality. A life with no frustrations. No responsibilities. Now that I have it, I understand the doctor's answer. Because you either live life, bruises, skinned knees and all, or you turn your back on it and start dying."

Pike's musings were dropped so he could appear to have learned nothing from his experience. The emotional growth gets delayed until the end of "The Menagerie." The editing was necessary, but it also makes Pike look like more of a sourpuss than Roddenberry intended.

Vina tells Pike that the Talosians scanned her thoughts and dreams as to her perfect man. That is why they picked Pike for her. She says, "I can't help but love you. And they expect you to feel the same way." He lets down his guard and admits that he is attracted to her.

As Pike confesses his intrigue, the camera zooms out from a close-up of him to the same image on a screen with the main Talosian keeper and another looking on. It is a creepy sequence, showing how the captors were manipulating Pike. At the same time, one almost feels flattered that they take such an interest in him.

Roddenberry also dropped the following dialogue in the transition from "The Cage" to "The Menagerie"; he directed both episodes. The keeper comments telepathically to the other Talosian, "A curious species. They have fantasies they hide even from themselves." Perhaps Roddenberry decided that this notion was implied and did not need to be said aloud.

The scene changes; Vina appears as a green slave girl, dancing erotically for Pike and some other men. He is titillated but leaves the room anyway.

A six-member rescue team enters the transporter on the *Enterprise*, but somehow only the two women dematerialize, Number One and Yeoman Colt. They appear in the cage with Pike and Vina. The Talosians tell the captain that he now has a choice amongst three females. Unaffected, the captain continues to keep his mind filled with anger and hate.

The Talosians are making their offer to Captain Pike even more tempting. He is now the only man amidst three attractive women, not an uncommon male fantasy. Some of the dialogue and reactions are quite amusing, in spite of the stereotypes. The situation arouses Pike, but he cannot let himself become aware of these feelings. He doubles his effort to fill his mind with hate so he can ward off the rising temptation he feels to give in to desire.

It is curious that Captain Pike goes right back to hating after his enlightenment in the picnic scene and his tenderness towards Vina. It now feels like Gene Roddenberry just threw in Pike's reflection on life to force him to show some growth. It is also odd to have such a moment in the middle of the story, as opposed to the end. In any case, I do not think much is lost by omitting the dialogue because it feels like his self-reflection hasn't changed anything.

Pike captures the keeper as the Talosian quietly opens a panel into the cage. The group and their hostage flee to the planet's surface. Once there, they are still unable to contact the *Enterprise* and escape.

Captain Pike offers to stay if the Talosians will release the two female officers. Number One insists that it is wrong to create a race of slaves and sets her phaser to explode and kill them all. She deactivates the charge when two other Talosians arrive, bringing with them some new information about the history of humanity.

The Talosians are shocked to learn that humans despise captivity, even when pleasant and benevolent. Pike and the others are therefore useless to the Talosians and are allowed to go free.

Why does Pike offer to remain on the planet if the Talosians free the two female crew members? If he is so horrified by this world, why would he agree to stay under any circumstances?

Captain Pike's proposal confirms the suspicion that secretly he is tempted by Vina and by life on Talos IV. Making this phony grand sacrifice would allow him to remain and indulge his fantasies, but it would appear as if he were doing so strictly to save the others. Instead of admitting that he felt all mixed up inside, he could maintain the illusion that he was acting altruistically. This self-serving pseudo-sacrifice does not turn him from a troubled soul into a heroic figure.

Tempting as the fantasy world may be, it would not be healthy or natural for Pike to stay on Talos IV. He would be stuck forever in the role of a child, dependent on the Talosians for all his needs. Instead of facing his adult responsibilities, he would be running from them. Pike would be living in a world of make-believe, denying that he is a fully-grown man.

It is also unhealthy for him to deny his fantasy life and longings, even if they seem childish and irrational. Everybody dreams of a world like Talos IV, where we could create whatever reality we choose. This sense of omnipotence takes us back to the first months of life when it seemed like we could fashion anything we wanted with our thoughts alone. We have a hungry longing to recapture that lost paradise. Captain Pike is so frightened by his inner child that he runs away. It would not have hurt him to have a little more fun. Instead, he fills his mind with such violence and hatred that it blocks out everything else.

I expect that NBC rejected this pilot film because it suggests that our fantasies are depraved and we need to fight against them. This attack on whimsy is not the message that fans want to hear. Viewers turn to television and movies to indulge their dreams, not to denounce them.

> Number One and Yeoman Colt beam up first, giving Pike a few minutes alone with Vina and the Talosians. In reality, the spaceship's crash landing eighteen years prior maimed and disfigured Vina. After revealing her true appearance, the keeper gives her beauty back to her—and more. Captain Pike watches as Vina and a fantasy version of him walk happily hand-in-hand back to the entrance and descend underground.

"The Cage" contrasts with "Shore Leave," in which Captain Kirk and the others enjoyed their brief taste of infantile omnipotence in adult form. Unlike Pike, they embraced the temporary escape from it all and looked upon their short respite with fondness.

Let's now look at "The Menagerie," the episode starring Captain Kirk and the other *Star Trek* regulars that NBC used to frame "The Cage." The plot is forced, but it does confirm some observations made about Captain Pike and radically changes the ending.

The Menagerie

The *Enterprise* receives a communication from former Captain Christopher Pike to divert immediately to Star Base Eleven. When they arrive, nobody knows anything about the message. Captain Pike could not have sent it because he is now completely disabled. He is confined to a wheelchair, unable to move or speak. During an accident, Captain Pike voluntarily exposed himself to radiation to rescue some other people.

Captain Pike's heroic act shows, again, how he takes responsibility for others as a way to hide from his longings to be dependent and carefree. These childlike wishes are so frightening to him that he goes to the other extreme. He sacrifices himself to rescue other people. He tries to prove to himself and the world that he lacks any concern for his wants and needs. How could anyone suspect he wishes to be a kid when he is selflessly putting himself in harm's way?

The self-sacrifice not only covers up his desire to be nurtured but it also satisfies the wish for dependency at the same time. Now that he is disabled, other people will be forced to provide for him. He no longer has the responsibilities that he found so troubling. Captain Pike's altruistic act shows how a deed can express an unconscious wish and simultaneously defend against it. His gallantry suggests he cares nothing about himself, that he lives to serve those in need. At the same time, he injures himself so severely that he will be profoundly reliant on other people for the rest of his life. He satisfies his unconscious wish in this tragic, self-destructive manner.

I am not criticizing this fictional hero for his bravery or martyrdom. Indeed, people who risk their own life and safety to aid those in peril deserve our thanks and admiration. What I am saying, however, is that it would be better if Captain Pike, and people in general, are aware of and comfortable with all the emotions, dreams, and longings that they feel inside. There should be no shame linked with the lingering traces of infantile omnipotence we all carry with us into adulthood. This legacy is a part of who we are. In the privacy of our minds, a rich fantasy life deserves celebration.

Spock kidnaps Captain Pike and illegally takes over the *Enterprise* while Kirk is off the ship. His goal is to transport Pike back to Talos IV. Captain Kirk and Commodore Mendez catch up with the *Enterprise* in a shuttlecraft. Spock places himself under arrest. He pleads guilty to mutiny and will face the death penalty if the *Enterprise* enters the Talos star system in violation of General Order VII. As part of the proceedings, Spock presents a video of Captain Pike's adventure on Talos as evidence.

The Talosians invite Captain Pike to come back to Talos IV for the remainder of his life, and he agrees. He and Vina are reunited. Starfleet drops charges against Mr. Spock after they receive the same transmissions seen aboard the *Enterprise*. They approve of Pike's return to Talos IV.

Is Starfleet one or two words, "Starfleet" or "Star Fleet"? Sources vary, but I consider a scene in "The Menagerie" the definitive statement on the matter. Commodore Mendez unseals a document for Kirk to read regarding Talos IV. On the cover, it states in all caps, "Top Secret For Eyes of Starfleet Command Only." The first page of the document uses the noun "Starfleet" three times, written as one word. Starfleet is "Starfleet."

The framing story fundamentally changes the ending, making the episode more palatable. Captain Pike, who repudiated his fantasies the first time he was on Talos IV, now embraces them. He can stay with Vina, which is what a part of him wanted to do all along. Initially the persecutors and villains, the Talosians are now the saviors. They are interested in Pike for who he is, not for whatever labor he might supply. The Talosians' motivation is now humanitarian.

This new ending gives a more upbeat message: we can enjoy our fantasies even if they are entirely unrealistic. Kirk looks on with some envy as Pike walks back into his dream world, where anything is possible by merely wishing it. "The Menagerie" uses the final footage on Talos IV differently than "The Cage." As Pike walks with Vina at the end, it is not her imagined version of him; it is the real Christopher Pike eighteen years later restored to full health in mind and body.

We all know that we cannot reject everyday reality and live in a world of fantasy. An escape to that degree borders on madness. However, it is stifling to hide from our imaginings as Captain Pike did the first time he was on Talos IV. It is fun and exciting to live out our whims via television, movies, and other art forms. As long as we remain aware of what is real and what is pretend, indulging our fancies can be enchanting.

Chapter 4: Captain Kirk's Magic

We discussed how infants feel all-powerful and how unconscious longings to recapture that experience play out in *Star Trek* episodes. This chapter will examine how Captain Kirk embodies the sense of infantile omnipotence and how this aspect of his character makes Kirk captivating to fans. His ability to revive a sense of invincibility in viewers makes him an appealing hero. Kirk portrays the stage of infantile omnipotence in three ways: his ability to master any problem, his driving need to remain in control of situations, and his relationship to the *Enterprise*. We will discuss each of these points in turn.

Captain Kirk is a robust and commanding character. During his career, he saves the human race several times over. He defeats a plethora of malevolent forces, talks several computers into killing themselves, and initiates fundamental shifts in other cultures despite the Federation Prime Directive of noninterference. His power and ability seem almost godlike. Captain Kirk can trounce any enemy, solve any problem, and overcome any obstacle. His list of accomplishments makes an impressive resume.

Kirk's extraordinary abilities parallel infants' belief that they have complete control over the world. When babies wish for something and it suddenly appears, they conclude that it was their command that caused the event to happen. Their conception of cause and effect is still archaic and naïve; they wildly overestimate the power of their mind.

Throughout life, we continue to suspect that our thoughts and desires can control reality. Young children demonstrate this belief with their faith in magic, chants, and other superstitions. The tendency is also present in adults, mostly at an unconscious level. We continue to think that our brainwaves can magically control the world, even though we know that this is absurd. We saw this theme in two *Star Trek* episodes in the last chapter; it appears in others as well. In "Plato's Stepchildren," the people of planet Plutonius have telekinetic powers that allow them to move objects at will. Trelane, in "The Squire of Gothos," creates planets out of nothing and controls the *Enterprise* crew with childish notions and role-playing.

Captain Kirk resonates with the sense of infantile omnipotence that remains unconsciously present within us. We all want to command the world, change it to our satisfaction, solve any problem, and come out on top. Identifying with Kirk, we vicariously participate in his triumph over the adversaries and complications that face the *Enterprise*. Captain Kirk takes us back to the time when it seemed that we did have complete mastery of the world. Audiences enjoy the feeling that anything is possible, merely by wishing it.

Characters from other television shows, movies, and literature also resonate with this unconscious sense of omnipotence. The stereotyped western hero is an example, killing two dozen people with one six-shooter while simultaneously evading a small army of villains. James Bond is a modern version of the larger-than-life hero. Going against billion-to-one odds, he always wins out. Superheroes also owe their popularity to our wish to identify with all-powerful beings; typically, these characters have an Achilles' heel to make them more relatable and enhance the dramatic tension.

Control

Captain Kirk's personality drives him to stay in control of situations at almost any cost. This trait frequently appears throughout the series. A good illustration occurs in "This Side of Paradise," which we will discuss in the next chapter. In this episode, spores take over the minds of the crew and induce a state of perfect serenity. Kirk cannot tolerate this "happiness" if it means he is no longer in complete control of himself and the situation. Of all the crew, he alone has the willpower to drive off the spore's influence without any help. Everybody else seems willing to live under their spell.

Kirk's account of how he dealt with the Kobayashi Maru simulation of *Star Trek II: The Wrath of Khan* is another illustration of his controlling personality trait. The movie opens on the bridge of the *Enterprise*; in the captain's chair sits Saavik, a young female Vulcan commander. The ship receives a distress call from a damaged Federation freighter, the *Kobayashi Maru*, within the Neutral Zone. Though entering the Neutral Zone is a violation of the treaty with the warlike Romulans, Saavik decides to attempt a rescue. Romulan warships surround the *Enterprise* and attack without hesitation. The ship is on the verge of utter annihilation when the front of the bridge opens. Admiral Kirk enters, revealing the scene to be a simulation; it is a test of leadership. How would a potential captain respond in a "no-win scenario?" The commanding officer can either ignore the freighter's distress call or answer it and get blown to bits.

Several times, Lieutenant Saavik asks Admiral Kirk how he handled the Kobayashi Maru. Eventually, he tells her. He reprogrammed the computer so he could complete the simulation successfully. "I don't believe in a no-win scenario," he explains to Saavik. Starfleet gave him a commendation for original thinking.

Even in a recreation, Captain Kirk feels compelled to stay in control of the situation. His character drives him to find a solution where none exists, to defeat the most formidable enemies and to turn a seemingly hopeless situation into a success. He cannot tolerate feeling weak or helpless.

This personality trait reactivates our unconscious sense of omnipotence. Throughout our adulthood, we still wish we could control everything around us. This feeling originates in infancy but persists throughout life to different degrees. Over the years, we learn that there are many things beyond our influence. It is still fun to dream that we have total power over the world.

Captain Kirk's personality enhances the viewer's sense of control. The audience knows that Kirk will feel compelled to triumph over whatever predicament arises. He will not allow events to get away from him. James T. may be temporarily vulnerable and helpless at the beginning of the episode, which enhances the dramatic tension. By the end, he always has the upper hand.

Because viewers enjoy identifying with Kirk, his driving need to stay in command is never challenged by those around him. The negative side of this personality trait is left unexplored until the *Star Trek* movies. Neither the *Enterprise* officers nor the viewers seem interested in questioning his judgment. The crew wishes to believe that their leader is infallible; viewers also suspend any criticism of his decisions. By the end of the episode, everyone seems happy and satisfied. If there were disagreements during the crisis, they no longer seem to matter. There are no after-action reports. Things have turned out well, and life aboard the *Enterprise* is back to normal.

Though he occasionally makes some questionable judgments, Kirk rarely faces any criticism of his decisions or the adverse consequences that may result from them. His most indefensible action during the original series occurred in "Let That Be Your Last Battlefield." In that episode, the *Enterprise* encounters two alien men who are half black and half white. Though one is considered a criminal and the other a police officer, both seethe with hatred toward each other. Bele, the law enforcer, asks Kirk to take them to their home planet, Cheron. After consulting with Starfleet, Kirk advises Bele that he must go through diplomatic channels. Dissatisfied, Bele takes over the *Enterprise* with his formidable mental powers and sets a course for Cheron. Kirk initiates the ship's self-destruct sequence. He will destroy the *Enterprise* unless Bele returns control to him immediately.

To say that Captain Kirk was overreacting would be generous. Bele did not want to harm the ship or the crew. When they had reached Cheron, Bele would have freed the ship. Losing control, even temporarily, is intolerable for Kirk. At the last second Bele gives in, so Kirk wins the test of wills. Nevertheless, there was no justification for putting the ship and the crew at risk. This confrontation was unnecessary, and hundreds of people would have died if Bele had not capitulated. In spite of this action's recklessness, nobody challenges Kirk. In a real-life situation like this, the crew would be angry about their unwarranted brush with death, and there would be an administrative review of Kirk's actions.

Viewers accept Kirk's decisions because of their wish to identify with an authoritative and unbeatable character. I am not implying that *Star Trek* should be more realistic; expecting this would take some fun out of the series. The observations are meant to explain why the captain appeals to audiences.

Now I Know Why It's Called "She"

The third way that Captain Kirk portrays the stage of infantile omnipotence is in his relationship with the *Enterprise*. The ship represents Kirk's mother. I am using the term "mother" over the gender-neutral word "parent" because the dialogue in some episodes refers to the *Enterprise* as "her" or "she." The quote above this paragraph comes from "The Naked Time." The starship metaphorically plays many of the roles a parent does with small children. Kirk is enmeshed with the *Enterprise*, almost symbiotically. This attachment parallels children's profound bond with their moms.

The ship's life support systems refer to the vital functions of mothers with their youngsters. Both provide food, warmth, and protection in a potentially hostile world. The ship seems big and mighty to the crew, as a caretaker appears large and resilient to small children. With a woman's voice, the ship's computer provides an endless source of information, as adults seem to know everything to their young offspring.

The *Enterprise* protects Kirk and the crew as they explore the galaxy. Similarly, parents protect children as they discover their surroundings. Kirk investigates strange new worlds and new civilizations, but the ship is always in the background. Safety is only a transporter beam away. Young children venture out but are within the sphere of their mothers' protection. Wandering away from her, they test things out on their own. They always return to Mom for food, emotional support, and protection from danger.

Symbolically, Captain Kirk has his mother with him at all times, to protect him and provide for his needs. No matter how old we get, this fantasy will always be appealing. Even as independent, responsible adults, we dream of being held and protected. We long for a parental figure to provide for us.

Captain Kirk also commands the *Enterprise*. As infants conclude that they control the world, Kirk masters the ship that represents his caretaker. To a degree, he decides where the starship will go and what it will do. Kirk's position recreates children's impressions that they can control the people and things around them with their thoughts and wishes.

Though less intense, the rest of the crew have a similar relationship with the *Enterprise*; it represents a caretaker, so the crew members seem perfectly happy and content to be aboard her. Trapped in a steel hull for many months of the year, nobody ever complains. The *Enterprise* NCC-1701 of the original series does not even have any windows other than the bridge viewscreen. The work is tedious, yet nobody longs for home or a more traditional life. Symbolically, they have Mom with them all the time, and that seems enough. The *Enterprise* holds, feeds, and protects them, and so they are happy.

CHAPTER 5: PARADISE

In Chapter 2, we discussed the terror and paranoia infants endure when they are frustrated and in pain. The following section examined the stage of infantile omnipotence, the power and euphoria little ones feel when their parents provide what they need. These opposites are two vastly different feelings and experiences. How do infants make sense out of these extremes? How do they put these contradictory views of reality into a cohesive whole?

Children traverse three stages as they integrate their disparate views of the world. In the first phase, infants experience a global sense of merger and satisfaction alternating with a realm of deprivation, disconnection, and fear. They do not understand themselves as separate from the world around them. "This Side of Paradise" and "The Return of the Archons" illustrate this first phase. Youngsters then come to see themselves as separate from their surroundings before they can integrate nourishing and frustrating aspects of people into a single mental image. Thus in the second phase, kids see themselves as two different people and others as split personalities as well; this period is discussed and illustrated in Chapter Six. Chapter Seven looks at the final phase when children bring together the alternating images of a positive and negative self and a gratifying and depriving other.

Initially, infants do not understand that their moments of satisfaction and frustration belong to the same world. Instead, they believe that they live in two separate creations, one good and the other evil. Experiences involving aching or agony are part of the depraved cosmos, while pleasant stretches are part of the benevolent one. They do not realize that these contrasting realities are two different sides of the same realm. Infants detach and isolate the safe world from the dangerous one. In their minds, children magically jump back and forth between universes depending on how they feel at the time.

Separating the world into good and bad, aptly termed "splitting" in psychoanalytic thought, is a healthy, expected development in young children. This sorting of experiences into positive and negative is how infants create order out of their sensations and the world in which they find themselves. They segregate moments associated with pleasure from those linked with pain. Throughout life, we have an innate drive to understand what goes on around us; children are no different in this regard. Relegating their experiences into alternating virtuous and evil camps helps them organize the world and feel that they understand it.

Black-and-white thinking is intrinsic to human infants' makeup and is a necessary part of development. (In adults, this dichotomous thought process can be a problem; we'll discuss this issue later.) Babies' feelings and senses are their reality. Their joy and pain are undeniably real, while the natural laws of the universe are beyond their comprehension. They use their emotions to construct a model of the cosmos.

Though infants distinguish between unpleasant and satisfying experiences, they initially cannot differentiate what is a part of them and what belongs to the world around them. Physically, they do not understand what their bodies can do or what separates them from the rest of their environment. Mentally, they do not realize that their emotions do not extend beyond themselves and are not felt directly by the people and things in their lives. The distinction between themselves and the rest of the world has no meaning to babies. They have no sense of what are sometimes called "boundaries," what divides their body and emotions from the outside world. The ability to distinguish me from not-me will develop over time; it is not automatically present at birth.

A real-life example will show how infants lack a sense of their physical boundaries. When my daughter was a month old, she occasionally would grab her hair, pull it, and then scream. She had no idea what was happening. She could see her hands when they were in front of her, but she did not know that they were a part of herself. Further, she did not recognize that the little strands she felt with her hands were a part of her body. The scalp from which she felt the pain was also a mystery to her. She had not yet learned what things are a part of her physical makeup, how they work, and how much control she had over them. Distinguishing her body from the rest of the world was incomprehensible at that early age.

The chapters on projection and infantile omnipotence both illustrate how infants misconstrue the origin of their emotions. They believe that their rage arises outside themselves, rather than recognizing that it comes from within. When infants are content, their happiness seems to fill the universe and bestow godlike powers upon them. They cannot comprehend that their feelings are contained in their mind and do not control the rest of the universe. An emotional border between themselves and the world has not yet developed.

Because of their blurry physical and emotional boundaries, newborns feel fused with the world. Their caretakers are the most critical part of their environment, so infants commonly feel merged with them. Within their minds, they have a combined image of self and parent. Mom and Dad are a part of them, and vice versa. They do not feel separate or distinct from the adults around them.

Returning to a state of fusion with a life-giving parent is often equated with paradise. Throughout the rest of our lives, we long for the oneness we felt at that early age. The feeling of union with the rest of creation is one of humanity's most meaningful experiences. We dream of blissfully merging with a nurturing parental figure who will care for us.

Although appealing in many ways, this fantasy of union is also terrifying. Becoming a part of a larger whole would mean losing our individuality, our autonomy, and our identity—things we cherish. We would melt into an enormous conglomerate, sacrificing the things that make us uniquely who we are. Both the intriguing and the frightening side of this fusion fantasy can be found in *Star Trek* episodes, as we shall see.

Because children divide the world into good and evil, and cannot distinguish between their self and the rest of the world, they face two vital developmental tasks. First, they must recognize that they are separate, distinct individuals; youngsters need to grieve the illusion of merger with Mom and Dad. Second, they must learn that there are good and bad sides of everybody and everything. We will discuss these two developmental tasks in more detail.

Children must learn that they are physically and emotionally distinct from the rest of the world. Gradually, they discover what separates the inside of their body from the outer, and what their extremities and other parts can do. They also learn that their moods arise from within themselves and that other people may feel differently than they do. Children have to take ownership of their state of mind, rather than attributing it to others. Just because the child is angry does not mean the whole world is dangerous.

After children have a sense of boundaries, that they exist in the world but are distinct from it, they still have two opposing mental pictures of themselves. They continue to sort their experiences into those associated with satisfaction and pleasure as opposed to times when they feel hurt or upset. They see themselves as separate people at different times, depending on how they are feeling at that moment. At this stage, youngsters also have discrete good and bad images of other people. They see an adult as two different individuals depending on whether they perceive him or her to be friendly or mean.

The disparate images of oneself and others need to be brought together and integrated into more realistic pictures that have both positive and negative qualities. The loving self-identity and the hateful one need to call a truce and begin working together. The mental split must heal, mixing the desired personality and the frightening one. Youngsters grow to understand that there are good and bad aspects to all people, including themselves. They integrate the disparate images of the world into one whole that has attractive and unwelcome traits simultaneously.

My daughter illustrated the struggle to join contrasting images of me soon after her second birthday. Every morning for a couple of weeks she would say, "Two daddies! One daddy goes to work, and one daddy comes home." Notice also that she had not grasped the role of pronouns, repeating "daddy" three times as part of just twelve words. Within her mind, there were two pictures of me, one loving and the other cruel. The mean father left in the morning, making her feel angry and forsaken. When I came home at night, I was the caring dad. She felt happy and excited, and we would have fun playing together.

After a few weeks, my daughter had combined the two incompatible mental images of me. She stopped saying, "Two daddies." Rather, she would ask, "You come home tonight, Daddy?" She was beginning to understand that the awful parent who abandoned her in the morning was the same one that came home at night to love and play with her. I could both hurt her and bring her joy. Her struggle to integrate the good and bad was not over, but she had taken a big step. Note that once I became a single person in her eyes that she was able to use the pronoun "you."

The tendency to split our view of people and the world into good and evil remains present throughout life, despite our later emotional growth. These familiar phrases capture this inclination: black and white, us and them, all or nothing, guilty or innocent, you're with us or against us, wrong or right, friend or foe, and so on. Often in movies and literature, the protagonist is the good guy or gal; the villain is evil. Politically, the propensity to see issues or parties as black or white is ubiquitous.

In reality, most matters are complicated. Only in rare circumstances is one side wholly right or noble and the other entirely wrong or depraved. Most problems are thorny and involve many different factors and considerations. A more mature approach takes a balanced look at all the concerns involved in an issue.

With that said, I have come to think that black-and-white thinking deserves more of our respect. Not only was it normal at one time in our emotional and cognitive growth but it was also necessary. Any young mind that could not distinguish between moments they liked and those they did not would be profoundly disturbed indeed. In Cognitive Therapy, all-or-nothing thinking is called a "cognitive distortion." I understand the reason for this label, but what it misses is an appreciation for what dichotomous reasoning initially gave to us. It was the first way that we made sense of the world and brought order to chaos. I have come to view black-and-white thinking as more of a starting point than a distortion.

It is harder to integrate the two sides of issues when we are upset. When there are intense feelings involved, people are at risk of splitting the world into friends and enemies. We regress. After the storm, however, progress can begin again.

We can condense the developmental ideas discussed in this chapter into three periods and two steps. The first step is between phase one and two; the second one occurs as children transition from stage two to three. In the first phase, infants divide the world into good and bad but feel fused with the people and things around them. The second period occurs when children learn that they are separate, autonomous individuals, but they still split the images of themselves and others into two—one warm, fuzzy, happy, and satisfied, and the other hungry, upset, neglected, and angry. During this second stage, there are independent images of a friendly self and a hostile one, and separate warm and dangerous images of others. The third phase is when young people combine the good and bad imaginings of the same person into a cohesive whole. In healthy development, children reach this third stage around age three to four. At least during calm moments, they have an integrated view of themselves and the world.

There are *Star Trek* episodes that illustrate each of these three phases; we will begin with the first.

This Side of Paradise

Captain Kirk, Mr. Spock, Dr. McCoy, and some others beam down to Omicron Ceti III expecting to find the colonists dead. An expedition arrived three years previously, before the discovery of berthold rays. This radiation is harmless in small doses but is deadly over a period of months. The settlement seems deserted, until the group leader, Elias Sandoval, greets them warmly and informs them that all the colonists are alive and healthy. He says, "We have harmony here. Complete peace."

The planet represents the parent in this story. We have seen this metaphor before, in "The Apple" and "Shore Leave." The colonists and the *Enterprise* crew portray the children.

The settlement on Omicron Ceti III is only three years old, suggesting that the conflict portrayed in this episode originates in the early ages of life. In a sense, the colonists were "born" into their new world just thirty-six months previously to build a new civilization, just as babies enter the world at birth and begin constructing a new life.

There are two conflicting sides of Omicron Ceti III. The berthold rays make the planet toxic, but it is simultaneously protecting the settlers from this deadly reality. The nurturing and protective aspects of the environment reflect the positive image children have of themselves and others; the dangerous and lethal risks posed by the radiation mirror the mental images of an aching and angry self in a world of venom and monsters.

Kirk wants to learn why the settlers are still alive. Mr. Sulu discovers that there is no other animal life on the planet besides the immigrants. McCoy determines that the colonists are all in perfect health, too perfect. Traces of Sandoval's childhood pneumonia have miraculously disappeared, and his appendix has grown back. Kirk demands an explanation, but Sandoval says the matters are unimportant.

Kirk advises Sandoval to prepare his people for evacuation. The leader tells the captain that they are in no danger. They will not leave.

Here again, we see the planet's extremes. The absence of any other animal life is a reminder of the deadly berthold rays. On the other hand, something about the place shelters the colonists from the danger and restores them to pristine health. They live in a world of ideal peace and love. These opposites depict the all-good and all-bad images of the world formed by infants.

One of the colonists is Leila Kalomi, a beautiful botanist who was in love with Mr. Spock six years previously on Earth. She offers to show Spock the reason for the settlers' good health. She leads him to some strange looking vegetation, explaining that it gives "life, peace, and love." A plant sprays Mr. Spock with spores which cause him pain. Spock's distress alarms Leila, as humans aren't affected this way. The torment subsides, and the spores take over Spock's personality.

He first words to Leila are, "I love you. I can love you." They embrace. They look at the clouds, reflect on the beauty of rainbows, and climb trees together.

There are some delightful scenes in "This Side of Paradise." Spock's transformation is a sight to behold, as are the dumbfounded reactions of Kirk and McCoy.

The spores induce fusion with the perfectly nurturing side of Omicron Ceti III. The planet, the plants, the migrants, and now Mr. Spock all become interconnected and mostly indistinguishable. This episode depicts the state of merger we all felt during our first weeks of life before we understood the boundaries between our self and the world around us.

United with the benevolent side, Sandoval sees only the positive aspects of their situation. He dismisses the dangers posed by the berthold rays and says the issues raised by Captain Kirk are inconsequential. He can neither acknowledge the peril nor integrate it into a total picture of the situation.

The spores then swallow Mr. Spock into the hive. Like the colonists, he becomes united with the wholly munificent side of Omicron Ceti III. He leaves his worries behind as he enters a dominion of peace and love. Anything hazardous about the situation is forgotten. There is only desire and tenderness between him and Leila; all obstacles and conflicts have magically disappeared.

Mr. Spock's metamorphosis depicts the joy of becoming one with an all-good creation. Sickness, pain, and worry are gone, as if these things belong to another universe. We all have a nostalgia for this symbiotic period of life when we felt a blissful unity with the cosmos. The fantasy of returning to this state has an unmistakable charm.

Though Spock has gained a type of happiness, there are also things he has lost. He is missing the pleasure of his adult role and responsibilities. He enjoys his duties as science officer; the position is vital to his sense of identity. Looking at clouds is whimsical, but there is much more involved in adult life. He is forfeiting the challenges and satisfaction of being second in command of the *Enterprise*.

Spock has also lost his autonomy. Once the spores take over his personality, he can no longer decide for himself what he thinks and what he wants to do. He is no longer an individual. His identity has dissolved into the collective.

Why does Spock feel pain when the spores spray him? His anguish expresses the sting of giving up his autonomy, but this is not the complete answer. The human crew members also give up their independence, yet they do not feel tormented. Why is Spock the only one who feels this agony?

The pain inflicted by the spores shows how difficult it is for Mr. Spock to accept his wishes for intimacy with others. More than anybody else, Spock tries to deny his yearning for love and togetherness. He vigorously represses these desires and feels a bite when the spores challenge this repression. In later chapters, we will discuss why these emotions are so threatening to the Vulcan.

> Before Kirk can arrange for the settlers' evacuation, the spores infect everybody aboard the *Enterprise*. The entire ship's complement beams down to the planet. A plant sprays Captain Kirk as well, but it does not affect him. Spock and Sandoval try to convince him to stay. Spock says, "It's a true Eden, Jim. There's belonging, and love."

> Kirk responds, "No wants, no needs? We weren't meant for that. None of us. A man stagnates if he has no ambition, no desire to be more than he is."

This segment summarizes the central conflict of this episode. On one side is the longing to regress to a blissful state of fusion with a powerful and loving provider. The crew's exodus from the ship and Spock's appeal for Kirk to join them express this wish. Captain Kirk, on the other hand, represents the desire to preserve autonomy and separateness. He enjoys his adult responsibilities and does not want to surrender them. His strength of will keeps the spores at bay.

> Alone and despairing aboard the *Enterprise*, a plant resprays Kirk. This time, he responds like the others and prepares to beam down to the planet. Just before engaging the transporter, he has a surge of anger about the situation, which drives off the spores' effects. Kirk has found the answer; hostile emotion destroys Omicron Ceti III's hold over people.

> Captain Kirk lures Mr. Spock up to the *Enterprise* and then insults him. Spock tries to laugh off the abuse, but Kirk persists until Spock is enraged and attacks. As Kirk had planned, Spock's anger frees him from the spores' control.

The scene with Kirk and Spock in the transporter room is another gem. The plot summary above barely captures the power of this well-crafted episode; it also skips over some flourishes. If readers have never seen "This Side of Paradise," it's well worth viewing.

Anger destroys the spores' effect because it shatters the illusion of perfect bliss and belonging. The spores only allow feelings of love, peace, and togetherness. They embrace the fantasy that no other reality exists. Under their control, the colonists maintain an impression of paradise. When Kirk forces Mr. Spock to get angry, the illusion falls apart.

In psychoanalytic terms, life on Omicron Ceti III is a regression to a stage of splitting the image of self and the world into opposites. Once again, Captain Kirk is on the side of emotional growth. He fights the childlike fantasy and struggles to be a full adult, then helps his friend and second officer do the same.

> Kirk and Spock adjust a transmitter to emit an irritating signal, hoping this will stimulate anger and fighting on the planet below. Their strategy works. After a few brawls, the crew and the colonists break free of the spores. Sandoval says with resentment, "We've made no progress here. Three years wasted!"

> Back aboard the ship, McCoy remarks that this was the second instance when people were thrown out of paradise. Kirk boasts that this time humanity walked out on its own. Mr. Spock says poignantly that for the first time in his life he had been happy.

Though it is idealistic, life on Omicron Ceti III remains alluring to the *Enterprise* crew, and to us as viewers. Dr. McCoy calls it paradise, while Mr. Spock laments that he was truly happy there. We all have an unconscious wish to merge with a strong and loving provider and to pretend that our antagonism and pain do not exist.

In the end, the crew must give up utopia. They return to their adult lives aboard the *Enterprise*, with all the joys and hardships that this entails. Sandoval realizes with sadness that they had made no advancement as a settlement. Kirk is proud that he and the crew walked away from this so-called paradise of their own free will. Though it is normal to feel emotionally fused with a life-giving parent during our early childhood, it is not healthy for this to continue into our adult years, at least not all the time.

There are moments when it is enriching and harmless to lose our identity to some extent. This immersion happens when we become engrossed in a good movie or book. We get so invested in what is happening to the characters that we temporarily forget who we are. A healthy loss of separateness also can occur during intimacy with a trusted partner, and in profound spiritual experiences.

In mature sexual relationships, the physical and emotional boundaries between a couple become blurry. Partners feel like they are merging with or dissolving into one another. Each lover's identity fades into the background as the two people become one. This melding is a temporary and reversible regression to the stage when the boundaries between oneself and others were indistinct. Experiences like this include some of life's most blissful moments and are often said to be beyond words. To a large extent, these occasions are indescribable because they take us back to a time in life before we understood language.

Spiritual experiences also offer a temporary regression to a state of fusion. Descriptions of these moments often involve feelings of oceanic oneness with the cosmos or being a part of a larger whole. This boundarylessness leads to a sense of communion with nature, the universe, and God for those who have a relationship with Him or Her. These experiences are often transformative to people who have them and have a profound impact on their lives.

We will now turn to another episode that involves losing our identity and becoming part of a larger entity, but this time the experience is terrifying.

The Return of the Archons

The *Enterprise* travels to Beta III to investigate the fate of the USS *Archon*, a Federation ship that disappeared in the vicinity a century ago. Lieutenants Sulu and O'Neill are on the planet's surface running for their lives. Several menacing figures pursue them, each one wearing a hooded robe and carrying a long staff. Sulu calls the ship for an emergency beam-up, but this takes a few seconds. O'Neill runs off, and one of the robed figures zaps Sulu just before the *Enterprise* engages the transporter.

When he materializes on the *Enterprise*, Sulu is not himself. He does not know who he is and does not recognize Captain Kirk. He has a blank, pseudo-contented look on his face; he speaks of "Landru" and being "of The Body." Of the planet, he says, "It's paradise, my friend. Paradise!"

How can Mr. Sulu call this planet a paradise? The hooded figures look like angels of death and stalk their victims with an eerie calm. They transform Sulu into a mindless automaton with no trace of his former personality. In what way is this a utopia?

Returning to a state of fusion with a commanding caretaker is often equated with paradise. Sulu loses his identity and becomes part of the larger whole. He returns to the early stage in life before children could distinguish between themselves and the world and people around them. Sulu becomes united with The Body, just as infants feel fused with their parents.

The reference to "The Body" confirms our suspicion that this episode depicts the early infant/parent relationship. Mother and her body play a vital role in babies' lives. Infants recently came directly out of their mother's womb at birth. Their food, warmth, and comfort as a neonate come primarily from Mom's body or a surrogate. Infants initially think that they are physically a part of their mother and that Mom is a part of them.

In both "This Side of Paradise" and "The Return of the Archons," the *Enterprise* crew members merge into a conglomerate, yet the mood of these two episodes is very different. Life with the spores on Omicron Ceti III overflows with love, peace, and belonging. Though it is not realistic, it is still enticing. In contrast, Sulu's fate on Beta III is grotesque and terrifying.

The reason that the professed paradise in "The Return of the Archons" is so ghastly is that The Body completely obliterates Mr. Sulu's persona. At least the spores allowed limited expression of one's unique character. The Body permits none. Sulu now thinks, talks, looks, and behaves exactly like everybody else. Nothing remains of his former self.

These two episodes show how we long for, but also fear, the state of fusion with a caretaker. Though they love and protect us, parents are also the source of primitive dreads and anxieties. We fear that the commanding caretaker will swallow or consume us. They might wipe out our identity and digest us like food. These terrors originate during infancy and live on in the unconscious mind throughout life.

> Kirk, Spock, McCoy, and a few others beam down to the planet to investigate. The inhabitants are cordial, but have Sulu's mindless expression and lack any genuine warmth or individual identity. A stranger asks if they have come for "Festival." Before they discover what Festival is, the clock strikes six in the evening and the holiday begins.

> Suddenly, the people go on a destructive and sexual rampage. They scream at the top of their lungs, destroy property, and fornicate with the nearest man or woman. The landing party escapes from the madness into a boarding lodge.

What does Festival add to this story? How do we understand this crazy, unrestrained behavior?

The holiday rampage and the contrasting meek behavior at other times depict how infants split themselves and the world into all-good and all-bad. The peaceful and congenial side of the inhabitants is cutoff from their aggression and sexual appetites. The instantaneous transformation when the clock strikes six dramatically portrays this division. The populace shows either one extreme or the other, with nothing in between. How much more separate can you get? Just as anger could not co-exist with the spores in "This Side of Paradise," the animal instincts of Festival are absent from the people's quiet everyday monotony. On Beta III, these two sides of the inhabitants' nature have separate lives which are detached and alien from one another.

Not only are the people different during so-called "Festival" but they are also destructive, oversexed maniacs. Why is their behavior so extreme, other than the fact that it makes for a more dramatic story?

The people behave like infants during the debauchery. They express their most primitive urges without any thought or restraint. When babies are angry, they immediately translate these feelings into actions. They flail their arms, their faces become red, and they scream uncontrollably. During Festival, the townspeople express their instincts just as rapidly and urgently. They do not consider the consequences of their actions. Their appetites are naked and exposed. The citizens show none of the self-control needed to live in a civilized society.

The absence of children in the episode is another indication that the townspeople represent youngsters themselves, not mature adults. They do not have offspring because they are fixated at an early stage of emotional growth. The typical grade -school student has a more mature grasp of life than the grownups in this society.

> Inside the inn, an old man becomes suspicious that the newcomers are not of The Body; he goes to get the lawgivers. At six o'clock in the morning, Festival ends as abruptly as it started. The citizens revert to their previous docile state. Kirk questions his two hosts about their culture, but the authorities interrupt.

> The lawgivers are the hooded figures who attacked Mr. Sulu. They kill one of the innkeepers and tell the landing party in a computer-like voice that they will be "absorbed." They order Kirk and the others to follow them. On behalf of all the landing party, Kirk refuses to go. The lawgivers freeze temporarily, as they are unprepared for outright defiance.

Captain Kirk's disobedience confuses the entire system. The lawgivers do not understand Kirk because they cannot comprehend that he is a separate individual with his own thoughts and ideas. Self-determination is foreign to them.

The term "absorbed" aptly describes the process of having our identity stolen from us and melting into a conglomerate. Our vital personal essence would dissolve within a vast reality. "Absorbed" captures the terror of losing who we are. Our distinctiveness would perish. Freedom would be nonexistent. Autonomy would be meaningless. The Body would digest us, tearing us into tiny, disconnected pieces.

At some level, we all fear that a giant of some sort will devour us, but to some people, it seems as if it is really happening. When persons become psychotic, i.e., lose touch with reality, they often feel like they have been absorbed. Their physical and emotional boundaries seem to liquefy. When in the grips of psychosis, some people will cut their skin just to reassure themselves that there is a boundary between the inside and outside of their body. When people hallucinate, they confuse what is going on in their minds with the sights and sounds of the outside world. They see and hear their thoughts and feelings. Similarly, when people believe nonsensical, delusional ideas to be valid, they confuse their thoughts and fears with what is real. They misinterpret words and events to fit their distorted view of the world. Their inner fantasies and external reality merge into one.

> Reger, the surviving innkeeper, is not of The Body and leads the landing party to a secret hideout. Once they are safe, Reger describes the planet's history. Long ago their society was plagued by war, injustice, and other evils of civilization. Landru eliminated society's vices through blind obedience and complete control. The "Archons," visitors from the lost Federation ship, were either killed or absorbed.

> A holographic image of Landru appears, calls Kirk and the others an "infection" in The Body, and promises that they will be absorbed. Ultrasonic sound waves knock them all unconscious.

> When Kirk and Spock awaken, their communicators and phasers are gone; McCoy has been absorbed. The lawgivers take Kirk next. Marplon, a technician who is part of an anti-Landru underground, saves him. He returns the *Enterprise*'s equipment and guides Kirk and Spock to the Hall of Audiences where Landru appears. They blast through the wall and discover that Landru is a computer. Before they can destroy the mainframe, it neutralizes their phasers.

> Captain Kirk convinces Landru that it is harming The Body by stifling creativity. The computer is killing the people it meant to rescue, Kirk argues, so it must die. Landru self-destructs, leaving the inhabitants to fend for themselves for the first time in their lives.

The resolution favors psychological growth and independence. The frightening yet carefree fusion with Landru is over. The people will have to learn to choose for themselves. This self-determination will be challenging, but there will be rewards. Captain Kirk leaves a team of experts on Beta III to "help restore the planet's culture to a human form."

"This Side of Paradise" shows us how much we long to feel fused with a powerful caretaker. "The Return of the Archons" reminds us that this fantasy is also horrifying. Both episodes recognize that this early childhood fixation must end if we are going to advance and grow.

"The Return of the Archons" contains the first reference to the Federation's Prime Directive which prohibits Starfleet from interfering with the internal development of alien civilizations. When Kirk concludes that Landru must die, Spock reminds him of the directive of noninterference. Kirk responds, "That refers to a living, growing culture. Do you think this one is?"

As a literary device, Spock's mention of the Prime Directive is meant to foreshadow the coming confrontation. Later in the episode, Landru says that "the good of The Body is the Prime Directive," which then allows Kirk and Spock to make their argument about creativity. The parallelism also serves to juxtapose the Federation's respect for autonomy with The Body's top-down, autocratic control. Landru's best line is, "I reserve creativity *to me.*" If it wants to be a good dictator, it needs to learn how to obfuscate.

One never knows what elements in an episode will be carried forward into future adventures. For better or worse, the Prime Directive did become a fixture throughout the original series and the rest of the *Star Trek* franchise. I applaud the idea that we should think twice before trying to impose our values on other people, privately or as a nation. Nevertheless, the notion of noninterference was troubled from the beginning. Just establishing contact with a society is interference of a sort; the encounter changes both civilizations. By some counts, Captain Kirk violated the Prime Directive eleven times, and there were no instances when strict adherence to the principle led to a good outcome. It is okay to discard ideas that no longer make sense.

CHAPTER 6: SPLITTING

As we discussed in the last chapter, infants cannot distinguish themselves from the environment around them. At first, they cannot differentiate me from not me. The ability to discriminate develops gradually during the first year of life. The physical and emotional boundaries that separate them from the rest of the world become evident in their minds only after several months. Fantasies about losing these personal boundaries are both enticing and terrifying.

After children can differentiate me from not me, they still divide the external world into all-good and all-bad. They build their mental picture of their surroundings on their feelings, which range from intense anger and pain to euphoric satisfaction. Therefore, they create two distinct images of reality within their mind. Hostility, frustration, and deprivation permeate one realm, while the other is enjoyable and pleasing. Mentally, these vastly different worlds are cutoff from one another. Infants believe that they live in two opposite, alternating universes.

Children also have two different pictures of themselves within their minds, one virtuous and the other depraved. One self-image is happy and loving, while the other is enraged. These disparate selves exist independent of each other.

Similarly, youngsters at this stage have good and bad images of other people. They believe that they have two different, independent mothers and two fathers. One set of parents is loving and warm while the other pair is angry and attacking. Splitting people into two images is common in literature and fairy tales, such as the fragmented personality of *Dr. Jekyll and Mr. Hyde*. The good witch and her nemesis in *The Wizard of Oz* represent the loving mother and the evil one.

This chapter explores how splitting people and the world into virtuous and corrupt appears in *Star Trek* episodes. The characters are either honorable and righteous or decadent and debauched, but they never lose their unique, individual identities. There is no merging or absorbing into larger organisms. The distinction between self and other is clear. "Mirror, Mirror" is a straightforward example of splitting into good and evil. "The Man Trap" also illustrates this idea, but in more subtle ways. Finally, we will discuss Dr. McCoy's difficulty recognizing both sides of himself and other people.

Mirror, Mirror

> Kirk, McCoy, Scotty, and Uhura meet with the peaceful Halkan council to negotiate a dilithium crystal mining agreement. The Halkans are leery; Kirk assures them that the Federation would never resort to force.

> The landing party beams up to the ship, but an atmospheric disturbance causes them to materialize on a barbaric *Enterprise* in an alternate universe. Spock readies to exterminate the Halkans for their defiance.

This powerful opening establishes the wickedness of the parallel *Enterprise* with a few simple visual cues and action. The *Enterprise* flips from moving to the right to heading left. The transporter materializes the landing party with a splotchier visual. Uhura's uniform shows her midriff; the men have sashes, and they all carry daggers. There are decals on the walls of Earth with a knife down the middle. The foreign salute is reminiscent of fascist regimes. Spock has a beard. He scolds Lieutenant Kyle for the transporter problems and demands the technician's "agonizer," which Spock uses to torture him. Spock orders Sulu to lock the ship's phasers on the Halkan cities, and says, "Regrettable that this society has chosen suicide." All of this is contained in just ninety seconds of film.

In an age of jaw-dropping special effects, the introduction to "Mirror, Mirror" shows how simple elements and a strong narrative can deliver a punch that is often lacking in modern big-budget blockbusters.

> Life aboard the substitute *Enterprise* is treacherous and cruel. Officers have henchmen and are perpetually engaged in bloody power struggles. It is common and expected to move up in rank through assassination. Kirk has orders to destroy the Halkans and take what the Empire wants.

The same time that the familiar Captain Kirk and the others arrive in the alternate creation, their vicious counterparts materialize on the original *Enterprise*. They are crude, savage, and vulgar.

The civilized and barbarous versions of Kirk and the others eventually return to their respective homes. Before he leaves the parallel world, Kirk persuades the bearded Mr. Spock to guide the evil *Enterprise* on a more humane path.

The split between good and evil is unmistakable in this episode; it is the central premise of the story. The original *Enterprise* is civilized and progressive. Captain Kirk negotiates with the Halkans as equals, demonstrating the Federation's benevolence. He respects the high council's doubt and caution. The parallel *Enterprise* is cruel, dramatized by the crew's brutality and violence and the orders from the Empire to kill the Halkans for their resistance.

Unlike the episodes in the last chapter, the characters are unique individuals. Captain Kirk is Captain Kirk in both universes. He is a separate person. The crew does not merge with a collective being, benign or otherwise, and no alien force takes over their minds. They are split into two contrasting parts, but there is no loss of personal identity.

This narrative portrays a mental age of roughly one to two years old. At this stage, children have established a sense of personal boundaries but still sort the world into all-good and all-bad extremes. They have two different images of the people in their lives, just as there were different copies of the familiar *Star Trek* characters in this episode. At this rudimentary stage of life, youngsters live in parallel universes and jump back and forth between them depending on how they feel.

The next developmental step is to combine the contrasting images of people into one idea of real persons with both strengths and weaknesses. This advance, however, does not occur in this episode. The virtuous and evil characters are separate at the beginning of the adventure and remain so to the end. The two halves do not come together.

The final encounter between Kirk and the alternate Mr. Spock signals hope. The captain persuades his parallel science officer to guide the barbarous *Enterprise* down a more enlightened path. If Spock can do this, he could temper the Empire's extremes and move it in a progressive direction. The civilized Captain Kirk would have softened the malice of the parallel reality.

This episode's emotional power comes from the terrifying transformation of the *Enterprise* and its crew. The safe, protective, familiar starship home is now a dangerous place. Spock, Sulu, Chekov, and the other characters that viewers like and admire are now venomous predators. The transmutation reawakens childhood memories of our mother or father morphing from a loving parent into a treacherous and vile one. When adults get angry, children think that the kind versions have disappeared and threatening imposters have taken their place. To youngsters, this transformation is as sudden and extreme as that in "Mirror, Mirror."

The child's goal is to get the caring parent back, just as Captain Kirk aims to get back to the virtuous *Enterprise*. Through this episode, we relive the terror, fright, and panic of watching a loving parent turn into a ferocious pretender. When Kirk and the others materialize back home, we re-experience the satisfaction and relief we felt when the gentle and warm caretaker returned. The plot summary above skips many twists and other details, which can be savored and enjoyed by streaming the episode one more time. "Mirror, Mirror" is one of *Star Trek*'s best.

"The Man Trap" also illustrates splitting into good and evil. It portrays a creature that transforms itself from a beautiful woman into a hideous monster. Dr. McCoy plays a central role in this adventure; the action will provide insight into his personality.

The episode has some artistic flaws. There is one major inconsistency in the plot, which I will comment upon. The dialogue is stilted at times, and the pace is ponderous. There are hints of misogyny, or at least reflections of the male-dominant culture of the 1960s when the original *Star Trek* debuted. At the same time, *Star Trek* broke new ground by casting an African-American woman as the *Enterprise* communication officer, Lieutenant Uhura, who plays a significant role in this adventure. Though it was not first to be filmed, "The Man Trap" was the first episode aired, on September 6, 1966.

The Man Trap

Captain Kirk, Dr. McCoy, and Crewman Darnell beam down to planet M113 to bring supplies to a husband and wife research team investigating the ruins of an ancient civilization. The mission is routine, except that the wife of the scientific team, Nancy Crater, was once in a romantic relationship with Dr. McCoy.

When Mrs. Crater arrives, each member of the landing party sees a different woman. McCoy greets the Nancy Crater he used to know, who appears about twenty-five years old. Captain Kirk observes a more age-appropriate image of the same woman, while Crewman Darnell sees a voluptuous young blonde. Mrs. Crater goes to find her husband and seduces Darnell into following her.

The ancient civilization suggests that this episode will depict issues from a primordial period of our life, childhood. McCoy's past relationship with Nancy Crater also indicates that the story will dramatize something from our past, and will concern a romance.

Our earliest passion is for our adult caretakers. They are our first loves. They feed, groom, comfort, and play with us. We naturally have strong feelings of affection for them. The ancient culture and Dr. McCoy's past involvement suggest that the action will depict the relationship with our parents from an early period of our life.

Though Kirk, McCoy, and Darnell each see a different version of Mrs. Crater, the copies are all attractive in their way. So far, she represents the mental image of an appealing woman. Dr. McCoy perceives the girlfriend he once knew. To Captain Kirk, she is a motherly figure. Crewman Darnell sees a sensuous woman his own age. From what the men can tell, there is nothing disagreeable about her. She is a reflection of the visitors' expectations, wishes, and memories, rather than a genuine person with her own stable, unchanging traits.

In contrast to the visitors from the *Enterprise*, the viewer must suspect that there is a dark side to this creature. There is something sinister about its ability to look differently to various people and its seduction of crewman Darnell. Kirk and McCoy are not yet aware of these eerie qualities.

Appearing as three different women, though thought-provoking, is a weak spot in the narrative. The creature will change its identity several more times, but in no other scene does its form vary amongst people in the same room. This inconsistency is confusing. Is the creature changing its appearance, or is it invading the minds of the people around it? The ambiguity weakens the episode. If it could simultaneously manipulate two people in different ways, it could have prevailed in the final confrontation with Spock and McCoy. In either case, whether it changes forms or just tricks people telepathically, it seems to take on the facade of what the visitors expect or want to see.

Professor Crater arrives. He is an irritable recluse and demands that Kirk and McCoy leave immediately. After calming down, he agrees to a physical exam.

Nancy Crater screams, and the three men run to investigate. Darnell is dead, with small pieces of some poisonous vegetation in his mouth. He also has several red rings on his face. Obviously shaken, Mrs. Crater says that Darnell ate the plant before she could warn him it was deadly.

Something killed Darnell, and there is more to the story than what Mrs. Crater has shared. A trained crewman would not stupidly eat an unknown plant from a foreign world. It is not clear what happened yet, but we must suspect that Darnell's seductive dream girl is responsible for the crime.

Nancy Crater, or what appears to be her, has two different sides to her nature. She can be beautiful and alluring or toxic and deadly. In altered forms, she represents both a warm, loving mother and her opposite. The viewer understands that there is reason to be alarmed, but Kirk and McCoy are not yet aware of her sinister, chameleon-like nature.

Dissecting reality into good and evil in this episode is not as recognizable as in "Mirror, Mirror," in which Captain Kirk and the others took on two distinct forms. "The Man Trap" deals with one creature, but splitting is still evident. The alien being is fragmented into two polarized parts; it can be attractive if not seductive, but it is also lethal. The divergent versions appear at different times, so people see only one or the other at any particular moment. Captain Kirk and Dr. McCoy do not yet suspect the dark side to Mrs. Crater because all she has shown them is the half that she wants them to see.

> Kirk and McCoy beam up to the ship. After some tests, McCoy discovers that the plant did not kill Darnell. Something sucked all the sodium chloride, or common table salt, out of his body. Humans die instantly without this essential mineral.

> Kirk and McCoy beam down to the planet along with crewmen Sturgeon and Green. Nancy Crater is not there, and Professor Crater runs off. While the captain and doctor search for the runaway scientist, the creature kills the two crewmen. It masquerades as Green and beams up to the *Enterprise* with Kirk and McCoy.

> Once on board the ship, the alien hunts for more victims. It becomes a handsome black man and almost seduces Lieutenant Uhura to her grave. It kills another crewman after Uhura gets away.

In this encounter with Lieutenant Uhura, the creature shows again that it can assume the appearance of somebody desired by its prey. It takes the form of Uhura's dream man; it charms her by speaking Swahili. She does not see that her prince charming is also a deadly menace. He is about to suck every bit of salt from her body, leaving her an empty, depleted carcass.

The creature becomes a desired man to Uhura rather than a sought-after woman. For her, as for the others, the monster can be wildly enticing one minute and deadly the next. The fantastic extremes of this creature dramatize the stage of splitting in our early life.

> Kirk and Spock capture Professor Crater. He tells them that the creature is the last member of an intelligent species that used to inhabit M113. It needed salt to survive; it murdered the real Nancy years ago to extract that substance from her. It has been playing the role of his wife ever since, as "it needs love as much as it needs salt." It does not wish to kill Professor Crater, who has willingly participated in this bizarre relationship.

The creature is the last of its race, a relic from a long-dead civilization. The ancient culture represents our early childhood, so the monster depicts a remnant or leftover from our beginning years. The alien being can alter its appearance, which personifies our tendency to split the images of people into extremes and reflects back to our first two years of life.

Why is Crater so cozy with this horrifying imposter? He even takes it as his wife, a delightfully creepy detail of this story.

The professor is comfortable with the creature because he is fixated at an early stage of psychological development; he cannot integrate the positive and negative aspects of other people into more well-rounded and realistic pictures. His mental handicap applies to his understanding of monsters as well as human beings. Crater is at ease with the creature masquerading as his wife because he can see only what he wants and no more. It appears to be Nancy, so nothing else matters. He is aware that it killed her, but this knowledge is compartmentalized and has no discernible effect on him. Well-adjusted persons can recognize both the strengths and weaknesses of people, even those they love. A healthy man could not overlook the history of his wife's murder under any circumstances. In contrast, Crater beds this eerie, homicidal, and vile creature.

The professor's reaction to Kirk and McCoy in the opening scenes confirms that he has trouble seeing others as complete persons with their strengths and weaknesses. He sorts people into friend or foe. He views the Starfleet visitors as enemies, denying their good intentions and their wish to be of assistance. Though they came to help, Crater belligerently orders Kirk and McCoy to leave the planet immediately. He treats the *Enterprise* officers like they are abusive, intruding attackers, rather than as a source of supplies, information, and companionship. Crater only sees the danger in them. He knows nothing about Kirk and McCoy but immediately assumes that they wish to irritate and torment him. He does not recognize that they also may have something to offer. To be fair, however, Crater was also trying to protect them.

Why is Crater such a spiteful man? How is this bitterness related to his difficulty perceiving others realistically? We are discussing a fictional character, but we can still wonder what sort of past could account for his personality.

We would expect that Professor Crater endured some severe hardships during his early life. He might have been physically abused, emotionally neglected, or abandoned in some way. To integrate the good and bad images of other people, children need warm and satisfying experiences to offset the frustrating and painful ones. If this does not happen, youngsters may conclude that the evil and cruelty of the world overwhelms anything decent. When the depraved side of humanity dwarfs our virtues, kids have trouble integrating the desired and terrifying images of other people into one. They fear that the malice is so intense that it will extinguish anything worthwhile.

Professor Crater and people like him become suspicious, angry, and avoid contact with others. The evil of the human race seems to overshadow anything worthwhile. In some cases, early traumatic experiences can permanently color how one sees the world. For Crater, even when well-intentioned people like Kirk and McCoy come to help, he belligerently pushes them away. He sees a universe filled with wickedness and so denies himself friendship and many other joys of life.

Now aboard the ship, Crater refuses to identify the creature. Kirk orders McCoy to give Crater a truth serum injection, but the imposter is now masquerading as the doctor. It kills the Professor and then seeks out the real Dr. McCoy, appearing again as Nancy. She begs McCoy for protection, explaining that Kirk and the others are trying to kill her. McCoy is not yet aware of what is happening.

Kirk enters McCoy's cabin with a phaser. He tells the doctor to move away from the enemy, explaining her true identity; McCoy does not believe it. He wrestles the weapon away from Kirk, giving the creature time to hypnotize the captain. It approaches Kirk for the kill, but McCoy still cannot shoot it.

Spock enters and frantically insists that McCoy fire the phaser. "I will not shoot Nancy!" McCoy answers. Spock tells him that the imposter is not who it appears to be and tries to prove it by striking it repeatedly across the face. Unaffected, the creature strikes back, sending Spock flying across the room. "Is that Nancy?" Spock asks.

Dr. McCoy still cannot bring himself to shoot. Only when it attacks Kirk and he screams out in agony can McCoy pull the trigger. The creature reverts to its original, hideous form as it dies.

Why does Dr. McCoy hesitate so long before killing the creature? What makes it so difficult for him to believe that what appears to be his former girlfriend is the murderer?

Like Professor Crater, Dr. McCoy still has difficulty integrating the good and bad images of other people within his mind. He cannot comprehend that the alien butcher is masquerading as Nancy Crater. This struggle explains why he waits until it is almost too late before he kills the creature. It is difficult for him to grasp that what appears to be the woman he still finds appealing could be the same living being that is leeching the salt out of its victims. The two images are separate in his mind, and it is agonizing to bring them together. Even when Mr. Spock strikes the alien across the face with his superhuman strength, Dr. McCoy still cannot take action. Looking bewildered, he stares on passively. Only when Kirk is near death, does McCoy overcome his resistance and fire the phaser.

Throughout the series, Dr. McCoy usually sees people and events in either a friendly or critical light, depending on his gut emotional reaction. A black or white thinker, he often has difficulty bringing opposing perspectives together into a balanced view of situations. Like Crater, he can appear stuck at the stage when we divided the world into positive and negative. It is no accident that he is the one who struggles with killing the salt vampire, rather than Captain Kirk or Mr. Spock. They more readily recognize that the thing that appears to be Mrs. Crater is the alien being in disguise. In contrast, Dr. McCoy struggles to put these two disparate images together.

"The Man Trap" portrays the most dramatic instance of McCoy's struggle with this issue, but his inclination for splitting comes up throughout the series. He rarely sees situations in their entirety; instead, he sees disconnected bits and pieces. What he thinks is common sense sometimes shows a poor understanding of the complexities involved. The solutions he proposes can range from simple-minded to preposterous.

His difficulty integrating the disparate sides of people and situations also explains Dr. McCoy's emotional intensity. Most issues in life are complicated; there are many different perspectives and few clear-cut answers. When people have a well-integrated and mature grasp of matters, they can appreciate conflicting viewpoints even if they do not agree with them; they tend to be more level-headed and restrained. If, on the other hand, you can only see one side of an issue, it is easy to be self-righteous and intense. When persons see their position as entirely right and the opposing viewpoint as unquestionably wrong, they can be zealous, attacking, and unreasonable. McCoy's inability to integrate the many sides of a problem, or to assimilate the good and bad images of himself and other people, leads naturally to his unrestrained sentiment.

Dr. McCoy's splitting is also evident in his relationship with Mr. Spock, who he often sees as malevolent. Nobody has an entirely accurate view of another person, but McCoy's image of Spock is more distorted than usual. According to the doctor, Spock is always insensitive and is cruel and immoral at times. McCoy denounces the Vulcan for being harsh and uncompromisingly ambitious, but neither of these accusations is true. Spock's emotionless objectivity is not same as ruthlessness, and he shows little ambition to command a starship. The other crew members do not share McCoy's view of the science officer. Kirk, Uhura, Chekov, and the rest appreciate Mr. Spock's abilities and contributions. They also see through the Vulcan's apparent insensitivity to the emotional life underneath. McCoy does not value Spock's noble side. He divorces any attractive qualities from the image of Mr. Spock he has formed in his head.

This negative view of Mr. Spock helps Dr. McCoy maintain a virtuous mental image of himself. He sees predominately corrupt qualities in Mr. Spock, making it easier to view himself as uniquely kind and compassionate. By magnifying Spock's flaws, Dr. McCoy avoids looking at his own. Neither his self-image nor his appraisal of Spock is balanced.

If McCoy were a real person, I would suspect that his wish to see only virtue in himself influenced his decision to become a doctor. As a physician, he cares for others, eases their suffering, and helps maintain their health. Assuming the caretaker role supports his benevolent and altruistic self-image. During a crisis, McCoy always takes the side of the underdog. He sees himself as the one who is concerned most about others, while he considers Mr. Spock to be insensitive and cold. Dr. McCoy has not developed an integrated mental image of Mr. Spock, nor has he reached a fair-minded understanding of himself. If he could grasp this truth, he might realize that he shares some of the shortcomings that he ascribes to Mr. Spock. This idea frightens the doctor. The accusations he flings at the Vulcan represent parts of himself that he cannot see. It has been said that we condemn in others what we like least about ourselves.

Why doesn't Mr. Spock object to Dr. McCoy's attacks on his motives and character? He often corrects the doctor on some logical scientific point, but he rarely protests McCoy's condemnation of his personality.

The most dramatic example of Spock's lack of protest occurs in "The Tholian Web." Captain Kirk disappears into another dimension of space, and the crew presumes he is dead. McCoy mercilessly accuses Spock of delighting in Kirk's tragic fate, because the predicament leaves him in command of the ship. At the climax of one scene, an enraged McCoy twirls Spock around in his chair, intending to continue the verbal attack. Spock sits passively, not saying a word.

McCoy, not Mr. Spock, is heartless in this encounter. The doctor is grossly insensitive to the Vulcan's feelings and anxieties. Spock, despite his apparent lack of emotion, is coping with tremendous pain at the loss of his colleague and friend. McCoy is cruel and brutal, telling him that he is secretly delighted that Kirk is dead. Also, Spock must feel enormous apprehension about commanding the ship in Kirk's absence. The *Enterprise* is crippled and in an unstable area of space that is making the crew lose their minds. The Tholians are constructing an energy web to imprison the starship. McCoy is unable to recognize the burden of Spock's unsought responsibilities. He only sees his one-sided, menacing version of Mr. Spock, and is blind to the Vulcan's pain and trepidation.

Spock does not object to McCoy's mistreatment because their relationship helps the Vulcan deny his feelings. More than anything, Mr. Spock wishes to suppress his emotional reactions. Though his moods and sentiments seem evident to the other crew members, he tries to convince everybody and himself that he has risen above them. When McCoy overstates an emotional reaction or recommends a rash course of action, it makes it easier for Spock to argue for one-sided logic. Spock can disown any feelings, even if he sympathizes with Dr. McCoy's position to some degree. The relationship helps Spock maintain his emotionless facade.

Mr. Spock projects his sentimental, caring, and vulnerable side into Dr. McCoy and then repudiates it. McCoy, in turn, rejects his cold, insensitive, and aggressive self and attributes it to Mr. Spock. The doctor helps the science officer keep his feelings repressed. The help denying his emotions is what Mr. Spock gets out of the relationship. It is McCoy's intensity, which Spock seemingly dislikes, that keeps the two connected. Dr. McCoy expresses his passions so hysterically that it helps Mr. Spock keep his sentiments submerged. Each of them gets something out of the relationship. They project the part of their psyche that is most threatening into one another and then portray each other as biased or out of touch. Psychoanalysts call this phenomenon "projective identification."

Dr. McCoy and Mr. Spock are like some married couples, where one spouse is highly emotional while the other is controlled and stoic. The partners have an unspoken, unconscious bargain worked out; one expresses the feelings for both of them, while the other pretends to have no reactions at all. Each partner projects an uncomfortable part of themselves into the other, but they also become a container for something that their spouse wishes to disavow in him or herself.

In healthy partnerships, the strengths and weaknesses people bring with them can lead to mutual growth and better balance. Indeed, the Kirk/Spock/McCoy three-way partnership does work very well, but without Kirk, it falls apart. In "The Tholian Web" when the Captain was lost and presumed dead, it is the recorded "final orders" of Kirk, encouraging Spock and McCoy to work with each other, that saves the day. With cooperation between Spock and McCoy restored, they recover Captain Kirk from the unstable alternate dimension and free the *Enterprise* from the madness-inducing Tholian space.

Chapter 7: Good and Evil

As they grow, children learn that the good and bad mental images of themselves and others are two sides of the same people. This realization is a profound step in their psychological development. Before they reach this stage, youngsters think that they are two separate persons at different times, depending on how they feel. They also see parents in dualistic terms, depending on whether their mom or dad is satisfying or frustrating them at the moment. Gradually, children integrate the split images of themselves and others into more realistic views. The disparate mental pictures merge into single portraits that have both positive and negative qualities. This step commonly occurs around age three. As we saw with Dr. McCoy, however, even adults can have difficulty recognizing both sides of people. We all have some tendency to divide the world into good and evil, which is most likely to come out during times of stress.

A loving, nurturing home life during the early years helps children integrate the good with the bad. When their happy, satisfying experiences outweigh their frustrations, youngsters can more easily incorporate all aspects of people into one image. When they have confidence in the benevolence of the world, or at least in their immediate surroundings, boys and girls can accept the weaknesses in themselves and those around them.

Sadly, there is too much pain and frustration in many children's lives. Some youngsters are neglected, humiliated, abused, beaten, or mistreated in other ways. When this occurs, it is difficult for them to see both sides of reality simultaneously. They do not develop a basic trust that the world is predominately nurturing and safe. Why should they? When one has been abused or neglected, it is a stretch to believe in humanity's goodwill.

It turns out that even the most abused children have a benevolent image of the world, but they keep it hidden deep in their psyche. They fear that degeneracy will overwhelm kindness, so they keep the two separated mentally. In this way, mistreated youngsters try to protect what little compassion they see in the world. They fear that the wickedness is so intense and powerful that it would overwhelm and destroy decency if they ever tried to bring the two opposites together. They protect their warm images of self and others by keeping them split off from the wicked. The healthy growth toward integration gets derailed. It is not clear how much frustration or trauma is too much for a child to overcome; it varies with each person.

Dr. McCoy is a fictional character, but if he were a real person one would expect to find some hardship or trauma in his early life. Somebody in his past was probably cruel and insensitive to him at times. This presumed experience colors his view of Mr. Spock and makes it difficult for him to recognize the Vulcan's strengths.

The ideal situation for children is a home life where they are loved and supervised with kindness. This positive, healthy experience helps them bring together the two polarized mental pictures of themselves and other people. If the child's environment is one of caring and giving, he or she will feel comfortable integrating the bad aspects of others into a mature and balanced view. Youngsters will feel confident that the negative traits will not overpower the positive ones, or take control of themselves or their parents.

This chapter explores how *Star Trek* portrays the integration of good and evil. The most obvious example of this struggle occurs in "The Enemy Within." "The Devil in the Dark" and "And the Children Shall Lead" also show how love and understanding can temper and tame our tendency toward anger and hate.

The Enemy Within

A transporter malfunction produces two versions of Captain Kirk. One is meek, compassionate, and intelligent; the other is hostile and vicious.

The bestial Kirk goes on a rampage. He demands liquor from Dr. McCoy and sexually assaults Yeoman Rand. The benevolent Captain Kirk gradually loses his ability to make decisions. He needs his alter-ego to command the ship. The opposites cannot exist without each other. The good captain and Mr. Spock capture the depraved Kirk and use the transporter to put the two halves back together.

The transporter splits Captain Kirk in two, but the copies are not identical. In isolation, neither one is a complete human being. As in "Mirror, Mirror," one Kirk is caring and kind while the other is a ruthless barbarian. Unlike "Mirror, Mirror," in "The Enemy Within" the two Kirks come back together in the end. The transporter combines the gentle and hateful versions into one person, who has the capacity for both good and evil. This episode is psychologically more advanced than those in the last chapter because thoughtfulness, consideration, intellect, and restraint, along with vital energy, drive, and appetite, all merge back together into a cohesive whole. Kirk's positive and negative traits intertwine with each other once again, producing the Captain Kirk we know and love.

The evil Captain Kirk represents the "id," as Sigmund Freud described it. According to Freud, this part of the mind wants instant satisfaction of its appetites above all else. The id is self-centered. It cares only to satisfy its lusts, oblivious to the concerns of the society around it. The barbaric Captain Kirk behaves as the id come to life. When McCoy questions his request for liquor, Kirk threatens him. The evil Kirk hates the word "no" and is quick to anger. He wants what he wants when he wants it. When the degenerate Kirk assaults Yeoman Rand, he only wants to satisfy his sexual craving. Like the id, he does not consider her feelings or the professional, social, and criminal implications of his actions.

The wicked Kirk is also akin to young infants when their appetites have erupted. The depraved Kirk explodes with rage, as babies cry with their entire body until Mom and Dad figure out what they need and provide it. Parents attend to infants as quickly as possible; when there is a delay, babies let everybody know how unhappy they are. They scream, cry, flail their arms and legs, and turn red in the face. Like the bad Captain Kirk, hungry newborns want what they want right now, and become furious when it is not forthcoming. This characteristic lives on throughout life in the id, but it is mostly unconscious.

The virtuous Captain Kirk is like the part of the mind that Freud called the "ego." Over the years, children develop intelligence, compassion, the ability to cope with delay and frustration, and other capacities that keep them from acting like wild animals. Freud attributed these mental aptitudes to the ego, which strives to balance many different considerations at once. It tries to satisfy the id, but it also respects other people's feelings. It knows that indulging the id's desires may feel good for a few minutes, but will lead to painful repercussions. A part of the ego, called the "superego," determines what an individual feels is morally right and wrong. Chapter nine discusses the superego in more depth.

Freud believed that infants start out as all id. They want their needs satisfied instantaneously. They have no capacity for delay and no realistic understanding of other people.

Further, Freud wrote that the id provides the energy that motivates people in all aspects of life; it is like gasoline for a car. The engine and driver are akin to the ego. The gas supplies the raw fuel, but the driver and the engine decide where the car will go, how fast, and what route it will take to get there. Later in life, many of the id's wishes become unconscious, which helps the ego resist temptations. Similarly, a car's driver may forget about the gas tank during most of the journey, focusing on driving safely and getting to the desired destination. Even when motorists have other things on their minds, the raw fuel powers the vehicle.

"The Enemy Within" fits with Freud's ideas about the id. The id-like Kirk provides the oomph for the total personality. He goes on an enthusiastic tear, while the virtuous Captain Kirk becomes more anemic as the story progresses. The ego-like Kirk will die without his immoral counterpart; his darker half supplies vitality and motivation.

Psychoanalysts since Freud have modified the belief that the id provides all humanity's energy, but "The Enemy Within" is aptly consistent with this idea. The bad Captain Kirk supplies the gasoline. The kind Kirk controls and modulates the final behavior of the person, or guides the direction and speed of the car. The classic Freudian formulation still captures something vital.

"The Enemy Within" attributes Kirk's ability to captain the *Enterprise* to his debauched half, which recognizes the fact that commanding other people does take a certain amount of aggression. Issuing orders compels others to ignore their wishes and do as they are told. Demanding compliance is inherently a forceful act. If officers are going to be successful leaders, they must be comfortable with this degree of assertiveness. Good commanders strike a successful balance between their hostile wishes to dominate others, and their intellect, restraint, sensitivity, and wisdom; they are comfortable with their aggression, yet have control over it.

Poor leaders populate two ends of a continuum. At one extreme, they may be meek and tentative. These people are often uncomfortable with their anger; it frightens them, so they try to hide from it. Timid people are usually ineffective commanders, like the gentle Captain Kirk. In other cases, some officers are too comfortable with their belligerence and violent instincts, like Kirk's vulgar twin. They do not temper or restrain their hostility. Captains like this can be sadistic, impulsive, and dangerous. Neither extreme makes an effective leader.

Before leaving "The Enemy Within," I feel compelled to highlight an unfortunate scene in the epilogue. After the two Kirks are put back together, Mr. Spock teases Yeoman Rand that the animal-like Kirk showed some "interesting tendencies"—as if she might feel flattered that he tried to force himself on her. I expect that the producers of the series wanted to play up the romantic tension between Kirk and Rand, but this exchange is not the way to do it. Sexual assault is a violent crime; there is nothing flattering about it. Women recognize when men are treating them as objects. From a psychoanalytic point of view, the exchange is regrettable because it mistakes the primal drive for sexual satisfaction, a part of the id, for the mature, loving, and respectful attraction adults feel for each other when forming life partnerships, primarily the domain of the ego.

The teasing scene is also out of character for Mr. Spock. He sometimes pokes fun at Kirk and McCoy when they are trying to best him, but he does not go out of his way to needle people. Ironically, after just eight episodes, Yeoman Rand's character was cut from the series allegedly so Kirk could have unencumbered relationships with other women. Fans remembered her, however, and she appeared in three of the six *Star Trek* movies with the original cast.

In "The Enemy Within," the integration of good and bad is impossible to miss. The transporter puts the two sides of Captain Kirk back together. In "The Devil in the Dark," the synthesis is not as apparent.

The Devil in the Dark

> Miners on planet Janus VII search for a monster that has already killed fifty of their colleagues. The mysterious creature murders Schmitter, a miner who is standing guard; the others find his body "burned to a crisp."

At first glance, we might expect that this adventure will be similar to "The Changeling" and "The Doomsday Machine" discussed in Chapter 2. The *Enterprise* encounters a stunningly lethal force, which somehow represents humanity's anger. The enemy is ultimately defeated, which gives viewers hope that they can master their darker nature. This episode could easily follow that pattern. The monster that is killing the miners is horrifically deadly. The humans could destroy it and then feel good about themselves. In contrast, the unfolding plot and the analytic understanding of it will move beyond this developmentally primitive stage to more advanced issues.

> The *Enterprise* arrives to help. The settlement supplies large quantities of "pergium," an ore which is essential to the Federation.

The planet is a "treasure house of minerals," though the deposits are tough to extract. Appearing three months previously, the monster first attacked machinery and then started killing workers. The deaths began in the mine's lower levels and had been moving up.

Mr. Spock examines some spherical silicon nodules that are plentiful in the mine, but the frightened workers are critical of his curiosity. They complain that Spock should devote all his energy to the danger at hand. The miners seem hostile toward Captain Kirk and his party.

An alarm sounds. The creature has taken the circulation pump from the colony's reactor, which supplies their heat, light, and air. Without the stolen unit, the reactor will go critical in forty-eight hours, flooding the colony with deadly radiation. Captain Kirk and the miners must retrieve the device before time runs out.

Spock speculates that silicon, rather than carbon, is the central element of life on Janus VII. This fact would explain the absence of life-form readings and the creature's resistance to the miner's phasers. The landing party adjusts their weapons to target silicon.

Having joined the hunt, Kirk and Spock find the creature and injure it with their phasers. With corrosive acid, the life-form escapes by burning a tunnel through solid rock.

If the creature is the last of its kind, Spock argues, it would be a crime against science to kill it. He suggests that they capture it instead. Kirk rejects this idea immediately; the enemy will be shot on sight.

Three details suggest that this story depicts a more advanced stage of emotional development than the episodes discussed in Chapter 2, which illustrated infantile rage and projection. First, the adversary is a living creature, unlike Nomad in "The Changeling" or the planet-killing automaton in "The Doomsday Machine." Its chemistry is alien, and its purpose is still a mystery, but the antagonist is undoubtedly alive. As such, it is more complicated than an opponent representing unadulterated rage or some other isolated and discrete part of the mind.

The second reason to expect the creature to be more than pure evil is that its behavior suggests it has organized thoughts and intentions. It began by attacking equipment, as if trying to send a message. It moved on to killing workers, progressing up the mine's levels. Apparently, it wants the people to leave. Then, it knew the one indispensable apparatus to steal from the colony's reactor, which demonstrates intelligence and intention. Later we will see that it also has feelings; it can experience pain and anger, as well as motherly love. Though it is a silicon monster, it shares many qualities with its human enemies. The story reflects back to the time in development when children understand that they are distinct from the world, but do not see others as multifaceted people with both good and bad traits. To Captain Kirk, the attacker is a murderer and nothing more.

The third element that suggests that their adversary is more than a danger to be eliminated comes when Mr. Spock suggests they try to capture the creature rather than kill it. Spock's hesitance is the first indication that the life-form has any value or worth. Nobody suggested that the *Enterprise* spare Nomad or the Doomsday Machine, or show leniency of any sort. Spock values the strange animal of Janus VII as a unique life-form with intrinsic dignity. The humans should protect it if possible. Implicitly, Spock accepts that the creature cannot be all bad. It does not deserve to die if other options are possible. Life matters. Kirk is not ready to hear this perspective.

The disagreement between Kirk and Spock dramatizes the struggle between a primitive, paranoid worldview and a more mature, integrated view of reality. At first, the episode portrays the early developmental stage when children project all wickedness outside themselves into the environment. The creature represents this externalized evil, which then attacks the human miners. They must kill it, Kirk argues; it is that simple. Mr. Spock moves beyond this paranoid position by realizing that the silicon life-form is not necessarily bad; it is just an animal. He tries to reflect on all aspects of its nature. This open-mindedness causes tension between Spock and Kirk. The captain cannot comprehend why it might be desirable to capture the creature instead of slaying it. Fear dominates his thinking.

Spock's reservations also raise questions we face as citizens of advanced societies. As the dominant species on Earth, do we consider the welfare of all animals or run roughshod over them? Do we protect biodiversity? Do we live in harmony with nature, or destroy it to extract what we want?

> Meeting the creature when alone, Kirk does not kill it on sight as he had intended; he holds it at bay with his phaser. Over a communicator, Spock advises the captain to shoot. Kirk's life is in danger, the Vulcan argues, and he cannot take the risk. Kirk does not think that firing his weapon is necessary and decides to wait.

Kirk and Spock reverse roles. The science officer advises the "shoot first and ask questions later" approach, while the captain shows restraint. What can we say about this flip-flop?

As people, we are at risk of regressing to more primitive styles of thinking when we are frightened. More nuanced views can temporarily vanish when we feel under threat. Mr. Spock is now scared that he will lose his friend and captain, so his balanced objectivity briefly disappears.

Kirk's hesitation shows that Spock's argument about preserving life had an impact, even though the captain did not show it at the time. That conversation persuaded Kirk, at least enough to hold his fire while weighing his options. Mature, secure people change their minds when circumstances demand; this ability is a strength, not a weakness. Allowing oneself to be influenced shows openness. The back and forth between Kirk and Spock tells us that they are both struggling to keep their fear and anger from controlling their actions. The contrasting scenes demonstrate how people often do better as a team than any one of them would perform separately. When paranoia dominates Kirk, Spock is thoughtful; then when Spock is afraid, Kirk shows compassion.

Arriving a few moments later, Spock makes telepathic contact with the creature using the Vulcan mind meld. He learns that the "Horta" is the mother of her race. Except for one individual, the entire population dies every fifty thousand years. She must protect and guide the next generation. The silicon nodules scattered throughout the mine are Horta eggs, which the miners had been destroying with disdain. She is fighting back, as any mother would.

Obsessed with revenge, the miners demand the Horta's death. They club the *Enterprise* crewmen holding them back and go en masse to lynch the creature. When they arrive, Kirk tells them that they have been murdering her children. Calmer and ashamed, the settlers plead ignorance.

The Horta, her newborn children, and the miners all form a symbiotic relationship. The silicon-based animals tunnel through the rocks, and the workers use the passageways to mine new mineral deposits.

"The Devil in the Dark" dramatizes how children start with an alternating loving and dangerous image of a parent and then put these two representations together into a more realistic picture. At first, the creature is pure evil. Persecutory and deadly, it murders miners for no apparent reason. It represents a dangerous adult who lacks any virtue. We learn by the end of the episode that it also has an admirable side; it is a devoted mother. Her natural maternal instinct compels her to do what is necessary to defend her children. The Horta is both good and bad; she is an integrated mixture of traits and intentions instead of one extreme or the other. Her seemingly contradictory excesses are just different aspects of the same life-form. The episode begins in the earlier developmental stage when everybody and everything seems black or white, and ends with a balanced view of the world with shades of gray.

In a sense, the Horta becomes a caring mother to the miners as well. She helps them tap the treasure house of minerals and become rich. The miners achieve a happy coexistence with their former persecutor. This synergy is similar to a child/parent relationship. Mom and Dad are indeed a treasure house of riches to youngsters, providing food, love, protection, and comfort. As the miners rely on the Horta, so young children depend on their parents to provide life's necessities and blessings. In return, parents feel the joy and fulfillment that goes with raising children.

The ideas presented in the next few paragraphs may seem strange. These concepts originated with a British psychoanalyst named Melanie Klein. Beginning her work in the 1920's, she was one of the first analysts to work with small children. She talked to youngsters, as Freud did with adults, but she also played with them, basing her notions on the themes that emerged. Klein's ideas have many critics, but they do not need to explain everything to convey something meaningful. Her writing comes to life in "The Devil in the Dark."

Melanie Klein believed that children have a rich fantasy life from the day they are born. Because their understanding of reality is embryonic, these imaginings can, by adult standards, seem wildly fantastic. Klein realized that youngsters are intensely curious about their mother's body and develop fancies about what lies inside her. Since they are too young to understand anatomy and physiology, they form their own ideas instead.

Children fantasize that there are levels and passageways throughout their mother's insides, lined with eggs or embryos of some sort. Her body contains pathways and corridors littered with babies, hundreds of them. With this in mind, the mining colony is a metaphor for what lies within the physical form of Mom's body, from the perspective of young children. The excavation is underground, or inside the mother planet. The mine consists of passages, tunnels, recesses, and levels, which is what young children believe lie within their mommy's physique. The silicon nodules, or Horta eggs, litter all the spaces of the quarry just as youngsters picture that babies populate every nook and cranny of their mother's innards. As adults, we know that women possess millions of eggs, but these gametes all lie within the two almond-sized ovaries. In contrast, children create a fantastic picture of the maternal body teeming with eggs or babies in every corner.

All children become angry with their parents at times. This natural reaction is impossible to avoid, as any mother or father knows. Melanie Klein described fantasies youngsters can have when they are upset, which serve to lessen the sense of humiliation and powerlessness that they feel at those moments.

When angry, children dream of destroying their mother's eggs. They want to scoop the babies out of her body and kill them. In this way, offspring will exact vengeance for whatever harm they feel Mom has inflicted upon them. At the same time, this fantasy terrifies children; they do not really want to hurt their parents. Without understanding that thoughts alone cannot harm people, the revenge fantasy can be horrifying to young minds. All the more reason for adults to tend to infants needs quickly so they do not have to feel frightened like this for very long, and to be gentle, patient, and loving with toddlers and young children.

The miners were destroying the eggs of the alien creature, as youngsters angrily wish to massacre the tiny babies inside their mother's body. The men were living out an early fantasy of retaliation, by their attack on Horta fertility. No wonder they felt so guilty when Kirk told them what they were doing. When they learned that the silicon nodules were the Horta's eggs, they felt ashamed of the angry wishes they had as children, which live on in the unconscious mind of adults.

The fantasy that mother's body is overflowing with eggs or babies turns up again in the episode "The Trouble with Tribbles," this time in an amusing light. Tribbles are small creatures that look like furry little powder puffs with no identifiable heads, eyes, or other distinguishing features. This appearance is more like an egg than an animal, with no up or down, bottom or top. Once aboard the *Enterprise*, the creatures reproduce uncontrollably, turning up everywhere within the ship. They line the corridors and rooms of the vessel the way the silicon nodules fill the mining colony. Their rapid breeding soon reaches crisis proportions, forcing the crew to get rid of them.

"The Devil in the Dark" succeeds at the psychoanalytic level; it also is a morality tale for us as a society. Do we understand the motives of others who seem to be against us? When does a group of people become a mob? Are we good stewards of the Earth, including all its plants and animals? Do we live in harmony with nature, or damage it in our thirst for resources? "The Devil in the Dark" touches many themes at different levels all at the same time, making it a particularly well-written story.

The next episode, "And the Children Shall Lead," will further explore the struggle to integrate good and evil.

And the Children Shall Lead

After receiving a distress call from the scientific expedition on the planet Triacus, Kirk, Spock, and McCoy beam down to investigate. Professor Starns dies before their eyes, while everybody else is already dead. They find a poisonous capsule in a lifeless woman's mouth and thus presume that the scientists killed themselves. The landing party plays an entry from Professors Starns' log. Nervous and agitated, he exclaims, "The alien among us! The enemy from within! Must destroy ourselves!"

Suddenly a group of children appears. Not only do they seem unharmed, but they are happy and energetic. They sing and play "Ring Around the Rosey," encircling a bewildered Captain Kirk.

Professor Starns' reference to the enemy from within signals that this episode will focus on human anger and destructiveness. Though he says that an alien is the source of the evil, an external force is often a fictional device to explore humanity's dark side. Professor Starns' statement, "The enemy from within," may be an allusion to the earlier episode actually entitled "The Enemy Within," which we discussed earlier in this chapter. Captain Kirk confronts his savage instincts in that adventure, in the form of an evil twin.

The professor also says, "Must destroy ourselves!" The evil is so overwhelming that it drives Starns and the others to suicide. They have gazed on the naked depravity of their souls as if viewing Medusa's head of snakes. To wipe out their wickedness, they sacrifice themselves.

In contrast, the children are oblivious to this gruesome scene. They have witnessed the mass suicide of their parents, yet act as if nothing has happened. Though they do not show any fear or sadness, they must feel it at some level. Nobody can watch Mom and Dad kill themselves without feeling horrified. The youngsters are repressing these feelings. They split off this part of their emotional life and put it away somewhere. They are only in touch with the happy, carefree, and playful aspects of childhood. "Ring Around the Rosey," as a nursery rhyme, song, and game, is generally considered to be a reference to the European Black Death, though this origin is debated.

Puzzled and alarmed, Kirk, Spock, and McCoy wonder why the horrific experience has not affected the children. Did an evil force induce the suicides? Were the children involved somehow? The landing party and youngsters beam up to the ship. Kirk decides that the *Enterprise* will stay in orbit around Triacus until they find an answer.

Back on the ship, Captain Kirk joins the children for ice cream. He talks about their parents, probing for feelings of sorrow. The youngsters say that the adults dragged them to a "dirty, old planet." Parents like "stupid things."

Just as the children are on the verge of some sadness, Tommy Starns chants, "Busy, busy, busy." Distracted, the children get up to play. They ask for more ice cream, but Kirk replies that it would spoil their dinner. With loathing, Tommy says, "What did I tell you? They all say it."

Once away from the adults, the children chant an eerie incantation which summons an evil spirit. The apparition tells the children that their destination is a Federation settlement; they should not let Captain Kirk take them anywhere else. "No one will tell us where to go or what to do."

The children are the real source of this episode's evil, in the form of the dark angel. Society likes to think that children are all sweet and innocent, so this may be a disturbing understanding of the story. As we have seen in previous chapters, however, anger and hostility are part of human nature at all ages. We cannot jettison our aggression just by wishing it away. We manage our shadowy side by tempering it with love, compassion, and generosity.

Captain Kirk tries to help the children deal with their hidden grief by eliciting their affection for their parents. Tommy successfully short circuits this effort; he portrays Kirk as another frustrating, depriving parent. The youths' loving side is compartmentalized and out of reach for now. Notably, Kirk would have done better to have a ship's counselor talk to the survivors, as his skills with them are rudimentary at best. Kids hate it when adults say, "It will spoil your dinner."

Since the apparition personifies the children's anger, it tempts them with a secret wish from their darker nature. It says, "No one will tell us what to do." The angel will liberate the children from their bossy parents and their stupid rules. The children will submit to nobody.

Using mind control, Tommy forces Sulu and Chekov to set a course for Arcus XII, a Federation settlement.

Kirk and Spock learn that Triacus was home to a band of marauders who made constant war throughout that stellar system. Ultimately, they were destroyed by "those they preyed upon." Legend says that the evil is awaiting a catalyst to unleash it upon the galaxy once again.

Still thinking that they are orbiting Triacus, Captain Kirk transports two security guards down to the surface. Later he learns that the *Enterprise* is nowhere near the planet. Horrified, Captain Kirk realizes that they beamed two crewmen into space.

The children summon the evil angel as Kirk arrives on the bridge. The spirit tells its young followers that the enemy has discovered them. "Call upon their beasts," he tells the youngsters. "Their beasts will serve us well." Kirk gives orders to Sulu, Spock, and Uhura, but Tommy Starns controls their minds, preventing them from following these directives. With his evil power, Tommy magnifies Kirk's fear that he is losing command. Anxiety overwhelms and immobilizes the captain. Spock regains control of himself and gets Kirk off the bridge.

The children are now the masters. They have taken the next step towards unleashing their own beasts. Feeling oppressed and persecuted by the adults, they have turned the tables on the *Enterprise* crew. Now in control, they exact revenge for the years of subjugation and humiliation they have endured. For now, their kind and loving selves have vanished. The demonic force continues its rampage through the *Enterprise*, as it laid waste to the scientific expedition on Triacus. One might wonder if the children are past the point of no return.

Kirk and Spock fight off their beasts. They head for auxiliary control to regain command of the ship, but another one of the children controls the minds of engineers there. Scotty threatens to kill Kirk and Spock if they do not leave.

Chekov believes that Starfleet has sent orders to arrest Kirk and Spock. He and two security guards try to seize them, but the captain and the science officer escape.

Back on the bridge, Kirk plays a tape of the chant that summons the dark angel. The spirit accuses Captain Kirk of being gentle—a "grave weakness." With all the children present, Kirk plays a video recording of the youngsters with their families enjoying a playful afternoon on Triacus. The children smile. Next, the video shows the adults' corpses littering the ground in unnatural, lifeless positions. Then comes video footage of each parent's tombstone. The children cry uncontrollably. The evil spirit loses its power over the human offspring, turns hideous, and fades into nothingness.

The evil dissipates when it meets the children's better nature. Youngsters feel love and gratitude towards their parents, in spite of some frustration.

No person, child or adult, feels only hate; there is always a mixture of affection and irritation toward the people in our lives. Resentments aside, the children also feel warmth and fondness for their parents and sorrow at their loss. Kirk uses the video to bring these repressed feelings to the surface. The children had temporarily forgotten that their parents could be loving, playful, and generous. The ferocious anger cannot survive when it meets love and caring—so the spirit evaporates. It is a personification of the children's rage. When their positive life force tempers their fury, the malevolent ghost loses his power.

In the final minutes of "And the Children Shall Lead," the youngsters take a big developmental step. They integrate the giving and depriving images of their parents together into one. The children become whole people, with feelings that range the entire spectrum of human emotion. They also see adults as complete persons, with moods of their own. The children can now mourn their parents' deaths.

From a sociopolitical point of view, we should all be on guard for evil spirits like that in "And the Children Shall Lead." The dark angel magnified the children's indignation to the point that it overshadowed everything else; there are people and forces in the world that that can wreak similar havoc in our lives. When misused or abused, alcohol and drugs magnify self-pity and resentment. Demagogues stoke their devotees' prejudice and bitterness. Ideological driven media on television and the internet seems to enhance and exploit people's darker natures. As Captain Kirk wondered what happened to the children's grief, we might ask ourselves if the people we follow and the substances and media we consume are helping us become our best selves— or are they degrading and using us?

CHAPTER 8: UNRULY KIDS

Children not only need to accept that they have a destructive side to their personality, but they also must control it. They cannot strike out, scream, or tear things apart every time they feel frustrated. How do young people develop control over their aggression?

Integrating the good and bad mental images of oneself and others is a crucial step in mastering hostility. When children recognize that the parent who frustrates them is the same person who loves and provides for them, they can soften their anger. It is easier for youngsters to snap at somebody if they think that person is all bad. It is harder when they realize that they are biting the hand that feeds them.

If emotional development proceeds on track, children integrate good and bad mental images between ages two and three years old. They learn that they have both an antagonistic, caustic side, and a loving and giving one as well. Still, they cannot always control their savage instincts, though they recognize them as part of their person.

During the early years, children are heavily dependent on their parents to help them control their aggression. Caretakers supervise their toddlers to protect them, but also to teach them the basic rules of living with other people. These expectations include: do not hit; be polite; do not scream; show consideration for others; do not tear things apart or break them; and so on. Parents maintain control over their children's aggressiveness using these basic guidelines. Moms and dads instinctively know that their children could go wild if not supervised and given a clear message about what conduct is okay and what is not. Youngsters need their parents to set limits for them if their behavior is going to remain within bounds. Adults step in when a child's actions go beyond what is acceptable.

In this chapter, we will discuss three episodes in which one or more characters lose control of their aggression, or exert little or no effort to contain it themselves. A higher authority, representing the parents, steps in to manage the situation.

"Where No Man Has Gone Before" portrays a man who stops making any attempt to restrain his brutality. It is the second *Star Trek* pilot film, produced after NBC rejected the original installment, "The Cage," which we discussed in Chapter 3. The network approved this subsequent attempt, and full-scale production of *Star Trek* then began. The episode features most of the familiar characters, except Dr. McCoy, who is not yet a member of the crew. The mood of the story is dark. NBC could have chosen to reject this installment as well, but it is different in that Captain Kirk acts bravely and heroically, in contrast to Captain Pike in "The Cage," who is irritable and petulant.

Where No Man Has Gone Before

The *Enterprise* finds a distress beacon, ejected from the earth ship *Valiant* two hundred years ago. From a message inserted into the device, Captain Kirk and his officers learn that the *Valiant* encountered an unknown energy field at the edge of the galaxy. Seven people died in the encounter; one crew member suffered injuries but recovered. The sequence of events afterward is unclear, but the crew of the *Valiant* frantically tried to learn more about extrasensory perception, ESP. Eventually, the *Valiant* crew blew up their own ship.

The energy field unleashed something dreadful aboard the *Valiant*. We will learn later that the awful force is humanity's own aggression and hatred. This evil either consumed the *Valiant*'s crew, or they deliberately destroyed themselves hoping to protect the rest of the galaxy.

To investigate further, the *Enterprise* travels to the edge of the galaxy and confronts the same mysterious force that damaged the *Valiant*. The energy field kills nine and shocks two crew members unconscious, Lieutenant Commander Gary Mitchell and Psychiatrist Elizabeth Dehner. When Mitchell wakes up, his eyes have an eerie silver glow; otherwise, he seems unharmed. Both Dehner and Mitchell had high ESP ratings before the encounter, suggesting that it made them more susceptible to the energy anomaly.

Mitchell develops fantastic powers. He reads minds, devours half the ship's library in one day, and moves objects with his thoughts alone. He treats his former friends with contempt, as playthings for his amusement. The bridge controls go crazy while Mitchell smiles demonically in his sick bay bed. His powers are growing at an exponential rate.

The same evil that erupted on board the *Valiant* is swelling within Gary Mitchell. The creepy change in his eyes represents this malevolence. He treats colleagues and former friends with scorn and disdain. Mitchell's ugly side is coming to the surface.

Mitchell freely accepts responsibility for his nastiness. We have seen other episodes that reveal how people can project their anger outside themselves into an external threat or split it off from the rest of their person. Mitchell does neither of these things. He never denies that the evil is a part of himself. Nobody attributes the malevolence in this story to a demonic angel, an alien probe, or any other external force. Mitchell's satanic side was present all along; the energy at the edge of the galaxy merely helped it come to the surface.

Though Mitchell takes ownership of his immoral self, he makes no effort to control it. He presumes that his newfound power gives him the right to mistreat others, trampling on their feelings and rights. We all have a savage side to our personality, but healthy adults can regulate themselves. Mitchell successfully contained his aggression before the *Enterprise* encountered the energy field. He is quickly losing this ability, exercising little or no restraint over his bestial impulses.

The new Gary Mitchell is similar to a three-year-old child. Most youngsters this age understand that they can be naughty at times, but they cannot always control this behavior on their own. They occasionally act impulsively and rely on their parents, teachers, and other adults to keep their conduct within bounds. Similarly, Mitchell accepts his depraved side, yet he does not have mastery over it. Because of his growing supernatural abilities, nobody can restrain Mitchell, and he can no longer do this for himself.

Mitchell's fantastic strengths dramatize another way that he portrays a three-year-old child, as youngsters this age still have an unrealistic understanding of their place in the world. They overestimate their importance, and dream of Godlike influence. Kids have fantasies of flying and other superhuman powers. Three-year-old children are still very egocentric; they think the world revolves around them. Though much more knowledgeable and sophisticated than infants, preschoolers' ideas and wishes can be extreme and whimsical by adult standards. These fantasies come to life in Mitchell. He can make anything happen with his thoughts alone. He can dominate others with a mere thought or punish them for their transgressions. Children sometimes dream of these imaginary powers to cope with feelings of helplessness and envy; other times their daydreams are just fun and fancy. In Mitchell's case, his menacing transformation is undoing all the self-control he had accomplished since childhood.

Spock warns that Mitchell is extremely dangerous and suggests that Kirk kill him "while you still can." The captain opposes outright murder but does agree to strand Mitchell on an uninhabited world. Kirk and others drug the superhuman lieutenant and beam down to a planet's surface with him. Now imprisoned behind a force field, Mitchell uses his telekinetic powers to strangle Lieutenant Lee Kelso with a cable, unlock his cell, and shocks Captain Kirk and Mr. Spock unconscious. Mitchell escapes with Dr. Dehner, who goes with him willingly as she has suddenly gained the same powers herself.

When Kirk regains consciousness, he follows Mitchell and Dehner with a phaser rifle. He orders the ship to leave in twelve hours if they do not hear from him, with the recommendation that Starfleet expose the planet to a lethal dose of neutron radiation.

Mitchell is telepathically aware of Captain Kirk's approach. He sends Dehner to talk with him, so she can see for herself "how unimportant they are."

Kirk appeals to Dr. Dehner for help. He reminds her that, as a psychiatrist, she should understand that people bury many ugly, savage things under the surface. Mitchell no longer needs to keep these dark instincts concealed, Kirk argues. Despite the superhuman powers, the captain adds, Mitchell is still driven by human frailties.

Dr. Dehner is about to agree with Kirk when Mitchell arrives, proclaiming, "Morals are for men, not gods!" He creates a grave and tombstone for Kirk and forces his ex-friend to pray to him.

Mitchell becomes more grandiose and cruel as the episode progresses. He shows less and less restraint over his hateful self and becomes increasingly alienated from feelings of love, friendship, and kindness. Any warmth, empathy, or compassion gradually evaporates. He has left his humanity behind. Mitchell is not going to suddenly have a moment of regret and pull back from the brink.

Mitchell is like an out-of-control child who cannot reestablish calm and self-control without help. Captain Kirk assumes the role of parent, who must step in to stop Mitchell's misbehavior. If Kirk fails, the Federation will irradiate the entire planet, killing everything. In either case, the adults will be in charge once again.

Spock's recommendation to kill Mitchell is a little out of character. "Where No Man Has Gone Before" was the pilot film, so I suspect that the producers and the actor were still in the process of sorting out Spock's identity. The Spock of later episodes may have come to the same conclusion, but would have done so more carefully and with the idea that preserving life whenever possible is logical.

> Alarmed by Mitchell's sadism, Dr. Dehner attacks him with her power. They shock each other until Mitchell's energy temporarily dissipates. Kirk kills Mitchell, while Dr. Dehner quietly dies.

Let's examine this episode and its ending from different viewpoints. At face value, the narrative is grim and pessimistic. It suggests that people would sadistically murder their best friends if given half the chance, which seems over the top. What constructive messages can we glean from this story?

From a psychoanalytic point of view, the adventure does metaphorically portray a situation we lived through as kids. Sometimes we lost control of our behavior, and the adults had to step in. As the resolution of "Where No Man Has Gone Before" involves killing Mitchell, however, the parallel of Kirk as a parent is disconcerting. Murdering misbehaving youths seems excessive. One could argue that Kirk represents the child, not the adult, who is fighting an abusive father figure in Gary Mitchell. In this scenario, Mitchell's death is still unnerving. Even traumatized children do not want to see a parent executed. "Where No Man Has Gone Before" is unsatisfying, from a developmental perspective. Other episodes, in contrast, will supply kinder answers to the allegorical question, "Is anybody going to control that child?"

The episode could be renamed "The Tragedy of Gary Mitchell." As in other tragic drama, the value comes from understanding the character's fall so we can avoid a similar fate in our own lives. So what does "Where No Man Has Gone Before" have to say to us as adults?

The episode reminds us that we need to keep our base instincts in check if we want to remain in a civilized society. Even as adults, we rely on the environment to help control our behavior to some degree. If we break the law, we know there will be some unpleasant consequences. This awareness helps us resist aggressive or illegal impulses. The looting that occurs during times of anarchy or natural disaster shows that adults do indeed need law and policing to keep their behavior within bounds. Without some adverse consequences for our actions, we may indulge our wishes to lie, cheat, steal, and destroy.

Even with law and government, some people cannot or will not control their aggression. Murderers, thieves, and other criminals must be incarcerated to prevent their dangerous and unlawful acts. The legal system is like a parent for these individuals. Society places external limits on their freedom because they act in socially unacceptable ways. For some, reporting to a probation officer is enough to deter any further lawbreaking. Others need continuous containment within a prison. Hopefully, when they complete their sentence, ex-convicts can then keep their actions within legal limits without constant supervision.

Most poignantly, "Where No Man Has Gone Before" is a cautionary tale about the abuse of power. Having the ability and opportunity to do something does not make it right. We always pay a price when we violate the rights of others or trample on people to get our way, even if we escape any apparent fallout. The cost is not always obvious and may not be evident until a series of similar actions pile up.

The price we pay for immoral behavior is that we lose touch with our humanity. *Homo sapiens* is a social, cooperative species; we thrive by working together on common goals, with caring and concern for each other. We celebrate together, and we mourn together. War occurs, but much more often it is avoided. Corrupt acts alienate us from our true self. We find this lesson in history, politics, religion, commerce, and other aspects of society.

Gary Mitchell's abuse of his colleagues isolated him from them and from his true nature. He drifted further and further away from his humanity until nothing was left. The person he used to be was gone. Community, belonging, cooperation, and caring were all sacrificed at the altar of narcissism and power. He thought he had become a god, but in truth, he had lost everything. The story takes these themes to an extreme, but it still speaks to us average people traveling through life. Our actions affect people. We cannot ignore our impact on others without losing a part of ourselves. Without a community, we are not complete people.

Like Gary Mitchell, the main character in "Charlie X" has difficulty controlling his anger and aggression. The tragedy is similar in some ways to "Where No Man Has Gone Before," but there are notable differences as well.

Charlie X

During a rendezvous with the cargo ship *Antares*, the *Enterprise* picks up Charlie Evans. He is the lone survivor of a crash on the planet Thasus fourteen years earlier. Three years old at the time of the accident, he is now seventeen. He survived on native foods and learned to talk by listening to the disabled ship's computer tapes. Though he speaks English well, his social skills are atrocious. He repeatedly intrudes while Captain Kirk and the *Antares* crew are talking. Kirk tells Charlie that interrupting is considered wrong. The captain of the *Antares* seems anxious to leave.

Though Charlie is physically seventeen years old, emotionally he is only three, his age at the time of the *Antares* shipwreck. He is impatient, impulsive, and awkward. He blurts out his thoughts without a filter and wants things to happen immediately. The interrupting demonstrates his inexperience with social etiquette and cluelessness regarding the feelings of others. But he also is enthusiastic and filled with childlike wonder, which makes him sympathetic despite his immaturity. Emotionally, Charlie is fixated at age three just as he was stranded physically on the planet Thasus at that early age.

By gently correcting Charlie's rude behavior, Captain Kirk acts like his father. Parents of three-year-old children must teach their youngsters how to behave in polite, acceptable ways. Kirk has already begun to do this with Charlie. The captain is not particularly skilled at it, but whom among us had perfect parents?

As he interacts with the crew, Charlie's lack of social grace is painfully evident. He clumsily asks Dr. McCoy, "Do you like me?" He is infatuated with Yeoman Rand and gives her some perfume as a present. This gift suggests some supernatural powers, as there is nowhere that he could have obtained this gift. Trying to escape gracefully, Yeoman Rand tells him to meet her in the rec-room after her shift.

When he arrives in the lounge, several people have assembled. Lieutenant Uhura sings a teasing song about Mr. Spock and then turns her attention to Charlie. Her song angers him. With some unknown power, he takes away Uhura's voice. No one suspects that Charlie is the cause of her sudden laryngitis.

Charlie temporarily wins the admiration of Rand and the other crew members by doing some amazing card tricks, illusions so inexplicable that they should have aroused some suspicion.

Like a three-year-old child showing off, Charlie feels terrific when he receives the attention and applause of the others. He is happy when he is center stage. Charlie especially wants Yeoman Rand to smile with admiration and praise, the way a mother approves of her son and thinks everything he does is brilliant. Charlie is yearning for the parenting he never received.

While Charlie is on the bridge, the *Antares* calls Kirk with an urgent warning, yet the freighter explodes before they can convey the reason for their alarm. Charlie seems amused by the tragedy and comments, "It wasn't very well constructed."

The dietary department calls over the intercom and tells Kirk that the meatloaf has turned into live turkeys. Charlie laughs under his breath.

Why hasn't somebody deduced that Charlie is causing these strange events? He has created perfume out of nowhere, done impossible card tricks, blown up the *Antares*, caused Uhura to lose her voice, and turned processed meatloaf into live turkeys. Even Kirk and Spock do not seem suspicious of him.

Since Charlie represents a three-year-old child, the crew's selective vision parallels society's wish to deny the hostility and rich fantasy life present in children. Youngsters this age have imaginings about everything that Charlie is doing in real life. They dream of fantastic powers and yearn to retaliate when they feel hurt or ignored. Like parents who see their children as sweet and innocent, Kirk and Spock are blind to what is happening. They must find it distasteful to think that Charlie is behind these inexplicable events.

Notice also that Charlie does not deny responsibility for his hostile acts. He keeps his culpability secret, but he is not remorseful or conflicted about what he has done. In truth, he seems quite pleased with himself. Charlie is fully aware of what he is doing. He doesn't pretend, even to himself, that someone else or an alien force is responsible for what is going on. He knows that this ugly half is a part of him, as are his more likable qualities.

As a three-year-old child, Charlie wildly overestimates the power of his thoughts and is naïve about how to live in harmony with others. Though he recognizes the aggressive side to his person, he has little control over it. He quickly lashes out when he experiences hurt or gets angry. Feeling wounded and rejected by the *Antares* crew, Charlie kills them in retaliation, hoping to soothe his injured self-esteem.

Charlie asks Mr. Spock to play a game of chess. Spock offers to teach him, but Charlie impatiently insists that he knows the rules. Charlie loses after only a few moves. When Spock leaves the room, Charlie furiously reduces his opponent's chess pieces to smoldering lumps of melted plastic.

Like all children, Charlie is envious of adults. The power and knowledge of grown-ups seem fantastic to little ones. They wish that they could miraculously know everything that adults do and have all their abilities and know-how. Charlie desperately wants to beat Mr. Spock at chess from the very first time he plays the game. If he could win, he would not feel as envious of Mr. Spock's experience and skills. This childish petulance is why he refuses any instruction from the Vulcan; if Mr. Spock helped him, it would deny Charlie the triumph he seeks to counter his painful feelings of inadequacy. Humiliated when he loses the game, Charlie takes out his anger on the chess pieces. He wants them to feel as beaten as he does. Young children often attribute human qualities or vulnerabilities to inanimate objects.

> Charlie pours out his love for Yeoman Rand. He says he is "hungry all over" for her and offers to give her the entire universe.

Charlie does not want a girlfriend; he wants a mother. Despite his lofty rhetoric, he cares very little for Yeoman Rand. Charlie has no idea what she is really like, what she needs, or whether she is interested in him. He can only think about his own desires and needs. He longs for a mother who will care for him twenty-four hours a day without demanding anything in return. He craves praise and admiration, which would boost his fragile self-esteem. He is not capable of seeing Yeoman Rand as a person in her own right, independent of what he wants from her.

Charlie's declaration that he is "hungry all over" supports the idea that Charlie wants a mother/child relationship with Yeoman Rand. Charlie wants Yeoman Rand to feed him the way mothers nurse their little ones. Nourishing youngsters is a profoundly important part of the mother/child relationship, from birth onward. Throughout the rest of our lives, hunger is closely tied psychologically with our longing for Mom. Charlie's appetite is for food, love, praise, and the other nurturing that mothers provide. Charlie also wants Yeoman Rand sexually, but this desire is a minor factor for now. He yearns for the loving parent he never had.

> Yeoman Rand asks Kirk to speak to Charlie about his crush. Kirk tells Charlie that Rand does not share his feelings for her. The boy is devastated; he feels like the world is ending. Kirk becomes impatient and scolds him, "There are a million things in this universe you can have, and there are a million things you can't have. It's no fun facing that, but that's the way things are." So, "Hang on tight and survive. Everybody does."

"Crush" is an apt word for Charlie's affection. Yeoman Rand probably felt suffocated under his needy demands, and Charlie was bound to feel deflated. Another name for a crush is "puppy love" as it resembles the worshipful adoration of a young pup. The word "infatuation" implies an idealized view of somebody else. All three terms have derogatory connotations, implying that the feelings are shallow and transient; in fact, the emotions are powerfully and compellingly deep and real. Just reflect back on your own life. Do you remember feeling like your world was ending when an adored person was indifferent to you? Scenes in "Charlie X" are some of the hardest to watch in the original *Star Trek*. Charlie embodies the unrequited love of a neglected toddler.

Kirk is correct in his feedback to Charlie, but he is impatient and expects the boy to condense fourteen years of growth into a few minutes. The situation is not going to end well.

> To help Charlie discharge some tension, Kirk takes him to the gym for a lesson in martial arts. Again, Charlie wants to do it perfectly from the beginning. He tries to throw Kirk to the floor before he has any skills at all. Kirk gently takes Charlie to the mat while an onlooker chuckles. Charlie is furious. "Don't laugh at me!" he screams. Using his powers, he makes the man vanish. Finally recognizing Charlie's danger, Kirk orders him to go to his quarters accompanied by two security guards. Initially defiant, Charlie bows to Kirk's will. The captain learns that all the phasers aboard the ship have disappeared.

> Charlie comes to the bridge. He shocks Lieutenant Uhura, prevents Sulu from changing the *Enterprise*'s course heading, and forces Mr. Spock to recite poetry. Kirk orders the youth to leave the crew alone. Charlie obeys. Spock points out that the boy will soon refuse to back down.

Captain Kirk's disapproval helps Charlie restrain himself some. He looks up to Kirk as a father and wants his support. Charlie's wish to please the captain, however, will only go so far, as Mr. Spock asserts. Without the ability to win a power struggle with Charlie, Kirk's control over the boy will evaporate. As a three-year-old child, Charlie cannot control himself all on his own, and Kirk's ability to influence him is quickly fading.

Parents must impose their authority periodically to help children keep their behavior within appropriate limits until they can do this for themselves. Often a verbal reprimand will get youngsters to behave, but sometimes other measures are needed. A "time-out" involves separating a child from the location where the unwanted conduct occurred, to a space with little stimulation so the child can settle down. The time-out place can be a corner, a chair, and sometimes a separate room. Alternatively, adults can change the activity associated with the misbehavior, usually to something neutral or even tedious. Time-out is a method of discipline as well as a way to help children develop the ability to calm down on their own and avoid acting on urges that will cause problems. For the strategy to work, however, the adults need to be bigger than the kids. Size matters.

Captain Kirk does not have the leverage to compel Charlie to behave himself. They are roughly the same size, and Charlie's supernatural powers make him a giant next to Kirk. So far, Kirk has relied on the boy's wish for approval, but it will not be enough to control Charlie indefinitely. Captain Kirk is simply not big and strong enough to make the boy comply.

> Angry from the confrontation with Kirk, Charlie turns a woman crew member into a lizard. He enters Yeoman Rand's quarters without permission and tries to force himself upon her. She slaps him harshly. Furious, Charlie makes her vanish.

> Spock and Kirk lead Charlie into a room guarded by a force field, but this does not contain him. Charlie makes the entire wall of the detainment cell disappear. In retaliation, he transforms a young woman into a debilitated old lady. When he hears another woman laughing, Charlie erases her face, leaving a featureless area that is unable to talk, see, or breathe.

Not only is Charlie angry, but he is also intensely envious. He craves the social grace and professional competence of Kirk and the others, but all the power in the universe cannot bring him these things. He remains socially inept no matter how hard he tries, and this makes him furious. Learning social and vocational skills takes time and work, but Charlie is so envious he wants to do everything instantly. He feels humiliated and enraged that others can do things that he cannot.

The horrifying things Charlie does to the women illustrates the damaging power of envy. He cannot have what he wants, so he retaliates by depriving others of the good things that they have. He destroys one young woman's beauty, turns another into a lizard, robs a third of her laughter and her face, and makes Yeoman Rand disappear. Charlie inflicts these atrocities on the others so they are no longer happy and competent, and no longer rouse his envy. In a sick way, destroying the good in others makes Charlie feel better. He is envious of the *Enterprise* crew, but he is not resentful of a green reptile, a faceless person, or somebody who no longer exists.

Like Charlie, small children are also envious of their parent's power and abilities. To comfort themselves, youngsters have fantasies of robbing adults of everything good. This way, their moms and dads would no longer have anything to covet. Unlike Charlie, however, real children cannot make their fantasies come true.

In healthy homes, parents put the welfare of their children above almost everything else. As a result, kids get frustrated and envious a relatively small amount of the time. Envy is a painful and corrosive emotion. With nurturing, love, limits, and guidance, youngsters do not have to feel this agony for much of their day. Also, by encouraging children's education and growth, we give the message that someday they will be grown up. In time, they will enjoy the skills and freedoms of adulthood. Desire is less painful if offspring know that the things they crave will someday be available to them.

> The arrival of a Thasian spaceship interrupts a final confrontation between Kirk and Charlie. A race of pure energy, the Thasians gave Charlie his powers when he crashed on their planet so he could survive. They apologize that they did not learn of his departure sooner. They bring back Yeoman Rand and the other *Enterprise* crew that Charlie harmed, but they cannot restore the Antares. Charlie will go back to Thasus with them.

> Begging to stay, Charlie promises never to misbehave again. Despite the danger, Kirk argues that the boy needs to be with his own kind. The Thasians know that this is impossible. He will always use his powers.

The Thasians finally get control over Charlie and his outrageous behavior. Like any good parent, they are firm and clear; he will not be allowed to harm others. Unlike Captain Kirk, the Thasians can ensure that Charlie obeys. The boy still needs this external control to keep his conduct in check. If the Thasians were to leave, Charlie would quickly act up again.

Charlie is a tragic figure. He is physically an adult but lacks the psychological and social tools he needs to deal with real-world responsibilities and situations. Without superpowers, he could eventually learn these skills, but as long as he can soothe his hurt immediately by lashing out this growth will be impossible.

As a consultant at a juvenile prison for nine years, I saw many teenagers like Charlie. These youths often lacked the basic skills needed to succeed in society. They had poor control over their conduct, so eventually got into trouble with the law. Social awkwardness and confusion about how to behave were common issues, along with a variety of other problems.

Juvenile offenders often come with histories of profound abuse and neglect. Their caretakers may have beaten or sexually abused them. Alcohol and drug abuse has multilayered and harmful effects on family members, even those who are not using the substance. One or both parents may have abandoned the children or might have been incarcerated themselves, currently or in the past. Some families let their children run wild. Other adults place too much responsibility on kids before they are ready to handle it.

Inevitably, some children grow to adulthood without the skills to control their behavior and build a satisfying life of their own. In these cases, society must intervene and insist that these youngsters keep their conduct within acceptable limits. This external control does not feel like help to them, but it is necessary. Their lives will go nowhere until they can keep their behavior within bounds.

"The Squire of Gothos" is similar to "Charlie X." It features Trelane, an adult with fantastic powers, who is emotionally a three-year-old child. Trelane lives alone on a planet and studies Earth's history. Holding Kirk and the *Enterprise* captive, he treats them like toys for his amusement, rather than as people whose freedom and dignity deserve respect. The situation is like a game to him. Despite his interest in humanity's past, his grasp of people is superficial. He mimics Earth customs without any genuine understanding, as children imitate the adults around them.

Narcissistic and cruel, Trelane believes the universe revolves around him, and he utterly disregards the rights and wishes of others. He kidnaps Captain Kirk, conducts a mock trial, chases him down like an animal, and almost murders him. Trelane's parents, two disembodied masses of energy, finally appear and stop him from harming Captain Kirk any further. Like Charlie Evans, Trelane accepts the aggression within himself, but he exercises little restraint over it. He desperately needs his caretakers to keep an eye on him.

Trelane's parents should have stepped in sooner. They prevented Trelane from killing Kirk, but they allowed him to trample on the captain's rights, feelings, and dignity. The out-of-control behavior is harmful to Kirk, but it is also damaging to Trelane himself. Cruelty and abuse degrade the perpetrator as well as the victim. Human children must learn that others have independence and worth, that getting along with people is necessary to be happy and prosperous. Trelane will not learn this if his parents permit his sadism to go unchecked. In "Charlie X," the Thasians came as soon as they realized that the boy was gone; they apologized and tried to reverse the damage.

In contrast, Trelane's parents do not explain what took them so long. They hardly seem concerned about their son's unruly behavior; obviously, humans are inferior. The maternal pulsating splotch says, "If you cannot take proper care of your 'pets' you cannot have them at all." Mommy and Daddy show up primarily because it is time for their special boy to come in for the day. When Trelane protests, the blobs of energy tell him to stop whining, or he will not be able to make any more planets. Trelane is like the rich kid, whose punishment is to fly on a commercial airline instead of the family jet. His elitist progenitors are not correcting his behavior; they just hate the pouting. Good parenting involves setting a good example, and these two super beings score a two on a scale of one to ten.

"Errand of Mercy" also depicts how parents need to take control when their children's aggression gets out of hand. The story has political overtones; we will discuss these issues as well.

Errand of Mercy

War erupts between the Federation and the Klingon Empire. The *Enterprise* arrives at the strategically located planet Organia, home to a peaceful and primitive culture, to offer protection and form an alliance.

Captain Kirk and Mr. Spock beam down to the planet and find that the inhabitants are curiously uninterested in them. Trefayne, chairman of the Organian high council, eventually shows up and welcomes them. Kirk meets with the ruling committee while Spock does some investigating. Spock discovers that the culture is stagnant; they have not advanced for over ten thousand years.

Kirk explains the Klingon menace to the Organian council, a group of elderly, mild-mannered men. They are pleasant, discount any danger, and respectfully decline Starfleet's offer of assistance. Kirk gets angry with the Organians for their apparent naïvety.

A fleet of Klingon warships arrives. The *Enterprise* leaves orbit suddenly, stranding Kirk and Spock on the surface. Kirk says, "I told you so!" to the Organian council, but they remain unconcerned.

The ancient culture and the elderly council both allude to the parental role the Organians will play. Kirk, the Federation, and the Klingons represent the youngsters who lose control of their hostility. The Organians will eventually intervene and manage the situation. Like good moms and dads, they will not allow their children to fight.

There are two other ways that the Organians represent decent parents. First off, the stability of their culture mirrors the steadiness found in healthy homes. A dependable, predictable, and calm home life provides the solid foundation youngsters need to face the stresses of the world and reach their potential. Frequent moves and changes in caretakers are very disruptive to children, as are confusing and inconsistent rules. Organian culture is the epitome of consistency. Kirk and Spock criticize the society as stagnant, blind to its advantages. They misjudge the Organians in more ways than one, as we shall see.

The second way that the Organians represent good parents is by their calm approach to conflict. The men on the council look like loving and kind grandfathers. Kirk becomes irritable and contemptuous, yet the Organians do not act angry in return. They remain tranquil in spite of Kirk's harsh criticism. Good parents realize that their children will get upset at times. While adults get annoyed, they should not let their ire take control of the situation. This unruffled approach helps children feel secure and protected.

Kirk misreads the Organians for the second time, misinterpreting their composure as weakness. He fails to consider that the Organians may know something that he does not, just as youngsters cannot always appreciate that their parents may have a broader idea of the world and what a given situation might require. Kirk quickly jumps to conclusions. He lets his hate for the Klingons dictate his thoughts and actions.

It needs to be said, in spite of the allegory in this episode, that sometimes moms and dads are wrong. Sometimes adults are a little off track; in other cases, their stewardship is inexcusable. Father does not always know best. As a society, we have a legacy of downplaying or ignoring child abuse and neglect. We victimize youngsters a second time when they ask for help, and we blame them for what happened. Thankfully, we are making some progress as a culture. In spite of setbacks, our collective attitude is progressing in regards to the mistreatment of children and other vulnerable people.

Kirk masquerades as an Organian, Spock as a Vulcan trader. A Klingon tyrant, Kor, takes control of the planet with an occupation army. Like Kirk, he loathes the complacent attitude of the council.

Kirk and Spock blow up a Klingon ammunition dump, attempting to show the Organians that they can fight back. The council scolds Kirk for this act of violence and implores him never to do anything like it again.

Since they bugged the council chamber, the Klingons learn that Kirk and Spock are responsible for the sabotage. Kor takes them into custody. He gives Kirk twelve hours to tell all that he knows, or they will extract the information with the Klingon "mind sifter," which permanently scrambles the brain. Kor also promises to dissect Mr. Spock.

Miraculously, Trefayne walks past the Klingon guards and rescues Kirk and Spock from their prison cell. The Organian leader explains that he and the council could not permit the Klingons to harm them. Kirk shows no gratitude or astonishment at this escape. Against the Organians' advice, he and Spock take their phasers and plan to capture Kor.

Neither Kirk nor Spock is curious about their baffling rescue because hatred clouds their minds. If they reflected on what happened, they would realize that the Organians are more resourceful than they appear to be. Kirk continues to despise the soft-spoken men of the ruling council even though they saved his life.

Kirk's lack of gratitude does not upset the Organians; they stay calm despite the captain's condemnation and contempt. Similarly, parents can best handle tense situations if they remain composed when their children are angry. Of course, adults also get upset. There is no way to rear offspring without feeling frustrated and impatient at times, yet ramping up the conflict to even higher levels accomplishes nothing. Caretakers can temper the intensity of their children's outbursts by staying cool. It is better to deal with underlying issues after everybody has calmed down.

Recognizing that anger is a natural human emotion can help parents remain calm when their youngster throws a tantrum. Like anybody else, children can become hot when they do not get what they want. Sometimes moms and dads need to step in to interrupt a behavior, but more importantly, they should teach children how to manage their feelings in constructive ways. Time-outs teach kids that a few minutes away from a situation can calm things down. As adults, just taking three deep breaths can detoxify many stressful moments. Youngsters can draw images that reflect what they feel inside or point to a picture of a face that matches their emotion. Sometimes caretakers can encourage young ones to switch what they are doing, directing their energy into more constructive activities.

Ideally, older children and teenagers learn to use words and language to express themselves and describe how they feel. Parents can encourage this skill by listening, by giving their offspring a voice. Letting youngsters speak their mind does not mean that adults need to acquiesce to childish demands. Hearing the kids out costs nothing and can pay handsome dividends. Idyllically, Mom and Dad also share their views and sentiments honestly with each other in conversation, thus modeling this talent for children. There are many reasons why both youngsters and adults can find it difficult to talk honestly about themselves; a fuller discussion of these factors would take us too far afield. Nevertheless, the best outcome is when children can express themselves verbally and in writing, with clarity, conviction, and openness.

This segment dramatizes a third way that the Organians represent good parents; they step in only when necessary. The Organians allow Kirk and the Klingons to handle their affairs as much as possible. They only interfere when somebody is about to get hurt. Caretakers should give children a chance to settle their conflicts but should intervene if violence is about to erupt. Good parenting is a balancing act. Moms and dads protect their children at times, but in other situations, they allow kids enough freedom to make mistakes. The Organians are sensitive to both sides of this equation.

Kirk and Spock capture Kor in his office. Several Klingon soldiers storm the room, yet nobody can use their weapons. Inexplicably, the phasers and Klingon disruptors radiate tremendous heat, making them useless. The combatants cannot fight with their fists either, as their bodies generate the same hotness if touched by another. In space, the Federation fleet arrives for battle, but neither they nor the Klingons can use their armaments.

The Organians tell the group that they have stopped the war. Kirk and Kor are furious, and demand that Trefayne allow them to handle their own affairs. Standing firm, the Organians refuse to let the violence go any further. Trefayne asks Kirk if war is really what the captain wants. The Organians transfigure into their true form; they are beings of pure energy, who have developed beyond the need for physical bodies.

Back aboard the *Enterprise*, Kirk feels embarrassed about his reaction to the Organians. He was furious with them for stopping a war he did not want.

The Organians finally step in and control the unruly children. They allow events to develop but intervene before combat begins. Parents sometimes must do what they feel is best for their children, even if it makes their youngsters furious. The Organians oppose violence and stop it, knowing that Kirk and Kor will be enraged. Since the Organians are bigger and stronger, they have the final say.

The episode ends on an optimistic note, as Captain Kirk reflects on what he has learned. He realizes that his aggression was out of control. He was not thinking clearly or considering any options other than fighting. Even the inexplicable rescue from prison did not arouse his curiosity or assuage his appetite for combat.

On a sociopolitical level, does "Errand of Mercy" advocate pacifism, the opposition to violence under any circumstances? At first glance, it may seem that the answer is yes; the episode appears to support the view that countries must avoid war at any cost, even when facing evil as great as military occupation by the Klingons. On reflection, however, I do not think that the episode is saying that war is never justified. It raises a different, more important issue.

"Errand of Mercy" asks the question, "Is war really what you want?" How many times in history have people rushed to war, even welcomed it, with no idea what was coming? Combatants in the American Civil War expected that one battle would decide the entire conflict. In World War I, the Germans declared war on France in August 1914, convinced that they would be victorious in a matter of weeks and the troops would be home eating dinner with their families that Christmas Day. Again and again, leaders and citizens inflate the righteousness of their cause, underestimate the strength and resolve of their opponents, brim with overconfidence, and discount the human suffering on all sides. While true pacifism is not a viable position, in my view, there is hardly a more important question than: Is war really what you want?

Trefayne's query brings Kirk back to his senses. Freed from his bloodlust, the captain feels embarrassed about his thirst for war and controls his hostility better when he meets the Klingons again in "Day of the Dove." We will examine that episode in the next chapter.

Chapter 9: Conscience

How do children learn to resist their aggressive urges? After all, their parents cannot supervise them for their entire lives. What stops kids from beating each other up when adults are out of the room?

Children gradually develop a conscience, which then helps them control their behavior. This sense of morality is an inner knowledge of right and wrong, along with the desire to act accordingly. After forming a moral compass, youngsters are less dependent on their parents' constant observation. This chapter will discuss how children acquire a conscience and how *Star Trek* dramatizes this process. In "Day of the Dove" and "Arena," Captain Kirk fends off his violent instinct by doing what he feels is right. "A Taste of Armageddon" portrays the corrupted conscience of an entire culture.

At first, children behave themselves mainly to avoid their parents' reprimands. Fear of their caretakers' disapproval often stops young children from acting aggressively. They know that screaming and hitting will evoke the adults' ire. Understanding how much they rely on their moms and dads, kids do not act naughty because they do not want to lose their parents' love and support. At this stage, this fear does not reflect the presence of a conscience. Youngsters dread the adult's actual reaction, not a sense within themselves that they disapprove of their own actions.

Gradually, children internalize their parents to form a conscience. Within the youngster's mind are images of their caretakers, which praise good deeds and frown on misbehavior. The result is that kids do not always need adults around to keep their conduct in check. Mom and Dad may not be there to exclaim, "No, no!" but a voice inside the child's head says "no" instead. These mental constructs keep youngsters out of mischief even when nobody else is around. Just as children crave the approval of real-life people, they try to please the dictates of their developing conscience by behaving in sanctioned ways.

An example will help show how children form their conscience from experiences with their parents. When our daughter was about one year old, she had a lustful interest in our stereo equipment, which was within her reach. Our disapproval was barely enough to keep her from fiddling with the knobs. (Yes, I am aware that it was my wife's and my responsibility to childproof the room; this is painfully obvious in retrospect.) When we turned our backs, she raced to the equipment and excitedly explored the world of volume control, treble, and bass. It was only the fear of reprisal that kept her from doing the same thing when we were looking.

By age two, our toddler was behaving differently. She would approach the stereo equipment, tempted, but would stop and say to herself, "No!" She caught herself even when she did not know that my wife and I were watching her. Our prohibition against playing with the knobs had become a part of her psychic world. She provided the "no" for herself, from the memories of my wife and I within her mind.

This example illustrates two characteristics of early conscience formation. First off, we mostly experience guidelines about dos and don'ts in terms of language, as audible words. When we face a moral choice, we usually do not picture people, images, memories, colors, temperature, or other things. We think of the spoken words used to express the values and guidelines involved in the matter. It is impossible to know for sure what was in our daughter's head all those years ago, but I expect what entered her thoughts was not an image of me or her mom; more likely, what crossed her mind was the word "no." Just "no." The prohibition was now a part of her, somewhat independent of her mental images of us, her parents. Similarly, adults think of directives such as "thou shalt not steal" in terms of the words that make up the idea and what they represent. We forget who initially told us this prohibition, where we were when we heard it for the first time, what we were wearing, and so on. The commandment is now a part of us, as part of our make-up, as part of a moral compass.

Our daughter's example epitomizes a second feature of a developing conscience; the sense of right and wrong initially embodies concrete rules, not necessarily the principles behind them. She did not know why her parents insisted that she leave the electronics alone. It would have been absurd for us to explain the purpose of the controls, or how much the unit would cost if she broke it. These ideas are gibberish to a toddler. She initially learned to stop herself to avoid our displeasure and later showed the same restraint to secure the approval of her embryonic conscience. By following instructions, she wins our praise and the admiration of her budding moral compass.

As children grow, their conscience becomes more sophisticated. Through the grade school and teenage years, youngsters come to understand the principles and values underlying life's prohibitions. Their allegiance shifts toward abstract ideas, feeling loyalty both to specific standards and to the ethical principles that underlie these guidelines. Teenagers rebel against blind obedience as their critical thinking matures and they develop their own sense of morality. This stage of life can be hard for grownups, who may wonder what has happened to their compliant youngster. Despite their emerging independence, however, teenagers still depend heavily on their parents' values to help them determine their sense of right and wrong.

The concept of the superego is very similar to the idea of conscience, with one difference. We are consciously aware of conduct that we consider right or wrong; most people agree that murder is immoral, for example. Freud believed that there was also an internal rulebook that operates outside our awareness, a part that is unconscious. It maneuvers in the background, rewarding or punishing us based on whether we meet its unspoken code. For instance, say a mother lost her temper on a holiday when her young son was setting the formal dining room table; she screams, "You broke the fine china?" Later in life, the young man is inexplicably terrified to upset a friend of Chinese ancestry. The superego has an unconscious commandment, "Never break the China." This fictional example shows the importance of words to the superego, as well as how capricious these hidden expectations can be. Together, the moral guidelines we embrace openly and their concealed counterparts make up the superego.

Problems occur if the superego is over or underdeveloped. If the conscience is immature, children may lie, cheat, steal, fight, or misbehave in other ways. A stable, caring, consistent, and predictable home environment helps youngsters internalize a positive code of conduct, so they do not get in trouble when they start school.

The superego can also be too critical. In these cases, children develop a harsh and punishing inner voice, part of which is in their conscious awareness while another portion is not. Youngsters like this are often said to be too hard on themselves. They feel guilty about understandable feelings of anger and normal human desires. Sometimes, they even come to believe that they are worthless or wicked. Those who suffer from depression often have a severe and critical superego. A kind, safe, and nurturing environment during children's formative years can help prevent them from beating themselves up later in life.

The ideal superego lies somewhere between these two extremes. It helps us control our conduct to a reasonable degree, but without excessive guilt or self-criticism. A healthy conscience can be a source of self-esteem, as it praises us for living a moral life. We feel good when we do things well.

When we last left Captain Kirk, in "Errand of Mercy," he was eager to fight the Klingons. In "Day of the Dove," a similar situation arises, but Kirk handles himself differently.

Day of the Dove

The *Enterprise* arrives at Beta XIIA to investigate the destruction of a Federation colony. Kirk, McCoy, and Chekov beam down but find no evidence of a settlement or its annihilation. When a Klingon battle cruiser arrives, Kirk assumes that these adversaries destroyed the colony somehow, without leaving a trace. The situation is confusing, however, because the Klingon ship is severely damaged. Who attacked them, and how could they have mounted any hostility towards Beta XIIA?

Several Klingons transport down to the planet, overwhelm the landing party, and accuse Kirk of attacking their ship. Kang, the Klingon captain, strikes Kirk in the face and claims the *Enterprise* as compensation. An alien life force is watching these events, but both sides are unaware of it.

Chekov attacks the Klingons in a rage, accusing them of killing his brother. The Klingons torture Chekov until Kirk agrees to beam them aboard the *Enterprise*, but Kirk covertly signals Spock with his communicator. Spock beams up the *Enterprise* landing party first. Security officers disarm the Klingons when they materialize. Unnoticed, the alien life also beams up to the ship.

Spock determines that the Klingons were too far away to have destroyed the Federation settlement. Kirk agrees that there is no evidence that the Klingons are guilty. McCoy and Chekov do not want any proof. They erupt with hatred and do not look at the situation objectively.

Everybody in this conflict has a good reason to be angry. Kirk and the *Enterprise* crew believe that an enemy of some sort demolished a Federation colony. Simultaneously, an unknown assailant attacked the Klingon ship, causing extensive damage and heavy losses.

Neither side pretends that they are not fuming. Both Kirk and Kang freely express how agitated they are about what has happened. They do not project their rage into some outside person or force. Implicitly, they recognize that these angry feelings are a part of themselves.

The whole group is losing control of their antagonism and hatred. From the first, the Klingons exercise little control over their hostility. They ambush the landing party, accuse Kirk of attacking their ship unprovoked, and torture Mr. Chekov. Captain Kirk's account does not interest them; the Klingons have already made up their minds.

McCoy and Chekov are also acting like enraged tribal warriors. They ignore Spock's assessment that the Klingons were too distant to have destroyed the settlement. Thirsty for vengeance, they are not interested in facts and express no sympathy for the Klingons, who have many dead shipmates aboard their crippled vessel. Blinded by hate, McCoy and Chekov cannot look at the situation objectively. Venom saturates their thoughts and actions. In contrast, Kirk and Spock stay level-headed for now.

> Unexplainable things happen aboard the *Enterprise*. Something disables subspace communication, cutting off outside contact. The ship alters course spontaneously and begins racing out of the galaxy at warp nine. The emergency bulkheads close, trapping four hundred crew members in the lower decks.

> Kirk suspects the Klingons are responsible for these events. He accuses Kang and strikes him across the face. As Kang recovers from the blow, all the hand phasers and other electronic devices magically change into swords. Equally armed, the Klingons and humans begin fighting.

These events aboard the *Enterprise* illustrate what happens to people when they allow their hatred and aggression to control them. Communication with others disintegrates, preventing any mutual understanding. People in this state of mind do not care about dialogue; they want revenge. Facts don't matter. Group members reinforce each other's resentments and become resistant to outside influences.

The *Enterprise* racing out of control dramatizes how people lose mastery of themselves when consumed with hate. Speeding toward the edge of the galaxy, the zooming vessel represents how people seeking retaliation can become blind to anything else. Vengeance can overshadow other options and goals, often leading to unnecessary violence. Oblivious to the collateral damage, combatants may destroy themselves or their society in a lust for revenge.

The four hundred crewmen imprisoned in the lower decks symbolize the civilizing human potentials that temporarily disappear. Reason, empathy, restraint, and other strengths are trapped and unavailable when our violent instincts reign supreme. Instruments of advancement and progress turn into primitive weapons of brute force. Taking the form of swords, hatred consumes everything good.

Kirk lets his animosity control him. Though he had previously listened to what Kang had to say and tried to stay calm, now he wants revenge. He strikes Kang across the face, telling the Klingon that he owes it to him because Kang hit him first on the planet below. This physical assault coincides with the moment when the swords appear, as Captain Kirk along with everybody involved abandon their commitment to restraint and clear thinking. Henceforth, violence will be answered in kind—an eye for an eye.

Kirk returns to the bridge. Obsessed with avenging his brother's death, Chekov sets off against the captain's orders to attack the Klingons. Sulu points out that Chekov is an only child. Spock discovers that there is an alien on board; his instruments pick up its life energy.

The Klingons capture engineering and cut off life support to every other section of the ship. Kirk tries to tell Kang about the alien, but the Klingon does not listen.

On the bridge, Scotty spews hatred for the Klingons and wants to slaughter them. When Spock looks at the situation objectively, Scotty attacks the Vulcan with racial hatred. He calls Spock a freak and tells him to go back to where he came from. Spock almost attacks Scotty, but Kirk intervenes. The three men use this experience to understand what is happening.

The alien has manufactured an artificial war. It magnifies the inherent hostilities between the two groups, compelling them to fight. The moment that Kirk, Spock, and Scotty recognize this fact, the life support systems come back on. Apparently, the mysterious energy wants both sides alive so they can continue fighting; it restores the humans' heat and air.

The alien reinstates the life support functions to keep the warring parties alive; the restoration is also a metaphor depicting the life-saving enlightenment that occurs in Kirk, Spock, and Scotty. After coming close to killing each other, they regain control over themselves and use their feelings of hatred to understand their predicament. This insight marks the moment that the starship's vital systems kick back on. By controlling their base instincts, working together, and reflecting on their actions, Kirk and his officers bring hope back to a situation headed for death and destruction. Restraint, cooperation, reason, and other strengths of humankind provide salvation from our dark side.

Kirk, Spock, and Scotty accept responsibility for their antagonism, which helps them regain control over themselves. The alien is magnifying the hate, but the innate human hostility was already there. Looking at oneself objectively is not easy; in this regard, the starship officers show their discipline and maturity. They realize that the aggression comes from their own psyche, which allows them to subdue it. In contrast, Chekov's hate is still out of control. In his mad lust for combat, he blames the Klingons for killing a brother who never existed. He does not realize that he is fighting his own demons.

> Chekov attacks a Klingon warrior and sexually assaults Mara, Kang's wife. Kirk and Spock arrive and pull Chekov off his victim. After much persuasion, Kirk convinces Mara that the alien exists and is manufacturing and feeding off the war. She agrees to help.

> Desperate because the ship's dilithium crystals are deteriorating, Kirk and Mara beam themselves into engineering. Kang ignores their explanation and begins a sword fight with Captain Kirk. When the mysterious energy becomes visible, Kang finally believes Kirk's story. He says, "Klingons kill for their own purposes," not at the whim of something else. The two leaders call a truce, and the group uses good spirits as a weapon to drive the alien off the ship.

The resolution of this episode represents a step forward from Kirk's encounter with the Klingons on Organia in "Errand of Mercy." This time, Kirk and the others did not need a parent to step in and stop them from fighting. They ceased hostilities all on their own, in spite of the creature's efforts to maintain the violence.

Kirk shows that he has a conscience, a healthy superego. He demonstrates his values of peace, cooperation, patience, and understanding. Without the intervention of a higher power, he regains control over his aggression. Kirk's moral compass tells him that it is better to resolve conflicts without fighting, and he risks his life to accomplish this. He does not need a stronger force, representing a parent, to make him behave. The Klingons also restrain their appetite for battle, albeit for different reasons.

"A Taste of Armageddon" portrays a culture that sanctions a particular form of violence.

A Taste of Armageddon

On route to Eminiar VII to open diplomatic relations, the *Enterprise* receives a communication from the planet to turn back. Ambassador Robert Fox orders Kirk to disregard the message and proceed.

Kirk, Spock, Uhura, and three other crew members beam down to the surface. The Ruling Council tells these visitors that Eminiar VII has been at war with its nearest planetary neighbor, Vendikar, for five hundred years. They warned the *Enterprise* to stay away for its own protection.

A Vendikarian attack interrupts the discussion; curiously, there are no explosions nor any other evidence of battle. Anon VII, the leader of the Eminian council, explains to the landing party that they fight the war with computers. The designated casualties then report to a disintegration chamber, where technicians kill them. Citizens obey willingly, without complaint. Individuals die, but the culture survives. The Eminians believe this is a better way to fight a war, but Kirk and his party are appalled.

Anon VII tells them that Vendikar used a computer simulation to destroy the *Enterprise*, meaning the crew must beam down for execution within twenty-four hours. Kirk and the others in the landing party are not designated casualties sentenced to die, but the Eminians hold them hostage to pressure the *Enterprise* to comply.

The Eminian culture endorses a peculiar kind of murder but otherwise seems quite advanced. In an incomplete and repugnant way, they have kept their aggressive tendencies in check, which has allowed them to progress in other areas. In spite of any apparent benefit to this computer warfare, the price paid is odious and abhorrent to Kirk and the other Earthlings. The citizens submit to disintegration like lambs to the slaughter. All life has value, self-aware beings above all else. To a newcomer, the Eminians appear to degrade life and civilization as much as they advance it.

Why are the Eminians so complacent about this revolting arrangement? How do we explain the blind obedience? Where is the resistance, the desire to change, the defiance?

The Eminians accept this voluntary extermination because their parents approved of it. For five hundred years, generations have supported the computer war. Children form their conscience primarily from the attitudes and values of their elders. The adults teach youngsters that the isolated violence of the disintegration chambers is not only morally acceptable, but it is also honorable and superior to the alternatives.

The Eminian conscience, its collective superego, approves of human sacrifice. The situation does not evoke a critical inner voice because the previous generation considered the practice ethically correct. Youngsters incorporate their parents' sense of right and wrong and carry it forward. In this bizarre fictional culture, offspring adopt the moral code taught to them, even if it means their death. If society says an action is just, and their caretakers agree, children fall in line.

In psychoanalytic language, the Eminian culture is fixated at an early stage of superego formation. Remember how my daughter obeyed the prohibition about touching the stereo equipment without understanding the reasons for it. The Eminian people are sheepishly following the rules their elders taught them. They have internalized the code of conduct as part of their self without question.

As healthy children grow, their superegos mature. Youngsters start to understand the ethical principles underlying the choices they face. Their views on right and wrong become more complex, showing a mixed commitment to specific guidelines along with unlying ideas regarding morality. Teenagers become willing to challenge and discard lessons spoon fed to them by the previous generation. In a sense, the Eminian culture never entered adolescence.

Though the disintegration booths in this story may seem unbelievable, history is rife with socially sanctioned violence in societies that are otherwise advanced. The Eminians' computer warfare is similar to a duel, in that murder in that context was acceptable to some people as long as it followed a set of orderly rules. Before the modern age, many cultures practiced human sacrifice. Slavery was endorsed by people who otherwise lived respectable lives, as judged by peers of their class. Government-authorized apartheid was a part of South Africa until 1991; the disgust of the rest of the world played a role in its demise.

In each of these cases, children grow up in a society that condones specific types of violence. A critical mass of the younger generation accepts the offensive behavior as morally just. Their conscience and superego do not object to the questionable practices, so they do not feel any guilt.

In spite of the challenges, people and societies do break out of old patterns. Children sometimes reject their parents' values, and cultures abandon the mores of past generations. This progress is often time-consuming and painful. Even when people adopt different values than their elders, they can carry remnants of the parents' prejudices. It can take a few generations for cultural shifts to solidify.

Anon VII tries to lure the *Enterprise* crew to beam down to the surface for execution. He fires on the ship when this strategy fails, but the *Enterprise*'s shields easily repel his attack. Kirk and the others break out of their holding area and destroy a disintegration chamber.

Anon VII captures Kirk and threatens to kill him if the Federation personnel do not surrender immediately. While the high councilman is talking with the *Enterprise*, Kirk issues general order twenty-four. The starship will destroy the planet in two hours if Anon VII does not release the landing party.

Spock and the others storm the council chamber, taking control of the situation. Kirk deliberately destroys the military computer. The Eminians must face the horrors of real war or talk to their enemies.

Angry, confused, and overwhelmed, Anon VII says that there can be no peace. The Eminians are instinctively a killer species, he explains. Unaffected, Kirk maintains that they can resist their violent instinct. While they cannot wish away their hatred and aggression, they can choose to control it nonetheless.

The Eminians open communication with the Vendikar Ruling Council for the first time in centuries. The two planets cease hostilities as they enter a dialogue.

Eminian parents taught their children that killing via disintegration booth is morally acceptable. Thus, their population does not feel guilty about the practice and lacks the motivation to change. The society's collective superego does not object. Anon VII argues that they cannot control their killer instinct, so it is preferable to contain it to an isolated part of their culture.

Kirk rejects outright the argument that violence is irrepressible. He scolds Anon VII; they can resist their hostile impulses. Murderous thoughts do not compel people to slaughter somebody in real life. The Eminians have a choice. They can continue their senseless war or open negotiations.

Good parents convey to their children what Kirk tells Anon VII; it is possible and expected that they avoid fighting and other violence. "He started it," is an excuse, as are: "I couldn't help it." "He deserved it." "I didn't mean it." "Everybody does it." "I was joking," and so on. Anon VII would argue that it is necessary for children to beat-up just one other kid, to get the aggression out of their system and to spare the rest of their buddies. Youngsters can avoid hitting, kicking, and biting if their parents expect them to do so.

When parents expect children to control their aggression, this standard gradually becomes a part of their persons. If violence is off limits, children will make this principle a part of their superegos. By the time young people become adults, they must control their behavior on their own. If they lack adequate self-control, they will have serious conflicts with others and their community.

When emotional growth is on track, prohibitions will gradually morph into positive values. For example, "do not hit" becomes "everybody deserves to feel safe." "Thou shalt not steal" transforms into "property rights are essential to civil societies."

Though the Eminians enter a cease-fire, negotiation and compromise are not yet a part of their value system. They agree to talk to Vendikar solely to avoid the atrocities of full-scale combat. Peace is not an end in itself. Anon VII prefers to continue the computer war, but that is no longer an option. He accepts dialogue with their enemy as a lesser evil, in comparison to the horrors resulting from conventional weapons.

The Eminians are similar to young children with an embryonic sense of right and wrong, who behave themselves just to avoid the ire of the adults. Anon VII is now doing the right thing, but only to avoid the metaphorical disapproval of a parent in the form of a giant bomb. In time, the culture may learn to value negotiation, dialogue, compromise, and peace all for their own sake. Similarly, though youngsters at first just want to avoid reprimands, later they embrace the moral principles needed to live in harmony with others. The value of nonviolence becomes a part of their superegos.

Regarding warfare in the twenty-first century, "A Taste of Armageddon" raises some troubling questions. The great conflicts of the 1900s involved total war on a scale never seen before. The full-scale destruction of armies, civilians, infrastructure, and the means of production left countries in ruin. Only a few decades later, there are computer-guided missiles with such precision that attacks are called "surgical" strikes. The United States has fought two simultaneous conflicts without a draft, rationing, war bonds, or an increase in taxes that would make the cost in dollars more apparent. In our personal lives, many of us have not had a friend, loved-one, or anybody we know killed or injured in our country's most recent wars. Are we sure that we are on the right course?

The next episode, "Arena," is similar to the last two but throws a little more light on how children internalize the values of their parents.

Arena

Beaming down for a routine visit to the Federation colony on Cestus III, the landing party finds the settlement in ruins. Within minutes, an unseen opponent fires artillery shells at the group from the surrounding hills. After Kirk strikes back with a sonic grenade, the enemy retreats to their spaceship.

The *Enterprise* pursues the attacking vessel into an unexplored sector of the galaxy. A mysterious energy stops both ships and disables their weapons.

The Metrons, beings from a nearby star system, will not allow what they call a "mission of violence." They transport the captain of each vessel to a barren asteroid, where the adversaries will do battle. Once one of the combatants is dead, the Metrons will free the victor's ship and destroy the loser's.

At first, this situation seems similar to the events on Organia in "Errand of Mercy," discussed in Chapter 8. In that episode, a parent surrogate steps in to stop the fighting. We might expect the Metrons to act similarly, forcing the adversaries to settle their differences peaceably.

Oddly, the Metrons' solution is no better than the problem they purport to solve. Violence will still decide the dispute, with tremendous loss of life on one side or the other. Their high-minded intervention seems pointless. Let's see where this story goes.

Kirk's opponent is a man-sized reptilian creature called a "Gorn." The alien is physically stronger than Kirk, but the captain moves faster and is more flexible. After several cliffhangers, Kirk defeats his rival by constructing a primitive cannon from the asteroid's natural resources.

Though the Gorn captain is wounded, Kirk refuses to kill him. During the contest, Kirk learned that the Gorns thought that the Federation outpost they attacked was on their territory. Kirk musters enough compassion to spare the injured commander's life.

A Metron appears; he is towering, radiant, and youthful, even though he is fifteen hundred years old according to time on Earth. Kirk's leniency surprises and pleases the Metron, who returns the Gorn leader to his ship and allows them to go on their way. The emissary praises the Federation captain for showing mercy. There is hope for Kirk's species, after all, the Metron adds. Though humans are "half savage," the two peoples may be friends after several hundred more years.

The Metron represents the parent. He towers over Kirk, just as human adults seem like giants to little people. Moms and dads are as ancient to youngsters as the Metron appears to be compared with Captain Kirk.

The Metron illustrates two ways that parents can help their children develop a healthy superego. First, the Metron praises Kirk for his restraint and compassion. He compliments the captain for showing "the advanced trait of mercy." There is promise for the human race, he says. Youngsters' first ideas about right and wrong form in direct response to what their caretakers highlight and revere. Adults reinforce and encourage some behavior with praise and admiration. If children keep their aggression under control, parents should applaud their patience and maturity. All kids crave their mom's and dad's approval and esteem; they will show more of the traits that elicit this attention. Youngsters need to hear when they are doing well; they deserve congratulations for a job well done. This encouragement helps them internalize their parents' values and develop a good feeling about themselves. As they grow, children rely less on the direct response from others and more on the regard of their superegos. They learn to supply their own approval.

Secondly, the Metron also makes a big deal about the reward Kirk and his descendants can expect in the future, that someday the two peoples will be equals. This feedback is a type of praise, combined with encouragement to persevere, and a qualified promise. Kirk may feel dwarfed and outdone by the Metron now, but eventually, they will stand side by side. Similar to the Metron, adults help children form a healthy conscience by highlighting how moral actions fit into the larger whole, and by reminding youngsters that they can expect good things to result, at least down the road. Even when the world does not support a person's ethical choice, a healthy superego will give that person strength; it will insulate him or her from the capricious attacks of self-serving critics.

"Arena" is a successful episode, but it has two notable flaws. I have already touched on the first; the Metrons' intervention is confusing and pointless. If they objected so strongly to violence, why did they use combat to settle the conflict? What was the purpose of interfering in the first place? In this regard, the Metrons are not acting like good parents. If two children are fighting, the adults should stop them. Youngsters must learn to resolve their conflicts with respect and cooperation. The Metrons' solution would be to put the two kids in a room by themselves and let them slug it out. In contrast to the Metron, human adults should be mindful of setting a good example, as youngsters quickly notice any hypocrisy. It is best to avoid spanking;

physical forms of discipline use aggression to teach children that violence is wrong, which confuses them and makes them angry. The tired phrase "do as I say, not as I do" does not absolve parents from their responsibility to set a good example.

The second weakness in this episode comes when Kirk decides not to kill the Gorn. Sparing his enemy is admirable, but Kirk's reasoning is muddled. The Captain implies that the attack on the Federation outpost was understandable because the Gorn believed that the planet was within their territory, so they were just defending themselves. Kirk is too forgiving. Even if the Federation was intruding unintentionally, this offense does not warrant the mass extermination of settlement personnel. Gorn lives were not in any jeopardy; perhaps they could have lodged a diplomatic protest. With a few adjustments, the teleplay could have addressed this problem. The writer was probably trying to give Kirk a reason to be sympathetic towards his opponent, but it almost sounds like the captain accepts all-out war as a legitimate response to trespassing. Also, the Gorn go on their way having paid no penalty at all, which almost guarantees that they will be back with a vengeance. Mercy and compassion are not the same as letting the accused off scot-free. We consider mitigating circumstances when sentencing, not when determining guilt.

CHAPTER 10: OEDIPUS REX MEETS EDITH KEELER

The preceding chapters have followed human development from birth to years three to five. By this age, children have a basic comprehension of how the world works. They know that people are separate individuals who have their attractive moments and their rough ones. By the time they start kindergarten, youngsters have reasonable control over their behavior and can mostly follow the rules of their household.

What, then, is the most prominent emotional struggle for children at this age? What issues are important to them?

Children three to five years old want to marry the parent of the opposite sex. In this chapter, we will see this wish in Captain Kirk's love for Edith Keeler in "The City on the Edge of Forever" and his longing for Rayna in "Requiem for Methuselah."

Before going further, let me be clear that I will be describing the dominant path of development in our society, that toward heterosexuality. The limited focus is not meant to exclude anybody or to disrespect those of different orientations. I am keeping the discussion narrow for the sake of clarity, and because the episodes portray Captain Kirk's relationships with women. The topic of homosexuality from a psychoanalytic point of view is beyond the scope of this book.

Preschoolers are very interested in love, their bodies, and sexuality. At times, they overflow with affection. Their curiosity about the birds and the bees seems limitless. They want to know where babies come from. Sometimes, they play doctor with their friends. The difference between the genders puzzles, frightens, and excites them. They crave knowledge about these questions and create fantasies to explain them.

Recognizing preschooler's sexual impulses alarms some people. Adults often think that children are innocent, meaning that they have no erotic thoughts or interest. This presumed indifference is a creation of the adult mind. Youngsters are very interested in sensuality. We often do not see this in our offspring because it makes us uneasy.

Children's genitals, like adults', are a highly sensitive and pleasurable part of their bodies. Expecting youngsters to have no thoughts or feelings about their privates would be naïve and unrealistic. They have many ideas and fantasies about their intimate areas and prize them as much as adults do.

Still, sensuality is only one part of a child's loving side. Because sex piques people's interest, it is easy to focus exclusively on this aspect of attachment. Other facets of amorous bonds include emotional nurturing and support. Learning, creating, and building things are also part of a child's affection. Collectively, Sigmund Freud called these qualities humanity's "life instinct."

Children long for the parent of the opposite sex and wish to marry him or her. Their moms and dads are the primary objects of their passion. This idea may appear shocking; upon reflection, however, it should seem obvious. Caretakers hold their youngsters, love them, play with them, guide them, and feed them. Naturally, boys and girls direct their desires toward the people who provide for them. Sons want to marry their mother and daughters their father. Later in life, children redirect these feelings towards people outside the family. For five-year-old kids, however, this shift is still in the future.

Freud discovered this incestuous childhood love affair. He called the constellation of thoughts, feelings, fantasies, and wishes associated with this stage the "Oedipus complex," named for the Greek tragedy *Oedipus Rex* or *Oedipus the King* by Sophocles. In this drama, the main character unknowingly murders his father and marries his mother.

Youngsters yearn to get hitched to Mom or Dad, but they do not really understand what love and marriage are all about. What they do know for sure is that they have intense affectionate feelings, and they want to express them somehow. Since their parents are already devoted to each other (in healthy homes, that is), children are left feeling frustrated.

My wife and I saw our daughter's Oedipal longings beginning a few weeks before she turned three. She would say that she is the mommy and her mother is the little girl. At other times she would climb into bed with us and tell her mom to go away. These are tender moments. It seems caring to reply, "Yes, and someday you will be married too. You will be a great mommy." Starting an answer with, "Yes, and someday you will . . ." affirms children's longings and dreams, while simultaneously encouraging them to be patient. Good things will come in time. This style of response is a variation of what is sometimes called " 'Yes, and . . .' thinking," which is a rule of thumb in improvisational comedy and sometimes in business brainstorming sessions. The idea is to accept what the speaker says no matter what, and then build on it. Negating what somebody shares can shut them down, making them unlikely to open up any further.

Many *Star Trek* episodes portray the Oedipal situation. We will discuss "The City on the Edge of Forever" followed by "Requiem for Methuselah."

The City on the Edge of Forever

As the *Enterprise* passes tumultuously through ripples in time near an unexplored planet, Sulu's control board overloads and knocks him out. Dr. McCoy gives him a small dose of the dangerous medication cordrazine. During more turbulence, McCoy accidentally injects himself with a hundred times the proper amount of cordrazine and becomes psychotic. He runs off the bridge shouting, "Murderers! Killers!"

In the transporter room, McCoy beams himself down to the nearby planet. Kirk, Spock, and several others follow him to the surface, hoping to recover the doctor. They discover a city of ruins ten thousand centuries old. One ancient structure is twenty feet tall and looks like a flattened, irregular ring; Spock determines that it is the source of the time displacement.

There are several clues here that this episode portrays a conflict from our past. The ripples in time suggest that the subject of the story will originate from another period of our life. The ancient ruins direct our attention to our primeval past, childhood. Something from back then threatens to erupt into the present.

Other details suggest that the past struggle is unconscious and dangerous. The time distortion knocks Sulu comatose, signifying that the action will symbolize issues that lie under the surface, outside our awareness. The temporal disruption jolts the entire *Enterprise*, graphically demonstrating its power. Dr. McCoy's madness is another allusion to the intensity of the conflict; it is enough to drive somebody crazy.

The ring structure speaks and identifies itself as the "Guardian of Forever." It is a time portal to the past and displays Earth's history as if it were a movie. McCoy suddenly comes out from hiding and jumps through the gateway into the past. Something he does back then dramatically changes the course of events because Starfleet and the

Enterprise no longer exist. Kirk and Spock follow McCoy backward in time, hoping to undo whatever the doctor has done.

Kirk and Spock arrive in New York City during the 1930s. After stealing some clothes, they hide from a police officer in the basement of a local building. Hearing a noise, the owner comes to investigate. It is Edith Keeler, an attractive and elegant brunette. Kirk confesses that they took the garments because they did not have any money. Without endorsing or criticizing Kirk and Spock, she offers them a job; Miss Keeler operates a mission and a soup kitchen.

Traveling back in time symbolizes returning to an earlier stage of life. *Star Trek* came out in the mid-1960s, about thirty years after the 1930s setting of this story. A human generation is about 25–30 years, so the episode takes viewers back to when they were young children and what they might have been struggling with back then.

Edith Keeler is a stand-in for Mom. She is the right age to be a parent, and her character makes her ideally suited for motherhood. Edith is kind, nurturing, and self-sacrificing. She does not flip-out when she learns Kirk and Spock stole some clothes. Instead, she gives them something constructive to do. She has devoted her life to the unfortunate and vulnerable, as mothers dedicate their lives to their children. Also, she's beautiful. Miss Keeler is one heck of a woman. Captain Kirk goes back in time and symbolically meets his mother.

Kirk and Spock eat dinner at the mission. An elderly beggar complains that they have to listen to "goody-two-shoes," referring to Edith. Kirk tells him to shut up, explaining to Spock that he wants to hear what she has to say. Edith gives a wide-eyed speech about harnessing energy, manned space flight, and other lofty visions. Captivated, Kirk says he finds her most uncommon.

Kirk is falling in love with Edith. Infatuated, he marvels at his sweetheart's forethought and dreams. He does not want to hear one word criticizing her. Kirk protects Edith when the beggar mocks her, as a youngster defends his mother from the insults of another boy on the playground.

Kirk and Edith get more involved with each other, while Mr. Spock discovers the root of the problem. Piecing together some equipment, he plays the video he recorded from the Guardian of Forever. He learns that Edith Keeler has two possible futures. Either she will lead a pacifist movement which delays the United States' entry into World War II long enough for Germany to develop the atomic bomb and prevail, or she will die in an auto accident. Somehow, McCoy changes history by preventing her accidental death. They must keep Dr. McCoy from saving Edith's life.

Kirk confesses to his Vulcan friend that he is in love with Edith Keeler. Spock warns that if he does what his heart tells him to do, millions will die who did not die before. "Edith Keeler must die," Spock says with certainty.

McCoy arrives. After sleeping off the cordrazine's effects, he wanders into Edith Keeler's mission. Kirk finds McCoy just as Edith is unwittingly walking in front of an oncoming vehicle. McCoy rushes to save her, but Kirk stops him. The car smashes into Edith, killing her. The time travelers return to their proper century.

Captain Kirk must sacrifice his longing for his beloved, as children must surrender their yearning to marry Mom or Dad. It is not possible for the captain and Edith to remain together. Neither is it conceivable for young boys to wed their mother, or girls their father. Youngsters must let go of their childhood passion, as Kirk stood by and allowed Edith to die. Kirk cannot have the woman he adores, and neither can an amorous young boy.

Ironically, Kirk's dilemma had an easy solution. Why not explain the situation to Edith and take her back through the time portal? Her disappearance would have the same effect on history as her death. Captain Kirk could have his dream girl, and Edith could see the future that so fascinated her.

This resolution would miss the point. Children do not want to surrender their love for Mom or Dad, but they have no choice. The episode captures the pain youngsters feel when they give up their first love. It is just as difficult for kids to make this sacrifice as it is for Kirk to let Edith perish. If the captain is going to get back to his adult life, he must follow Mr. Spock's advice. Similarly, if children are to grow up emotionally, they need to mourn and move on.

Kirk, Spock, and McCoy each dramatize a different facet of a youngster's longing for Mom or Dad. Taken together, the trio portrays the inner forces at work as children navigate the Oedipus complex.

Dr. McCoy represents the passion. His madness parallels how children feel crazy with desire and frustration. He desperately tries to save Edith, unconcerned with the effect on the rest of humanity. He personifies the wish to preserve the early attachment to Mom at all costs.

Mr. Spock represses any longings. As children must disavow their hunger for their parents, Spock does not once consider sparing Edith. He looks at the problem logically, devoid of emotion. Spock's advice is crystal clear: let her die. It is not possible to remain in the past and marry your mother. Life must go on.

Once again, Captain Kirk must weigh all the considerations and figure out what to do. Hanging on to Edith would short circuit humanity's future, as a childhood fixation on his mom derails a boy's growth and destiny. On the other hand, it hurts like hell to stand by while a vehicle runs over your girlfriend. In the end, Captain Kirk does what is right. Like children surrendering their early attachments, Kirk makes the sacrifice out of necessity.

"The City on the Edge of Forever" begs the question: if the Oedipal love is so consuming, how do children give it up? One can admonish people to "deal with it" when they face something challenging, but this rarely helps. Do youngsters just decide that they are being ridiculous? What factors are involved in letting go and moving on?

School helps children grow beyond their early childhood attachments. Their passion for Mom and Dad can now energize their academic, athletic, and other extracurricular pursuits. Learning new things and mastering skills are intrinsically rewarding. Team activities redirect youngsters from their immediate families to their peers. Athletics help kids get to know their bodies and develop their physical aptitude.

Other adults and children outside the family help youngsters detach from their parents. School-age boys and girls are less dependent on Mom and Dad, and have many other students and grownups in their lives. They learn to be companions, friends, and teammates. They can feel warmth, admiration, gratitude, and other emotions toward people besides their blood relations. A young boy's crush on his teacher is an example of how children can long for somebody outside the family. Peers become increasingly more important than they were before. Some childhood friendships last a lifetime. Unlike the physical longing kids have for their parents, their love towards another boy or girl can someday be consummated.

As adults, our work life provides a healthy, constructive outlet for our energy. A vocation helps us grow beyond our childhood attachments, and it also benefits society. Captain Kirk illustrates this healthy advancement when he sacrifices Edith and returns to his Starfleet responsibilities. He replaces his lost sweetheart with the joy of his command. He has surrendered his boyhood infatuation and substituted a mature role in the adult world.

The episode "Elaan of Troyius" also shows that Captain Kirk's passionate cravings can motivate his work life. In this adventure, Kirk falls for Elaan after he touches her tears, which act as an irresistible love potion. Kirk's consuming devotion to Elaan represents the longing of a young boy for his mom. Alas, Kirk must surrender Elaan to preserve galactic peace. When McCoy finds a remedy to the Troyian tears, Spock informs the doctor that it is unnecessary. Kirk has found his antidote in his devotion to the *Enterprise*. Like many of us, Kirk has channeled his vital energy into his work and other adult responsibilities.

In spite of later growth and accomplishments, remnants of the wish to marry Mom or Dad stay with us throughout life, mostly at an unconscious level. "The City on the Edge of Forever" resonates with this underground legacy present in us all. Unconscious desires do not listen to logic; contradictions do not bother them. They want what they want, despite obstacles or consequences.

There are many ways that people show their unconscious love for their parents. Some men and women marry somebody so similar to their mom or dad that it is eerie. Arguably, the best expression of this phenomenon is the 1911 hit song "I Want a Girl Just Like the Girl That Married Dear Old Dad." Others find a partner who is their parent's opposite; in these cases, the early attachment is still shaping the adult child's choice, paradoxically. Employees may seek the approval of people of both genders in authority, feeling they never got the affirmation they craved from their parents.

What remnants of the Oedipus complex can we find in Captain Kirk? Let's take a closer look.

Captain Kirk believes that his command precludes him from having a long-term relationship with a woman. In "The Corbomite Maneuver," he says, "I already have a female to worry about. Her name is the *Enterprise*." He feels married to the ship. In "The Naked Time," Kirk says, "This vessel. I give, she takes. She won't permit me my life; I've got to live hers." Of Yeoman Rand, he says, "Have you noticed her, Mr. Spock? You're allowed to notice her. A captain is not permitted."

There is no legitimate reason, however, why Captain Kirk could not sustain a long-term partnership with a woman. Many military men get married. They may spend extended periods of time away from home, but it is still possible to wed and have a family. The prohibition against marriage comes from within Kirk's psyche, not from his command. Something inside his head vetoes the idea of finding a lady friend. He cannot allow himself to have a genuinely devoted romantic relationship; his brief affairs throughout the series are no substitute for the companionship and intimacy found within long-term bonds.

In psychoanalytic language, we could say that Captain Kirk manifests some unresolved Oedipal issues. He has substituted his starship command for a female partner. Since the *Enterprise* is his mother ship, he gets to keep his childhood attachment in a disguised form. Kirk does not have room for a sweetheart of flesh and blood; the *Enterprise* is the woman of his life.

Some people seem to substitute duty of some sort for a romantic partner, like Captain Kirk. Others might call these folks "workaholics." To those people, and to anybody else who needs to hear it, let me set the record straight. Love, indeed, is the most important. Work is what you do, not who you are. You are lovable. You deserve balance, happiness, and the arms of a partner around you, if that is what you want.

Before leaving "The City on the Edge of Forever," there is a political question on the table. Does the episode make a case against *pacifism*, the opposition to war in any and all circumstances? (There are different types and degrees of pacifism; we are barely touching on this issue.) At face value, the story suggests that pacifism is not just naïve, it is dangerous. Edith Keeler's activism against the United States entering World War II led to a greater evil than would otherwise have been.

It is a stretch to say that this fictional narrative can support any particular ideology, in principle. One can create stories that depict any philosophy in a bad light. What the episode does convey, however, is that people in the 1960s were still recovering from the trauma of World War II. In that specific case, there is conventional wisdom that *appeasement* led to a delay in confronting the growing Nazi menace. There is a natural tendency to look back and wonder whether we could we have done anything differently.

So far, we have not discussed how the parent of the same sex affects youngsters' ardor. After all, the Oedipal situation involves three people. It is a love triangle—two male suitors and one woman, or vice versa. What role does a father have with his son and a mother with her daughter? No paternal figure appears in "The City on the Edge of Forever." Another episode, "Requiem for Methuselah," will shed light on this part of the picture.

Requiem for Methuselah

When deadly Rigellian fever infects the *Enterprise* crew, they rush to planet Holberg 917-G in search of "ryetalyn," the only known antidote. Soon after Kirk, Spock, and McCoy beam down to the surface, a mechanical device attacks them.

An older man named Flint stops the automaton before it hurts the trio, but he then demands that they leave immediately. Kirk explains the desperate need for the ryetalyn. Unmoved by the potential loss of life, Flint threatens to kill them if they refuse to go.

Kirk orders the *Enterprise* to lock phasers on their coordinates. He promises to devastate the entire area, including Flint, if he does not allow them to obtain what they need.

This episode portrays the conflict between father and son, Flint representing the older generation and Kirk the upstart offspring. All intra-family male relationships include some struggle and competition. The tension is inevitable. When boys are young, their strong and powerful fathers have almost complete control over their lives. The child accepts this situation because he knows how much he needs his dad, but he also resents it. Nobody likes to be told what they can and cannot do, including youngsters.

Boys dream of overthrowing their father, and taking his power and possessions for themselves. The fairy tale of "Jack and the Beanstalk" illustrates this wish. In the story, young Jack climbs the beanstalk and steals the giant's treasures, first the goose that lays the golden eggs and a then a harp that plays by itself. Woken by the harp's music, the ogre chases the boy down the beanstalk. Jack calls ahead to his mother to grab an ax, then uses it to cut down the massive vine, sending the giant crashing to his death. Jack and his mom live happily ever after with the stolen riches.

Notice in the fairy tale that Jack and the Giant do not reach a benevolent compromise. One of them has to go. What belonged to the big man now serves the boy. Also curious is what happens to Jack. He does not move out and find a bride. He gets to live forever in bliss with his mom! On the surface, an outcome like that seems strange, if not disturbed. When we view the message through the lens of the Oedipus complex, it all makes sense. The story resonates with five-year-old boys, who enjoy for that moment the symbolic victory over their father. They will eventually surrender their Oedipal longings, but not yet.

Fathers also feel ambivalence toward their sons. Dads feel pride in their boys' accomplishments, and pleasure that the family line carries forward. At the same time, men feel threatened by their male offspring. Their sons' growing strength and acumen come while dads are facing middle age. Is this child going to surpass or unseat me, he may wonder.

Sophocles' tragedy *Oedipus Rex* captures a father's anxieties, among other things. The Oracle at Delphi reveals that the King of Thebes is "doomed to perish by the hand of his own son." Frightened that the prophecy could come true, the sovereign sends his newborn son, Oedipus, to die. Through a series of events, Oedipus is adopted and raised by the King of Corinth, Polybus. Now a man, Oedipus asks the Oracle about his parentage and gets this reply: "You will mate with your own mother." Horrified, Oedipus leaves Corinth in a desperate attempt to prevent the revelation from coming true. Without knowing the identity of his natural father, the younger and stronger Oedipus kills him over a trivial dispute on the road to Thebes. Clever and resourceful, Oedipus then solves the riddle of the Sphinx, an accursed creature that was strangling all travelers attempting to enter Thebes. The Sphinx throws itself off a cliff, and Oedipus receives the hand of the Dowager Queen in marriage: his mother, Jocasta.

One can see the tragedy of Oedipus Rex from the perspective of different actors. From the father's point of view, the message is: This kid is a threat! He's going to grow up and kill me!

In spite of fears and anxieties, a father's job is to quietly soothe the emotional intensity between him and his son if and when it erupts. Boys rivalrous moments are fleeting; most of the time they adore their dads and want to give them a reason to be proud. Mature adults calmly wait out their youngsters' storms, secure in the fact that kindness, patience, and warmth is the true cement of the father/son bond. Grownups have the lion's share of the responsibility for staying composed, as they are bigger, have lived through their own childhoods, have more life experience, and have much more power than the youngster.

In "Requiem for Methuselah," both Flint and Kirk fuel the conflict between them, yet Flint is most at fault. What harm could come from allowing the landing party a few hours to collect the ryetalyn? His refusal shows a shocking lack of compassion and seems motivated out of spite. He sentences the *Enterprise* to certain death without a second thought. Flint is a bitter man. He fails miserably in his role as a father figure.

As sons and their dads get into power struggles sometimes, Kirk and Flint are locked in a test of wills. One of them will have to back down, or at least give a little. With our knowledge of the Oedipus complex, we know that there is another issue that creates a rivalry between the younger man and the patriarch in a home. The other contest is for Mom. Perhaps a woman will appear in the Kirk/Flint jousting match.

> Flint takes back his threat, apologizes, and invites the threesome to his home. M4, his robot probe, will gather the ryetalyn. Flint's remarkable possessions puzzle Spock. His book collection spans centuries. His artwork includes several unknown da Vinci paintings on contemporary canvas. Sheet music for an undiscovered Brahms waltz is on the piano.

We will learn that Mr. Flint is immortal. In the past, he has been the composer Johannes Brahms, polymath Leonardo da Vinci, and many other celebrated figures. The previous identities explain the unknown masterpieces in his home.

Flint's long life and his many talents exemplify how a young boy sees his father. To a youngster, forty years seems like an eternity. Flint's extended lifespan reflects a child's belief that his parents are infinitely old and will live forever. To young children, parents' many abilities seem fantastic. They can drive cars, use perplexing tools, lift massive objects, and perform many other marvelous deeds. Flint's extraordinary accomplishments symbolize fathers' remarkable talents in the eyes of their sons.

Flint discusses the visitors with Rayna Kapec, his beautiful young ward. Though he calls the trio selfish and brutal, he allows her to meet them.

Kirk and Rayna fall in love. They dance and share some intimate moments alone. Kirk cannot believe that Rayna is happy living with Flint and suggests that she leave with them. As they kiss, M4 enters and threatens Captain Kirk. Spock arrives and destroys the robot.

Flint explains that M4 thought Captain Kirk was attacking Rayna. It was just attempting to defend her. He says M4 is too useful a device to be without; within minutes, he creates a replacement.

Kirk's instant infatuation with Rayna is out of character. It is hard to believe that this is the same man who thinks of his ship above all else. He is chasing after Rayna while his entire crew is dying. He is provoking Flint, whose cooperation they need to obtain the antidote for the illness threatening the *Enterprise*.

Kirk's behavior is bizarre because he represents a boy aged three to five years old. His effusive longing captures a young child's passion for the parent of the opposite sex. A little boy wants his mom as much as Kirk pines for Rayna. World problems and lofty social issues do not concern youngsters, just as Kirk has almost forgotten that his entire crew is about to drop dead. Captain Kirk usually keeps the big picture in mind, yet in this episode, desire and rivalry cloud his judgment.

Amorous young boys want to steal their mother away from their dad. This competition is the earliest and the most defining love triangle of our lives. It is almost impossible to overstate the intensity of these feelings or the importance of this age in personality development. The initial, potentially cataclysmic confrontation between Kirk and Flint reflects the strength of this contest. Kirk has come to take something that belongs to Flint—first the ryetalyn, and now Rayna.

The Oedipal love triangle creates problems for both father and son. Young boys fear that Dad will retaliate for their wish to have their mom all to themselves. With terror, they realize that their desire puts them in direct conflict with a giant. Boys fear that their dads will discover their hidden fantasies and will strike back, as the Giant threatens Jack with the words, "Fee-fi-fo-fum! I'll grind his bones to make my bread."

The M4 probe represents the child's fear of retaliation. Just as Kirk kisses Rayna, M4 appears and almost kills him. Symbolically, Kirk indulges his forbidden Oedipal wishes, which risks fatal retribution. M4 embodies the dread children feel when they realize that they are competing with a parent. This understanding explains why another M4 appears so quickly. Since it represents the child's fear of revenge, a phaser cannot destroy it. Anxieties that arise within oneself cannot be wiped out by projecting them into a robot and then blasting it. The real issue is unchanged; the fear of reprisal is as poignant as ever. Thus, M4 reappears.

The challenge for fathers in the Oedipal drama is to stay calm, kind, and patient. Mature dads realize that their son's defiance, competition, and self-expression are often a necessary part of growing up. If parents give children some time and space to struggle with life's challenges, the inborn push to move on will work its magic. When conditions are right, people mature naturally. We inherited this gift from our forebears.

M4 also represents a sick father's jealous anger toward his son. It expresses Flint's rage at Kirk for the captain's interest in Rayna. Flint calls it "a very useful device" because it does his vengeful dirty work.

> Irate, Kirk challenges Flint's hold over Rayna. He begs her to come with him, saying, "You love me, not Flint!" Spock warns Kirk repeatedly that he is endangering himself and the *Enterprise*.

> Flint lures Kirk, Spock, and McCoy into his laboratory, where they find a series of Rayna androids. She is a machine created by Mr. Flint— his idea of the perfect woman. Feeling spurned by his creation, Flint was hoping that Kirk could awaken Rayna's emotions.

If Flint created Rayna, why does he need Captain Kirk to rouse her sentiments? Why didn't he just program her to adore him?

Flint cannot build an android that loves him because he feels that he doesn't deserve it. His inner sense of rottenness prevents him from achieving his dream. He feels unlovable and constructs a partner who cannot provide the warmth he craves. A woman who truly treasured him would contradict his sour self-image. Flint can believe that Rayna might fall in love with Kirk, but he cannot be sure she would do the same with him. He is a pathetic character, who thinks that he can only find warmth and caring by stealing it from somebody who deserves it.

If Flint were a real person, I would expect that there was little nurturing in his early life. When adults abuse or deprive youngsters, they can feel rotten, dirty, and undeserving. This negative self-image then affects how they live their lives. Sometimes, people who think they are unlovable will choose partners who are distant, unavailable, or even abusive. In this way, they reaffirm their unspoken belief that they do not deserve warmth, companionship, and affection.

Besides his relationship with Rayna, Flint expresses his self-hatred by the life he has chosen. His voluntary isolation masks the painful feelings that others do not love him or want him around. He scorns others, to master his fear that they will reject him. Flint blames the human race for his terrible feelings about himself; he thinks that deserting the everyday world will solve his problems. Regrettably, Flint cannot escape from his emotional suffering by running from humanity. His troubles go with him.

As a couple, Flint and Rayna dramatize a troubled husband and wife. Flint longs for Rayna's affections, but they are perpetually outside his grasp. Rayna signals that she is not truly happy with Flint, but her sense of duty compels her to stay with him. Flint hopes that another man will awaken Rayna's feelings for him, as a spurned husband may think that having a child will win the love of his wife. This plan cannot succeed. Children do not solve a couple's marital problems, just as Kirk does not unravel the troubles between Flint and Rayna. In fact, Captain Kirk is making things worse. When a child does not improve the marriage or adds more stress, Mom or Dad might openly or indirectly blame the youngster. Flint's rage toward Kirk is partly his anger that Rayna has not given him the devotion that he craves.

One can also see Flint as a father who raises a daughter to meet his own needs, rather than to prepare her to leave home and live her own life. Flint is a failure from this perspective as well.

Kirk is furious with Flint. The two men fight. Flint magically shrinks the Enterprise to a few inches in size and freezes everyone on board. Flint tells Kirk that it is time to join his crew.

Rayna enters the scene and is horrified. She feels responsible for the conflict between her two suitors. Unable to decide whether to stay or go, she short circuits and dies.

Kirk is in his cabin aboard the Enterprise. He feels tortured by recent events; several days without sleep have exhausted him. He finally dozes off saying, "If only I could forget." Spock uses the Vulcan mind meld on Kirk, and says, "Forget."

The father and son conflict escalates to mortal combat. Kirk wants Rayna, as a preschool boy longs for his mother. The ardent childhood wish enrages the spurned husband in the story, Flint. Insecure and jealous, he tries to intimidate, bully, and then murder Captain Kirk.

In a healthy family, the tension between generations does not get to this extreme. Mature fathers can accept some anger and rivalry from their sons without exploding. When Dad feels secure about himself and his marriage, he can be patient as his son works through his Oedipal issues. Time and natural growth will redirect his child's interests.

Fathers sooth their sons' intense emotions by remaining calm, yet firm. Children are sometimes overwhelmed by their anger and frustration. By staying relaxed, compassionate, and composed, parents can help their children regain control of themselves.

A healthy, devoted marriage helps parents deal with their children's Oedipal ambitions. A primary commitment to the spousal bond allows parents to keep their youngster in an appropriate position in the family. Kids must face the painful reality that their mom and dad have a relationship that is independent of them. They do not want to feel excluded, but they will accept it if they have no other choice. If caretakers are dedicated to one another, the children's Oedipal love will not rupture their adult partnership.

Working as a team when dealing with children enables parents to maintain a healthy household. Calm, consistent expectations and limits help youngsters manage their turbulent feelings, keeping the home pleasant and predictable. When Mom and Dad are working well together, they rarely use threats and hostility. Aggression and intimidation are signs of desperation and should signal the adults to re-evaluate what they are doing. Healthy partners will temper one another when child-rearing stresses get intense, as they can do. Together, a couple can balance out each other's extremes.

Problems will arise if a marriage is rocky. If the spouses do not support and nurture each other, then one or both of them may expect the children to fill their adult needs. In some cases, one parent might use a son or daughter to hurt the other; there are many variations on this theme. If the adults are divided, the kids might stir things up even more by pitting one partner against the other.

We discussed how school helps kids release their Oedipal desires and how work for adults carries on that role. The redirected childhood passions can fuel these healthy pursuits. Notably, after leaving Holberg 917-G, Captain Kirk is depressed, immobilized, and unable to fulfill the duties of his command. He cannot stop ruminating about Rayna and the conflict with Flint. What has gone wrong? Why can't Kirk channel his energies back to the *Enterprise* and her crew? Spock provides the answer when he erases the memory of Rayna from Kirk's mind.

Freud discovered that children repress the Oedipus complex as they enter their school years. They "forget" in the sense that they put it out of their conscious awareness. Before this age, a boy may freely tell his mommy that he is going to marry her when he grows up, or a girl may tell her daddy the same. Statements like these show that the youngsters are consciously aware of the wish; they put it into words. Later on, children do not typically make these declarations. Thus, Spock gives Kirk the subliminal command to forget.

A fundamental idea in psychoanalysis is that repression is more than forgetting. Not only are the memories, feelings, wishes, and fears buried outside conscious awareness, they provide the vital oomph that drives the person forward. In troubled people, the energy gets derailed and creates emotional problems. When growth is on track, the repressed stuff fuels learning, work, belonging, cooperation, love, and other things that combine to create a whole human being.

Repressing the Oedipus complex allows students to focus on school and their friends; it frees them to get on with their lives. Youngsters can invest their energy in academic, social, and athletic pursuits. Their childhood longings for their parents would be too distracting if they continued to be consciously aware of them. The fear of retaliation would make them constantly afraid, weighing them down.

Kirk and Spock illustrate how children navigate and tame the Oedipus complex. With the mind-meld, the Vulcan helps his friend and captain put Rayna, Flint, and the whole mess out of his awareness. Kirk can then resume his command with gusto. All these dynamics underlie and contribute to Spock's one word—forget. If the Vulcan wanted to be more precise, he would have uttered "repress" instead. For the sake of interplanetary diplomacy, I'll cut Mr. Spock some slack on this one.

Chapter 11: It is Better to Have Loved and Lost

This chapter will explore how Mr. Spock is like a grade school child. The episodes "All Our Yesterdays" and "The Naked Time" highlight this similarity. We will also discuss how the Vulcan culture depicts the struggles of children ages five to twelve.

By the time they start kindergarten, youngsters are competent in a variety of areas. They speak their primary language well. Their gross and fine motor skills are decent, at least in comparison to preschoolers. When instructions are simple and clear, kindergarteners can follow directions and procedures. Their view of themselves and the people in their lives is more or less realistic, and they can resist impulses to hit or to misbehave in other ways.

Usually, five-year-old children are primed and ready to enter school; they jump into this titillating new realm with enthusiasm. Kindergarten is an exciting time in their lives when their world expands a hundred-fold. They become a part of a classroom and other groups. Reading and writing open new vistas. Students develop and polish their physical skills. In addition to their immediate and extended families, other children and adults start to play a significant role in their lives.

In contrast to other stages of growth, there is little emotional turmoil during the grade school years. Children have left the tantrums of their early days behind, for the most part. They have repressed their wish to marry Mom or Dad, and the tumult of adolescence is still several years in the future.

Youngsters are relatively comfortable with their parents during their first years in school. They are still awed by adults' knowledge and skill. Seeking support and guidance from moms and dads seems natural. Their sense of identity revolves around their place in the family, and they have no desire to strike out on their own. Parents of school-age children often describe these years as a delightful time of life when there is little conflict with their offspring. The period is enjoyable for caretakers because young students are capable in many ways, but they are still mostly compliant and respectful. Kids can clean and dress with little supervision. They can follow instructions and can even help around the house. Young students strive to do well at school; since parents also want them to succeed in the classroom, the common goal helps maintain a bond and limit conflict.

Freud believed that the reason this age is calmer and more stable is that children have tamed their sexual and violent instincts. The impulses to act in forbidden ways are still present in youngsters, but they channel the energy into ventures more acceptable to society. For example, sports promote a healthy expression of antagonism and rivalry. Athletic competition is an enjoyable and productive outlet for pent-up frustrations. Unrestrained aggression is prohibited, like hitting another kid. In contrast, many sports celebrate the child's urge to fight. These physical contests give partial expression to the violent itch, bringing applause to the athlete rather than condemnation. Similarly, erotic feelings and curiosity energize learning in science and the arts. The world opens up to students like never before. The staggering depth and breadth of human knowledge mean that there is always something new to explore. Learning how things work has sexual overtones for both children and adults. Dance and other art forms give expression to sensuality in ways that are more than just acceptable; they are aesthetically transcendent.

Sigmund Freud coined the term "latency" for this stage of life because children's sensual and hostile urges hide under the surface. These issues are still present but are not currently active or dominant. The buried compulsions remain concealed or find a limited voice through sanctioned activities. Of course, grade school students still struggle with instinctual pressures to some extent. Latency is a relative term. Children this age still get angry at times and remain intensely curious about the birds and the bees. However, in comparison with the emotional intensity of a preschooler or the uproar of adolescence, latency is a peaceful time.

In some significant ways, Mr. Spock epitomizes a latency age child. As youngsters repress disagreeable urges, Mr. Spock blocks any and all emotion. He fears that anything less than total repudiation would allow his instincts to erupt to the surface. There is no doubt that his sentiments run deep. We have already seen his hunger for romance and belonging in "This Side of Paradise." The spores on Omicron Ceti III allowed him to show passion for

Leila Kalomi. In this chapter and the next, we will see more examples of both his love and his hostility.

Spock replaces his emotions with reason and science, as latency-age children channel their energy into school. His devotion to logic forms a blockade around the forces of chaos trying to break free from within him. Spock has reached a compromise that works quite well on most occasions; his objective, unruffled assessments play a key role in preventing many disasters. The Vulcan is a highly valued member of the team. Similarly, grade school students stay focused on their academics, hobbies, or other approved activities the majority of the time. Concealing a portion of their psyche has paid off handsomely. Emotions still erupt, however, even for youngsters navigating latency. Similarly, Spock's repression breaks down sometimes, as we shall see.

The history of Mr. Spock's home planet Vulcan also characterizes the repression of latency age children. The Vulcans were formerly a barbaric, violent people. Constant warfare threatened their very survival. On the verge of extinction, they disowned hatred and all other emotion. Collectively and individually, Vulcans embraced logic as their savior and their guide. From then on, rationality was the core of their identity. By dismissing their feelings as illogical, they mastered the forces that threatened to destroy them.

The Vulcan people's early history of instincts run wild parallels the first years of our individual lives, infancy through the Oedipal stage. Like the barbaric Vulcans, toddlers and preschoolers are aware of their emotions. Small children do not deny how they feel. On the verge of a tantrum, a two-year-old child doesn't say, "Who, me? Angry? Of course not. I didn't throw that block. It fell off the table." In fact, young kids experience their state of mind so directly that storms can overwhelm their ability to cope without help. Similarly, the Vulcans did not deny that it was their own warlike nature that threatened them. In spite of their awareness, however, they seemed unable to save themselves.

The Vulcans solved their problem by blocking all emotion, paralleling how latency-age children repress all the developmental stuff they have lived through so far. The repudiation of feelings allowed the Vulcan culture to progress; children's ability to ignore or conceal disruptive forces from within permits them to succeed outside the home.

In grade school children and Mr. Spock, the repressed issues are still present within the mind at an unconscious level. They stay in the background most of the time, outside of direct awareness. Ignoring feelings does not mean that they go away; it means that we have blocked them. Like tectonic plates that store energy as tension builds, repression can suddenly collapse, creating a personalized earthquake with many aftershocks.

The episode "All Our Yesterdays" illustrates the eruption of primitive instincts and the repression of latency. The title comes from a well-known oration from William Shakespeare's *Macbeth* (Act V, Scene V); we will touch on this below. The phrase "All Our Yesterdays" also implies that the story will say something about our past and will apply to everybody. Since it dramatizes the onset of latency, it is relevant to all beyond the age of five.

All Our Yesterdays

The *Enterprise* visits Sarpeidon, a world whose sun is set to explode in three and one-half hours. According to Federation records, an advanced people inhabits the planet, but the ship's censors reveal no signs of intelligent life. Kirk, Spock, and McCoy beam down to a source of power on the surface. They discover an extensive video library and meet its librarian, Mr. Atoz.

Atoz scolds them for being late and urges them to make their selection. The library contains thousands of metallic discs, each providing a visual display of some era of the planet's history.

While viewing a disc, Kirk hears a woman scream and runs to investigate. Without realizing it, he steps through a time portal into the past. Kirk finds himself in a city street in an era similar to seventeenth-century England, the period of history he was viewing back in the library.

Alarmed when the captain disappears, McCoy and Spock follow him through the gateway. They arrive in an ice age, five thousand years ago. The time machine sent them to the epoch that they were watching just before they stepped through it.

As in "The City on the Edge of Forever," the time travel denotes a journey to a previous period of our life. The past eons of the planet's history symbolize early stages of psychic development. Kirk does not go as far back in time as the other two, and his adventure will be less provocative.

McCoy and Spock arrive in a primitive era, which suggests that they will face a primeval struggle from childhood. Our first five years on Earth are prehistoric in that we retain very few conscious memories of them. Our mind does encode these primordial issues, however, but not as historical accounts using language and grammar. Our earliest memories are preverbal, consisting of vague feelings, images, or even body sensations.

Metaphorically, the ice-age connotes repression, the freezing of emotion, thoughts, memories, and wishes. We put things on ice to set them aside somewhere, at least for a while. Like food in a freezer, however, the meat is still there. We defrost it in small portions, amounts we can handle and digest. At other times, losing electricity causes all the stuff to thaw at once. Yikes! The allegory in "All Our Yesterdays" suggests that a frozen conflict from our past will melt, threatening to drown Spock and McCoy.

Kirk talks to Spock and McCoy through the time portal. The Vulcan's and the doctor's disembodied voices are evil spirits to the locals. A police officer arrests Kirk on charges of witchcraft.

McCoy passes out from the cold while he and Spock are looking for shelter. Led by a hooded figure, Spock carries the doctor to safety. The stranger, Zarabeth, is a beautiful young woman exiled from the future by a political tyrant. She tells Spock that she cannot return to the library or she will die. Moments later, she adds that Spock and McCoy also cannot go back, that they are now prisoners in the past. Spock accepts what she says as fact.

Spock changes. He becomes indecisive, frustrated that he cannot reduce their predicament to a rational equation. Though it contradicts his civilized Vulcan values, he enjoys eating animal flesh. He falls in love with Zarabeth. Carrying her in his arms, Spock basks in her beauty and kisses her passionately. He becomes enraged with Dr. McCoy and threatens to kill him.

McCoy deduces what is happening. As they are five thousand years in the past, Spock is reverting to the state of his barbaric Vulcan ancestors.

Spock is backsliding, a metaphor for returning to a prior stage of life. Typically, Mr. Spock resembles a latency-age child, who represses the sensual and violent leftovers from early years and devotes his life to school. He is regressing to a previous time in his Vulcan people's history and an earlier period of childhood when appetite, drives, desires, and emotion can erupt in a flash and overwhelm youngsters.

Spock loses his problem-solving objectivity because this skill is not present in the first stages of life. Critical thinking develops later, during the school years. Younger children haven't learned to separate emotion from a rational analysis of situations.

Like his violent ancestors, Spock's aggressiveness explodes. The predatory instinct of primitive hunters bubbles to the surface, as he devours a piece of meat. He grabs McCoy and threatens to kill him. Unlike a toddler throwing a tantrum, Spock has no parent-surrogate to keep him in line.

Mr. Spock's libido also detonates. Within minutes, his hunger for Zarabeth consumes him. Like a preschool boy, Spock wants her all to himself. That mettlesome doctor must go, even if the Vulcan has to murder him. The situation does not portray three mature adult people trying to figure things out; the volatile state of this trio goes way beyond awkwardness. The raw passion and danger reveal the intensity of that original love triangle, the Oedipus complex.

With some aid, Kirk returns to the library and forces Mr. Atoz to help him look for Spock and McCoy. Mr. Spock has regained some control over himself. Zarabeth confesses that she does not know if Spock and McCoy can return to the future; she is only sure that she, herself, cannot go back. The threesome sets out to look for the time portal.

Once through the gateway, Mr. Spock reassures Dr. McCoy that he has reverted to the present in every respect. Still, McCoy reminds him that "it did happen." Spock agrees that, indeed, it happened, but it was five thousand years in the past and Zarabeth is dead.

The *Enterprise* races away as the sun explodes and the planet disintegrates.

Spock returns to the latency stage of development. Once again, he can repress his emotions, deny that they exist, and get on with his Starfleet responsibilities. Spock leaves behind both Zarabeth and the Oedipal attachment to his mother. They are now distant memories. Science and logic become his partners, like before.

The time portal dramatizes how a struggle can arise in the past, yet continue to affect us throughout life. In one sense, Spock's affair with Zarabeth occurred eons ago. At the same time, she is only minutes away if Spock wished to return to her. All it would take is a few steps through the gateway. Similarly, childhood conflicts can seem so long ago that they should be irrelevant. At the same time, remnants of those years stay with us. We might view an issue from a safe distance at times, like watching a disc in Mr. Atoz' library. Other times, we get entangled. The gateway reveals how quickly and inadvertently this regression can happen and how much effort it can take to come back. The time portal tells us a vital truth: our past is long ago and right now. This statement is not a paradox because both perspectives are needed to know ourselves fully.

Why does Dr. McCoy tell Mr. Spock that "it did happen?" The good doctor can be a jerk sometimes. Even for McCoy, however, it seems heartless to rub salt into Spock's wound the instant they return to the present. The comment may be in response to the monologue in *Macbeth* which contains the phrase "All Our Yesterdays." Near the end of the Shakespeare's tragedy, Macbeth's crimes have erased all traces of humanity from his soul. The famous speech ends with his words that "life is a tale told by an idiot, full of sound and fury, signifying nothing." Comparing Spock to Macbeth is a stretch; one is a criminal, and the other is not. The similarity, however, is that Vulcan culture teaches that emotions "signify nothing." In other words, McCoy points out that our past matters, our attachments matter, our feelings matter. This time, Spock does not dispute the point. Zarabeth is dead, but she matters.

In spite of some plot holes, "All Our Yesterdays" is quite clever in its construction. One puzzle is: why would the *Enterprise* rush to visit a world three hours before its star explodes? They never explain their mission. With that said, the ending is brilliant in how it ties up loose ends. Notice that the time portal would have allowed Spock to go back and visit Zarabeth, even on a regular basis. He could spend his vacations with her, in a dank cave hiding from the frozen wasteland. This resolution would miss the point. Spock must mourn Zarabeth completely, for all time. Childhood must end. The narrative not only destroys the temporal gateway so that Spock's holidays are impossible, but it also obliterates the entire planet. How many ways can one say that there is no going back? At the same time, the world's disintegration was the reason why the inhabitants invented the time portal in the first place, to escape from their star going nova.

The next episode, "The Naked Time," is similar to "All Our Yesterdays" in that repressed emotions bubble to the surface.

The Naked Time

> The *Enterprise* arrives at the research station on Psi 2000 after reports that the planet is breaking apart. The landing party finds the personnel frozen to death after somebody turned off the life support systems. It appears that the scientists went insane before they died.

The order of events at the research station is: the planet is breaking up, the scientists go insane, somebody turns off the heat, and they freeze to death. Each step has an allegorical meaning, as does the full sequence. Without knowing more, we might speculate that an entire world going to pieces represents the fragmentation of our mind. Sometimes the eruption of concealed emotions and drives embodies a type of madness in which latency-age repression has metaphorically broken down. The naked instincts probably terrified one of the researchers, who tried to get the genie back in the bottle using mass suicide. Freezing to death could symbolize a desperate attempt to re-repress stuff that should not have thawed in the first place.

Whatever caused the craziness on the surface is sure to affect the *Enterprise*. We can expect that unconscious stuff will bubble, froth, then spill out all over the place.

> Without knowing, Lieutenant Tormolen brings the madness aboard the *Enterprise*. Overwhelmed by the researchers' deaths, he tries to stab himself. Lieutenants Riley and Sulu restrain him, but they contract the disease in the process. The infection spreads by skin contact.

> Mr. Sulu chases some crewmen down the corridor with a sword. Riley locks everybody out of engineering and pretends he is captain of the ship. Mr. Spock concludes that the illness forces "hidden personality traits" to surface.

At its essence, the illness attacks its victims' capacity for repression. Typically, people have executive control over the way they behave. Whatever distracting things they may think and feel, adults can still focus on the task at hand. The infected crew no longer have a filter. They can no longer push aside the disruptive stuff inside their heads. Their impulsive actions are reckless and dangerous. Without any moderating, their sentiments are gushy and extreme.

Mr. Spock is partially correct when he says that the disease reveals "hidden personality traits." Issues are certainly coming to the surface, things that typically remain concealed or in the background. However, the term "personality trait" refers to something different than what is evident in the story.

In psychoanalysis, a personality trait is a pattern of thought or action people display over time and across different contexts. It is not only a way that people respond to the world but also how they deal with unconscious forces from within. For example, Mr. Spock demonstrates the trait of intellectualization; he relies on reason and logic to understand his surroundings and fend off buried emotion and conflict. Consistently, Spock applies his brand of objectivity to whatever problem presents itself, whether the threat comes from his environment or his own psyche.

It is more accurate to say that the fictional illness forces naked drives and sentiments to the surface by removing the filter. The infection does not reveal methods of coping; it strips them away. Without their help, the victim is left exposed and vulnerable.

> The illness spreads rapidly, while the ship spirals down toward incineration in the planet's atmosphere. In engineering, Riley cuts off control from the bridge and is not making adjustments to stabilize the vessel.

> Nurse Chapel contracts the illness and confesses to Mr. Spock that she loves him. Overwhelmed, Spock leaves the room and cries uncontrollably.

> Captain Kirk and Mr. Scott break into engineering and retake control of the ship. Horrified, they discover that Riley has turned the engines off completely. The reactor needs thirty minutes to warm up, but the Enterprise has only half that time before it disintegrates. Their only hope is a risky technique, a sudden implosion of matter and antimatter.

> Kirk finds Spock and tells him what they need to do, but Spock does not listen. He sobs, ashamed that he never told his mother he loved her. He scolds himself for rejecting her human heritage. Even feelings of friendship for Kirk evoke shame.

"The Naked Time" reveals what lies below Mr. Spock's repression. The disease has stripped away his metaphorical clothing, leaving him exposed. Like the majority of young boys, Spock's first love is his mother. Without his defenses, the attachment comes quickly to the surface. As in "All Our Yesterdays," Mr. Spock has regressed to a developmental stage before latency. His emotions come out of hiding and smack him in the face, as if to taunt, "Where is your logic now?" Kirk quite literally slaps Spock four times before the Vulcan strikes back.

It is not surprising to find Oedipal struggles under Spock's surface; these issues are universal. What is unusual about Spock, however, is how he rejects any and all emotion out of hand. Not only does he disavow anger but he also banishes warmth and affection. He demonstrates this total repudiation of all sentiment when he walks out on Nurse Chapel after she just poured out her love. Why is he driven to repress and disown everything?

To answer these questions about Spock, we must first return to the Oedipus situation in general. We have learned that repression allows children to put the remnants of the complex out of their mind and school directs their energy outside the home. There is another factor that helps children move beyond their longing for the parent of the opposite sex.

Identification with their dads helps young boys give up their wish to marry their moms. Instead of competing with their father for her affection, they decide to become like him. If a son emulates his father, someday he can find a wife of his own. Like most people, if children cannot have what they want, they take the next best thing. Boys stop yearning for their mothers and start looking for suitable girls their age. They can marry their mom in a disguised form. Their father is no longer a rival; the son can stop fearing his retaliation.

Mr. Spock identifies with his father, and thus rejects all his emotions and his human heritage. Like all good Vulcans, Spock disavows his feelings and devotes himself to pure logic. Following in his dad's footsteps helps him give up his childhood longing to have his mom all to himself. Acknowledging emotion frightens him because it threatens the idea that he is a chip off the old block. Feelings evoke shame, which then drives the sentiment back underground.

In "The Naked Time," Spock cannot escape how one-sided he has been towards his parents. He rebukes himself for rejecting his mother's heritage. Perhaps for the first time, he puts himself in her shoes. It is as if he had been saying, "I love everything about Daddy and nothing about you." At the same time, embracing Vulcan culture like his father was a way to detach from his mom because he wanted her so much. Arghh! Did she know? Why didn't he tell her?

If Spock were a real person, the questions he asks himself in this episode could lead to some emotional growth. Self-reflection is tough, but the rewards can be great. How many times have we hurt the people we love without intending to, without considering how we might look in their eyes?

Rest assured that Mr. Spock will reclaim his repression and intellectualization by the end of the episode. He cannot change too much without losing the angst that makes him endearing to viewers.

> Kirk strikes Spock across the face, hoping he will come to his senses. Spock regains his composure, but then Kirk catches the illness. Kirk laments his devotion to the *Enterprise*, complaining that he lives "her" life and not his own. There is no room left in his life for a real woman.

This naked view of Captain Kirk's emotional life confirms what we discussed in the last chapter. Kirk feels so devoted to the *Enterprise* that his life does not seem his own. Stripped of his façade, he laments the sacrifices he makes. The Captain's insight is incomplete, however, because he does not grasp that his perpetual bachelor status is self-imposed. Getting close to a woman would involve some compromises, but it is possible. Other military officers get married, so can he. You're not *that* special, James T. Kirk. I can hear those who know him say that he "has a problem with intimacy."

> The *Enterprise* pulls out of the planet's gravity using the unorthodox antimatter technique, but the maneuver causes time to run backward. The crew corrects the anomaly by reversing the engines, but by then the ship has gone back in time seventy-two hours. Spock says that they have three days to live over again.

> Dr. McCoy finds an antidote to the illness and distributes it throughout the crew.

The time reversal is yet more evidence that the disease psychologically turns back the clock for the *Enterprise* crew. Kirk, Spock, and the others regress to an earlier age, temporarily losing the latency skills that keep disruptive unconscious forces at bay. Spock's comment about reliving three days alludes to reestablishing their mental equilibrium so that they can get on with adult life.

As a literary device, the antimatter time-warp maneuver was also meant to foreshadow or set the stage for future stories when the *Enterprise* might choose to return to the past. When Spock comments that they now know a way to journey back in time, Kirk responds that they may risk it someday. Later episodes, however, portrayed the *Enterprise*'s time travel as the result of a "slingshot" operation around a massive body like the sun or a black hole. This motif appears in "Tomorrow is Yesterday" and "Assignment: Earth," as well as the movie *Star Trek IV: The Voyage Home*.

As a student of physics, I would have advised *Star Trek* producers to stick with the antimatter implosion idea. The mechanics of a *gravity assist* or "slingshot" maneuver are fully understood and frequently used by NASA's and other countries' planetary explorers; there is no mystery. The procedure is used to accelerate a probe to a higher velocity; it has nothing to do with the flow of time. In contrast, it turns out that the mathematical description of antimatter is the same as regular protons, neutrons, and electrons going backward in time. According to the equations, changing a particle's electric charge from positive to negative is the same as reversing the flow of time. Does this fact reflect some underlying truth about the universe? Perhaps. Time will tell.

"All Our Yesterdays" and "The Naked Time" highlight the importance of repression by removing it. When all hell breaks loose, the characters must struggle to regain their sanity. Both stories reflect back to when we emerged from the tumult of our early life and started school. The years after that were exciting. We expanded our knowledge, developed our physical skills, and enlarged our circle of friends. The mild winds made for smooth sailing. It was the calm before the storm of adolescence.

CHAPTER 12: PON FARR

Adolescents face three developmental tasks: adjusting to the physical changes of puberty, forming an identity independent of their parents, and leaving home. While these struggles are overlapping, we will discuss them separately for the sake of clarity. Then, we will explore how these adolescent themes appear in *Star Trek*. Spock's mating instinct in "Amok Time" reflects the bodily transformation of puberty. "Journey to Babel" explores Mr. Spock's conflicted identity. "Who Mourns for Adonais?" portrays adolescents' struggle to leave home and build lives of their own.

Puberty brings dramatic biological alterations. Girls develop breasts and a rounded, shapely figure. Hair starts to grow in the genital area and under the arms. Menstruation begins, with ovulation and fertility around the same time. Boys grow whiskers, along with pubic and axillary hair. Their voices can get squeaky but then settle into the deep resonance of an adult man. The male sex organs mature, making orgasm, ejaculation, and fatherhood all possible. The word "puberty" refers to these physical changes, while the term "adolescence" encompasses all the bodily, emotional, social, and family issues that accompany this time of life.

Adolescents feel awkward about their changing bodies. Though formal sex education has helped prepare youngsters to some degree, puberty is still a challenge. The child's body goes through a metamorphosis. Girls become young women, and boys grow to be men. Since the maturation is evident to people around them, adolescents feel exposed, conspicuous, and vulnerable.

Mr. Spock's alien anatomy symbolizes the physical changes of puberty. Some of his non-human features are internal, like the green blood and the location of his heart. Other Vulcan features are visible to everybody. His eyebrows do not curve, and his ears form a point at the top. These anomalies make him stick out from the crowd.

At first, adolescents' changing bodies feel as alien to themselves as Spock does to the humans around him. Hypervigilant to how others react, teenagers often feel that they stick out as conspicuously a Vulcan. They can relate to Spock because they understand what it is like to be an outsider.

Spock's ears are particularly meaningful to adolescent boys, as they represent the growth and maturation of the penis. The vertical, stiff, pointy aspect of his ears suggests this connection. It is sometimes a laugh line to call something a "phallic symbol," meaning that it is a stand-in for the male sex organ. We should remember that there is a hint of truth in comedy. The male genitalia is on the outside of the rest of the body and is very conspicuous. Growing boys feel exposed and vulnerable. Will girls accept and admire them, or will they laugh? Will other men feel threatened by their ascendant virility? To make matters worse, teenage boys often have little control over their excitable penis. Erections can appear out of nowhere, at inopportune and embarrassing moments. This spontaneous combustion is distracting at best; it can also create abundant angst.

Along with the physical maturation, adolescents' sexual drive increases dramatically. Their interest in copulation grows as their genitals mature. Erotic thoughts and urges fill their minds. Anxious about their sex appeal, adolescents become hypersensitive to appearance and status. Typically, teenage girls focus on makeup, fashion, and popularity. Adolescent boys concentrate more on muscle mass, fast cars, sports, and other symbols of potency.

A brief aside is prudent at this point. There are many differences between male and female human beings, which have biological and cultural roots. A full discussion of this matter goes beyond the scope of this book. I am aware that some sentences express generalities which will not apply universally. This deficit seems unavoidable in a tome that just begins to touch on psychoanalytic ideas. I have no desire to pigeonhole anybody or impose a foreign agenda. I am also cognizant that the notions presented here are male-biased. The imbalance has four roots: our historically patriarchal society; the overwhelming dominance of men in the history of psychoanalysis along with their male focus; as a man, myself, I come with some baggage; and the lopsided appeal of *Star Trek* to men and boys. I am not saying that women do not enjoy *Star Trek*; my wife is an admirer, for instance. The fact remains that there are more male fans than female. I hope that people will just take in the concepts on their first reading. There will be time afterward for discussion, critique, expansion, and improvement.

Instinctual aggression also increases during puberty. Violence among teenagers is much more common than it is among latency age children. Adolescents can direct their hostility towards others, but also at themselves. Suicide is rare in latency-age kids, but it is a severe public health issue for teenagers. Boys are more openly belligerent, but girls also struggle with a surge of antipathy. Using language, people can express antagonism verbally and in writing. We inflict a lot of suffering through biting comments, put-downs, name-calling, mean-spirited sarcasm, and other attacks.

Adolescents must find a way to cope with their heightened sexual and aggressive drives. During latency, youngsters successfully repressed these impulses and devoted themselves to other areas. As teenagers, it is more challenging to keep disruptive forces underground or redirect them in constructive ways. Nonetheless, many of the same activities that helped children in grade school can aid the adolescent. Sports and other competitions provide a healthy outlet for anger and rivalry. Schoolwork and social activities channel energy into productive areas and keep young people connected to others in appropriate ways. Teenage boys and girls can gradually explore the mysteries of the opposite sex by dating.

A new coping mechanism appears during adolescence, called "asceticism." Psychoanalyst Anna Freud (Sigmund Freud's daughter) wrote about this phenomenon in depth. Asceticism in this context is the vigorous devotion to a cause or idea; it ranges from a strong interest to an all-consuming obsession. The principles involved can be moral, religious, artistic, political, dietary, or academic. Others might describe ascetics as fanatics or complain that they are on a crusade.

Asceticism helps some adolescents ward off scary sensual and angry thoughts and feelings. The exaggerated focus on a higher calling gives them an outlet and distracts from frightening impulses from within. Ascetics often defend against internal struggles by going to the opposite extreme. Teenagers who fear their hostility may respond by becoming pacifists. Opposing violence of any sort helps them keep their aggression in check. Those who loathe their sexual appetites might campaign against premarital sex, pornography, homosexuality, or other sex-related issues. Other people might wonder, "What are they so afraid of?" Asceticism contrasts with more mainstream values and beliefs because it can be excessive and inflexible.

From this perspective, Spock's logic-worship is an example of asceticism. He is a fanatic. What is so terrible about emotion, friendship, affection, and love? His extremism and rigidity empower Spock to keep his unwanted emotions under wraps. Intellectualization wards off the sentiments he does not want to experience. If his feelings threaten to emerge, he responds by becoming more unyieldingly rational. Underneath the surface, raw instinct pummels Mr. Spock. We saw his yearning for love and blissful merger in "This Side of Paradise." Episodes "The Naked Time" and "All Our Yesterdays" revealed the childhood attachments he has tried so hard to disown. "Amok Time" portrays the resurgent rivalries and swelling libido of adolescence.

Amok Time

McCoy mentions that Mr. Spock has seemed nervous and has been avoiding food. Kirk dismisses the doctor's concern until Spock throws a bowl of food at Nurse Chapel and threatens to break McCoy's neck. Without explanation, Spock asks Kirk to divert the *Enterprise* to his home planet, Vulcan.

The explosive opening parallels the beginning of puberty. Mr. Spock's fury portrays the teenage surge in aggressiveness. He can barely control himself. A disbelieving Captain Kirk wonders, "What happened to the Mr. Spock I thought I knew?" Similarly, dumbfounded parents might look at their budding adolescent and wonder, "Is this really my child?" The serene latency years are over.

After much persuasion, Spock finally tells Kirk and McCoy what is happening. He has entered "pon farr," the Vulcan mating period that occurs every seven years. He must return to Vulcan and take a wife, or he will die. Disobeying direct orders from Starfleet, Captain Kirk sets a course for Vulcan.

Pon farr speaks to the resurgent instincts of adolescence. Like his hostility, Spock's libido erupts. His drive to copulate takes over his person, drowning out all other considerations. Similarly, commanding new sensations and urges descend upon young teenagers. These forces overwhelm some adolescents, just as pon farr consumes Mr. Spock. The Vulcan's typical coping mechanisms no longer ward off his instincts. Logic fails him.

Pon farr's seven-year cycle happens to be the same amount of time as the latency period in children. This parallel hardly seems coincidental. The emotionally quiescent grade school period begins around age five and lasts to age twelve, more or less. Five years subtracted from twelve leaves seven years. Just as Spock had an 84-month period of relative calm, so children have a quieter seven-year stretch before adolescence begins.

Accompanied by Kirk and McCoy, Spock beams down to Vulcan to marry his beautiful betrothed, T'Pring. Both sets of parents arranged the marriage when Spock and T'Pring were children. T'Pau, a powerful Vulcan dignitary, presides over the ceremony.

Unexpectedly, T'Pring selects Captain Kirk as her champion, meaning that she prefers him over Spock and the two will fight in the Vulcan rite of "kal-if-fee." Not wanting to offend T'Pring, and to avoid the selection of another challenger who might really hurt Spock, Kirk agrees. After he is committed, the Captain learns that the combat is to the death. Kirk must kill Spock or be murdered by him. The tradition is a relic from ancient times when Vulcans battled for their mates.

During the ensuing contest, Dr. McCoy gives Kirk a "tri-ox compound" to compensate for the hot, thin Vulcan air. In reality, the concoction simulates death, making it appear that Mr. Spock has killed the Captain. With Kirk's apparent death, Mr. Spock returns to his former, calm self; the madness passes.

Spock asks T'Pring why she chose a champion and why it was Captain Kirk. She explains that she actually preferred another Vulcan named Stonn. She reasoned that if Kirk had won the challenge, he would have relinquished his claim to her, allowing her to marry Stonn. If Spock had prevailed, he would have released her because she dared to challenge him; in this case, too, she would be free to marry Stonn. Spock commends her for her logic. As he gives up his claim over T'Pring, he tells Stonn that "having" is often not as pleasant as "wanting." It is not logical, but it is often true.

When Spock returns to the *Enterprise*, he welcomes the news that Kirk is alive and well.

"Amok Time" depicts the Oedipal conflict. Spock is the son, T'Pring the mom, and Kirk is the dad. Spock longs to mate with T'Pring, yet she chooses another man. The rejection infuriates Spock, as a mother's rebuff stirs her son's rage. Spock wants to kill Kirk, who has transformed from a friend and benevolent father figure into his rival. Boys do not really want to murder their fathers; similarly, grief and guilt wash over Mr. Spock when he appears to have taken the captain's life.

Puberty brings the Oedipal conflict back to the surface after a latency of seven years. Teenage boys re-experience the desire for their mothers; girls feel similarly about their fathers. Quiescent feelings of jealousy and rivalry re-emerge. However, a lot has changed since preschool. The reprise of the Oedipus complex is different in many ways.

For the first time, adolescent boys may be physically stronger and more virile than their fathers. At the same time that these youngsters reach adolescence, adults face middle-age. Bodily strength and athletic ability peak in the 20s or 30s, so dads have typically passed their peak or will do so soon. In contrast, teenage sons explode with energy and their muscle power and skill are still in ascendance. When children were three years old, parents were bigger and stronger. For adolescent boys, it is now possible to best their father in competition. A similar situation exists for teenage girls. As they mature into attractive young women, their mothers face the issues of midlife.

Spock portrays the adolescents' growing strength and prowess by defeating Kirk, the father figure. Not only does Spock dream of killing his rival, but he also does it. Similarly, teenage boys are strong enough to actually hurt somebody if they do not watch themselves. They are not small, dependent children any longer.

Adolescent boys also have the physical equipment to have sex. (Acknowledging this fact is not an endorsement.) Copulation and fatherhood are not unachievable daydreams any longer; the possibilities are very real. Once children enter puberty, they have the biological capacity to reproduce.

The physical maturation and rising libido are exciting, but they also frighten adolescents. Teenagers may have leftover hostile and sensual urges toward their parents, but they do not want to act on them. They are also looking forward to when they leave home and leave the dependency of their youth behind them. The time has come to resolve the Oedipus complex in a more definitive and lasting way.

Adolescents direct their longings and rivalries toward their peers. Rather than pining for Mom, boys become intrigued with girls their age, and vice versa. Competition within social groups and on the ballfield replaces rivalry with their parents. Healthy teenagers become involved with one another and detach from their life at home. This shift tamps down Oedipal remnants and harnesses the energy for relationships outside the family.

Spock models how adolescents reject their Oedipal longings by relinquishing his hold on T'Pring. Even though he won the challenge, he turns her away. Similarly, adolescent boys abandon the childhood attachment to their mothers and ask out teenage girls. Should they stick with Mom? Like Spock, they say, "Thanks, but no thanks."

Spock tells Stonn that "having" is not as pleasant as "wanting." On the surface, this comment is a bit puzzling. I find that *having* a cozy home is much better than just *wanting* one. The comparison makes sense, however, in the context of the Oedipus complex. Often, what we most want when we are kids would not be good for us in the long run. From this perspective, having your Oedipal dream would mean slaughtering one parent and life-long enmeshment with the other one; Spock is correct to say that this would not be pleasant. "Wanting," in regards to the Oedipus complex, can be redirected and eventually blossom into a loving partnership with another adult.

Forming an identity independent of caretakers is another developmental task for adolescents. During latency, children define their self in the context of their family. If you ask grade school students who they are, they will tell you their names, who they live with, how old they are, and so on. Teenagers want to be more than just their parents' kids. They begin to resist their parents' ideas and ways of doing things. While still a part of a family, they also want to be separate from it.

Psychologist Erik Erikson coined the term "identity crisis" in reference to adolescents' struggle to discover and define who they are. The word "crisis" in this context does not imply that something has gone wrong. Teenagers must wrestle with these issues if they are to move forward. Labeling the task a "crisis" recognizes how disrupting and confusing the time can be and how deep the questions go.

As teenagers think more critically, they become poignantly aware of their parents' faults and weaknesses. Youngsters tend to idolize their caretakers during early childhood. They assume that their parents know what they are talking about. During adolescence, this illusion comes crashing down. Teenagers feel disappointed and angry that their parents are not perfect and all powerful. They feel betrayed. The letdown prompts adolescents to question their values and beliefs; they no longer accept what adults say on blind faith. Before agreeing to anything, young people want to think about it and decide for themselves. Challenging, probing, and testing authority is a healthy part of growing up, most of the time. Defiance can be frustrating for parents; understanding the struggle in the context of overall growth can be reassuring. Over time, the process of differentiation can be a valuable experience for both parent and child.

Abused and neglected youngsters face unique challenges. If young people see little in their caretakers to admire, they might feel adrift in a confusing world without knowing who they are. Traumatized children may end up behaving in ways that they despised in a family member, unsure how to escape the gravitational pull of dysfunction. Freud called this phenomena "repetition compulsion," in that the person acts out issues from their early life in their adult relationships. Overwhelmed with disappointment and anger, some wounded youngsters condemn everything about society with blistering ferocity. Abuse can make it difficult for them to distinguish the grownups who raised them from all adult institutions.

Ideally, adolescents can still rely on some adult guidance to get through the difficult years, with parents who are worthy of that trust. When things break down, teenagers can be vicious with their anger and indiscriminate when it comes to sex. Adults can help them avoid costly mistakes. Teens often resist it, but parents should remain involved in their children's lives, albeit at a distance. Some missteps are inevitable on both sides. I recall a learning module I completed at the recommendation of our insurance agent when our children started driver's education. The statistics showed that sixty percent of new drivers are involved in an accident of some sort within the first year. The message? Don't freak out. Car accidents are a part of learning to drive; some property damage is unavoidable. Hopefully, it will just be a fender-bender. It was sound advice and applied to other issues, unrelated to automobiles.

The adolescent's approaching emancipation adds fuel to the identity crisis. Teenagers grow increasingly aware that they will soon be out in the world on their own; they cannot rely on their parents' material support indefinitely. This awareness pushes them forward, even in the face of insecurity. Some questions demand answers Who am I and where am I going?

Parents can help adolescents wrestle with identity, but only to a point. The idea is for teenagers to discover themselves in distinction from their moms and dads, which requires some distance. When youngsters make choices based primarily on parental approval, they sacrifice some of their budding autonomy. When rebellious behavior is mostly about defying family, offspring lose focus on what they want for themselves..

Teenagers look to three groups of people to help discover who they are and who they want to become: to heroes and idols, to their peers, and to adults outside the family.

Adolescents idolize their heroes, then identify with the qualities they admire. These champions may be rock stars, athletes, prominent figures from the past or present, or even fictional characters. Teenagers no longer think that their parents are perfect, but they still can believe in their champions. It is easier to overlook faults when you do not live with somebody. At this stage, it is okay if youngsters' view of these people is one-dimensional. What is important is the qualities the child admires, imagined or not. Children strive to be like the people they idolize. Superheroes add another layer, symbolically compensating adolescents for their disappointments and their insecurities about growing up.

Adolescents also turn to each other for mutual help. They see each other in class, after school, at events, and in their homes. Cellphones and computers allow nonstop communication. There is a feeling of camaraderie that grows out of a shared struggle and experience. As teenagers detach from home, they can find a sense of belonging in various peer groups. They might gripe about parents, but this can help them figure out how they want to define themselves. Groups and friends are bouncing things off each other all the time. The feedback loop helps them figure out what character traits they esteem and who they want to be like. Ideally, schoolmates reinforce virtues in each other and support one another when branching out.

The importance of peers during adolescence also carries risks. Teenagers are exquisitely sensitive to whether they fit in. The needed distance from parents leaves them feeling shaky and vulnerable. Teens can reinforce each other's strengths or drag one another down. A child can fall in with the wrong crowd. Adolescents can be so desperate to belong that they lose their identity rather than find it. Social media in the information age is posing unique challenges.

Teenagers also identify with adults beyond the immediate family. They turn to teachers, school counselors, coaches, ministers, group leaders, their friends' parents, neighbors, aunts, uncles, grandparents, and others. When they see something they like, adolescents can integrate it into their own person. If somebody acts distastefully, children can use the experience as a negative example; "I never want to be like that." They can imitate grownups other than Mom and Dad without feeling smothered or controlled. Mentors do not threaten youngsters' autonomy and individuality the same way that parents do. Activities outside the home help young people figure out who they want to emulate. Regrettably, some trends in modern society seem blind to children's need for adults other than blood relatives, like online high school. Kids cannot pattern their identity after an electronic learning module, but they can model themselves on a respected teacher.

Discovering and defining who we are is often difficult, and continues throughout life. While adolescents focus their attention outside the home, adult children often look back and want to understand their roots. To know who we are, we need to grasp where we came from. Curiosity about our background does not necessarily mean that we approve of our parents' and other adults' decisions, just as interest in a country's history does not condone its actions. Sometimes people in their 30s and 40s find a new appreciation for their moms and dads, but not always.

In "Journey to Babel," we meet Mr. Spock's parents and will see how he struggles with his identity.

Journey to Babel

The *Enterprise* is transporting several delegates to a Federation conference on a planet code-named Babel. The Vulcan ambassador and his human wife arrive, Sarek and Amanda. Captain Kirk offers Mr. Spock as a guide, but Sarek requests someone else. Kirk suggests that Spock beam down to Vulcan while they are there and visit his parents. Spock replies that Ambassador Sarek and his wife *are* his mother and father. Spock and his father have not spoken in eighteen years. Sarek wanted his son to attend the Vulcan Science Academy, but Spock joined Starfleet instead.

Tension is high among the delegates. Sarek and the Tellarite ambassador, Gav, argue over a political issue. Gav almost attacks Sarek, until Kirk intervenes.

A small, unidentified spaceship follows the *Enterprise*; it is fast and maneuverable.

Babel in the episode's title alludes to the expansive collection of delegates with their competing politics and languages. The Tower of Babel narrative appears in the Hebrew Bible's and Christian Old Testament's Book of Genesis. In the account, all humanity is united, and everybody speaks the same language. They agree to build a tower tall enough to reach heaven and begin the construction. Displeased, God scatters people around the globe and confounds their speech. Since people now speak different languages, they cannot understand each other or cooperate on a development project or anything else. The Tower of Babel no longer threatens God.

Babel also alludes to the conflict between Spock and Sarek. Indeed, Mr. Spock is of two peoples, as he has both Vulcan and human ancestry. As in the Biblical story, the schism between father and son is so profound that it is as if they speak different languages and cannot communicate. Also, Sarek's harsh reaction by cutting off contact just because Spock decided something for himself is akin to God's response to humanity in Genesis; the Heavenly Father and the Vulcan father are saying in unison, "How dare you? Take this!"

"Journey to Babel" portrays the adolescent's struggle to form a new, independent identity; it also speaks to the competition between father and son, at least in this one fictional case. We will discuss both of these perspectives.

Spock's mother is from Earth and his father is Vulcan. The two civilizations have distinct histories, principles, and traditions. Spock's challenge is to take something of value from both parents and cultures. Simultaneously, he needs to look beyond his parents for role models and values he admires. Then, he can mix everything to create a unique, autonomous sense of himself.

Adolescents face the same task as Mr. Spock. There are always differences between parents regarding outlook, values, temperament, beliefs, mannerisms, and so on, even when both are Earthlings. Husband and wife have conflicting views on relationships, jobs, children, money, extended family, and other major and minor issues. Teenagers seek to internalize what they find attractive in each parent and avoid what is distasteful, to take what they like and leave the rest. Spock's mixed ancestry highlights this challenge, which helps adolescents relate. His fictional background is a literary device to convey to teenagers: we understand what you are dealing with.

Spock's solution is less than ideal. He over-identifies with his father and appears to disown his maternal, human heritage. He presents himself as Vulcan. End of story. Does he ever say that he carries within him the proud history of two great and distinguished civilizations? No. Spock embraces Vulcan's logic-worship without reservations. One might ask Spock: is it logical to accept logic as logical without logically refuting the logical logic against logic as logical?

At first glance, it is puzzling that Sarek is so angry with Spock. His son has internalized the Vulcan mindset so uncritically and completely that it seems Sarek would be pleased. The Vulcan father's ire is in response to Spock's choice of career.

Spock identifies with his mother indirectly by leaving Vulcan and immersing himself in the human culture of Starfleet. He chooses to live with *Homo sapiens* rather than Vulcans. Spock tells people that his decision emerged out of his scientific interests, but this is not the full story. He left Vulcan for the Academy to embrace his mother's heritage and discover the half-human part of himself that he has repressed.

Sarek sensed the unconscious meaning of Spock's commitment to Starfleet and felt threatened. Spock's service to the Federation spotlights his bond with his mother. With his actions, Spock celebrates Amanda's human heritage. Sarek is now the outsider. Spock shares an intimacy with his mother that his father will never know. The upstart whippersnapper has metaphorically kicked Dad out of the room. This hidden understanding explains why Sarek is so angry and unforgiving of Spock's decision. He fears that Spock's choice to work with humans is a threat to his marriage.

Sadly, Amanda does not recognize nor appreciate the meaning of Spock's devotion to Starfleet. In a disguised form, he is expressing his attachment to her, but she does not see it. Instead, Amanda feels hurt and offended because Spock comports himself as Vulcan only, not as human or even partly so.

Simultaneously, Sarek feels betrayed because Spock left Vulcan to live and work among his mother's people. Spock tries to please both his parents but ends up satisfying neither one.

Amanda and Sarek would have done better to respect Spock's choices. Parents should allow children enough latitude to form a unique identity. Teenagers need to establish their distinctive sense of self. Contrarians might object here and accuse me of imposing twenty-first-century liberal values on another civilization. The patriarchal alien culture esteems obedience, some could argue. To Vulcans, it is customary for fathers to choose their sons' careers. Who am I to say that they are wrong?

I would answer these critics that I do not claim any absolute morality. However, what I can say as a doctor of mental health is this: *if* we want people to be happy and balanced, *then* we will encourage them to choose their own path. *If* enthusiastic academics and inspiring leaders are vital to us, *then* we will accept some risky new directions. Some practices promote emotional health and growth, and others do not.

> Gav is murdered. Since the killer used an ancient Vulcan technique, Sarek is the primary suspect. Sarek collapses while Kirk is questioning him. McCoy determines that the ambassador needs emergency heart surgery. McCoy cannot perform Sarek's procedure unless Vulcan blood is available for transfusion. Spock offers to help, even though it is risky. A dangerous drug will boost Spock's production of blood; the surplus will go directly to Sarek during the surgery.

> Spock backs out at the last minute after an Andorian diplomat stabs Kirk. As the second officer, Spock feels that he cannot relinquish command while the captain is incapacitated.

> Amanda is furious. She implores her son to find his human half and save his father's life. Spock is frustrated that she cannot understand the Vulcan logic behind his decision. When Spock does not relent, his mother slaps him across the face.

Spock has mixed feelings about his father. Initially, he wants to save Sarek's life. A minute later, forget it. He claims that he is just being logical, but this argument is ridiculous to everybody but himself. Many officers are capable of commanding the *Enterprise*; only one person on board can supply Vulcan blood. Spock is of two minds. His initial willingness demonstrated his love; backing out conveys something else.

Ambivalence is a fundamental aspect of human relationships. Affection and frustration can exist side by side, as can other competing emotions.

Mixed feelings are especially prominent among adolescents and their caretakers. Sometimes, kids can't decide if they love or hate their moms and dads. They want to break away, but it is also scary. Parents also go back and forth. Adults sometimes say things like, "First I'll hug him, then I'll kill him." Spock's dilemma in the story speaks to teenagers because he feels torn in different directions.

Spock's stubborn refusal to yield expresses hostility towards Sarek, but it is also a tribute. In his mind, Spock may be honoring his father by demonstrating how far he will go to prove that he is Vulcan to the core. His duty-first approach testifies that he has disavowed any and all emotion. He is imitating the obstinacy he learned from his father. Even as Sarek nears death, Spock longs for his approval. It is as if the son is saying, "See Daddy, I'm uber-logical."

At the same time, Amanda is frantic. Does his mother's suffering count for nothing? She pleads with Spock to remember that he is human too. She reminds him of his childhood hurts, hoping to bring his feelings to the surface. His mother is right that there is a world of emotion behind Spock's rigidity, but a frontal assault on his defensive walls was not likely to succeed. She would have done better to start by approving of his devotion to logic in the abstract. When dealing with ascetics, direct challenges often send them deeper into their bunkers.

As in adolescence, Spock's family crisis is messy. Sarek, Amanda, and Spock misunderstand where each other is coming from. They hurt one another without intending to do so. Their motivations are confusing to others and sometimes to themselves. Hurt feelings go unspoken, then come out in other ways. Frustrated expectations lead to resentment and lashing out. "Journey to Babel" certainly fits in a chapter about adolescence.

> Captain Kirk feigns recovery and orders Spock to report for Sarek's procedure. Before Kirk can leave the bridge, the unidentified spaceship fires on the *Enterprise*. The tiny assailant evades the starship's counterattack. Vulnerable and desperate, Kirk orders the *Enterprise* to play dead. When the alien vessel closes in to investigate, the *Enterprise* destroys it. Both Sarek and Spock make it through the surgery.

With Captain Kirk back on the bridge, Spock can rescue his father without compromising his sense of duty. A lighthearted moment after Sarek's surgery suggests that an emotional logjam has broken for the family and relations will be better going forward.

"Journey to Babel" underscores the importance of talking with one another. The Biblical Tower of Babel narrative can be read many ways. One interpretation is that nothing can happen if people are not communicating in a language they can all understand. In the episode, Sarek's eighteen-year silence solved nothing. Son, mother, and father all felt wounded even though they tried hard not to show it.

Learning to talk about ourselves honestly is a critical life skill. Stuffing our emotions does not mean they are gone. Pretending is not a strength. It is hard to figure out who you are if you cannot speak your truth. At home and work, problems fester if they do not get discussed. Suffering in silence is rarely the best choice. Emotions are messages from our true self; when we listen, they teach us important things.

The third task of adolescence is leaving home. This issue is related to identity formation, but it focuses more on the tangible aspects of life: finding a place to live; working or going to school; paying bills; getting around; grocery shopping; cooking; staying in touch; and so on. Most young people achieve independence gradually. They take on more responsibility as their parents back out. Emancipation does not need to be abrupt or traumatic.

The episode "Who Mourns for Adonais?" touches on many themes simultaneously. It portrays a father dealing with the aptly-termed "empty nest syndrome" on an Olympic scale. From another perspective, it deals with time, change, loss, death, and legacy. The title is taken from the 1821 elegy "Adonais" by Percy Shelley, itself alluding to the Greek god Adonis. Both Shelley's poem and the myth are multifaceted; they can be analyzed on many levels, as can a juxtaposition of the two. A few paragraphs of introduction are warranted, even though they barely skim the surface.

Adonis was the mortal lover of goddess Aphrodite. He was vain and promiscuous, but incredibly handsome. Another deity (accounts vary) sent a wild boar to kill Adonis while he was out hunting. Taking pity on Aphrodite, Zeus raised Adonis from the dead and made him a god. Thus, invoking the name Adonis can refer to male vanity, attraction, untimely death, resurrection, and other things.

Percy Shelley composed "Adonais" after his friend and celebrated fellow poet John Keats died of tuberculosis at age 25. As a stand-in for Keats, the talented character Adonais of the elegy was taken at an early age, like Adonis. The persona speaking in the poem weeps with grief and calls all to join him, "Who Mourns for Adonais?" The mood transforms from despair to rapture with the revelation that Adonais achieves immortality with his words. He has become part of the "white radiance of Eternity. Like a star," the soul of the dead poet "Beacons from the abode where the Eternal are."

Who Mourns for Adonais?

The *Enterprise* is on a routine mission to investigate planet Pollux IV. A glob of energy appears on the viewscreen, hazy at first. As it approaches, it takes the form of a giant human hand. The thumb and fingers grab the *Enterprise* and hold it motionless.

The enormous hand suggests that Kirk and the others will face an adversary who represents a parent. To young children, grown-ups' hands seem massive and powerful, like the entity gripping the *Enterprise*. Adults can hold a child motionless if need be, as the hand of pure energy immobilizes the ship. The scene awakens unconscious memories in viewers of being physically or emotionally contained.

The head of an attractive, sophisticated man appears on the bridge viewscreen wearing a laurel crown. With hyperbole, he welcomes his "children." The long wait has ended. When Captain Kirk demands that he release the ship, their captor almost crushes it. This near disaster is Kirk's "first lesson."

Kirk beams down to the planet's surface along with McCoy, Scotty, Chekov, and Lieutenant Carolyn Palamas, an expert in ancient civilizations. The alien identifies himself as "Apollo," one of several space travelers who visited Earth five thousand years ago and were treated as gods. He tells Kirk that the *Enterprise* crew will stay on Pollux IV and worship him. When Kirk refuses, Apollo grows a hundred feet tall.

As the allegorical father, Apollo does not want his youngsters to leave home. Not only will the Earthlings remain, but they will also base their identity on their relationship with Papa. Kirk and the others resist, as they are fully capable of running their own lives. The landing party confronts the same struggle faced by every adolescent, to define themselves as more than just their parent's kid, and physically move out of the house. Apollo makes it clear that he is bigger and stronger, with his giant hand of energy and then by expanding to the size of a skyscraper. These demonstrations do not diminish Kirk's resolve, just as teenagers do not stop taking charge of their lives because their moms and dads have more authority and experience.

"Who Mourns for Adonais?" captures the adolescent struggle particularly well because of the complicated relationship of the *Enterprise* crew with Apollo. Whatever Kirk and the others think about it now, Greek mythology played a critical role at one time in our past. The Olympian deities were there at the dawn of Western Civilization; one could say that humanity grew up under their tutelage. Apollo was one of the more significant residents of Mount Olympus. He was the sun-god, radiating light and warmth for all life on Earth. As the spirit of prophecy, he was the immortal patron of the oracular city of Delphi. He was also the god of music, healing, and poetry. The world still turns to Homer's epic poems *Iliad* and *Odyssey* to understand our roots. The United States named its manned exploration of the moon, the "Apollo" program. In spite of this legacy, the fact remains that Kirk and the others have no interest in herding sheep or building temples.

Similarly, teenagers have a tricky balancing act in response to their parents. On the one hand, Mom and Dad brought them into the world, fed them, clothed them, played with them, protected them, and supported them. Even when adults fall short, just being there as youngsters grow up makes family significant; adolescents are aware of this truth at some level. At the same time, teenagers need to detach from their caretakers in preparation for leaving home. They get more involved with their peers, make their own decisions, and insist on more privacy. Their earlier years allowed them to get to where they are, but that does not mean that they want to go back.

Apollo has trouble letting his so-called children grow up or accepting that they already have done so. He feels hurt that the *Enterprise* crew members are capable adults and do not need the doting caretaking he wants to give. Some parents are like Apollo in this regard; they pressure youngsters to stay dependent because they want to feel important and needed. They look back with nostalgia to the simpler days when their sons and daughters were in grade school. Can't my child look up to me like that again?

One could say that Apollo is a pathological narcissist demanding worship or an infantilizing control freak, but this would miss the point. He is a sympathetic antagonist in spite of the bombast. Science fiction often exaggerates aspects of a character to highlight central issues or deal with them in metaphor. All parents have mixed feelings as their children grow up. Looking through our youngsters' baby pictures is bittersweet; we remember those days with fondness, but also face the truth that the past will never come back. Apollo is a dad who loves his kids but can't grasp that they no longer need him in the way that they used to.

Kirk and the others defy Apollo. Kirk says they don't bow to every creature that has a bag of tricks. Several times, Scotty tries to attack Apollo when the so-called god shows interest in Lieutenant Palamas. The four men try to provoke Apollo into killing one of them; this would drain his energy so that the other three could overpower him.

The family drama escalates. Events spin out of control, even though the Earthlings and Apollo share some regard for each other. What is going on?

If Apollo was there during our childhood as a civilization, what keeps the landing party from showing him some esteem? Why doesn't Captain Kirk thank Apollo for his contributions and calmly explain that they now prefer to govern their own lives?

Kirk and the others cannot give Apollo any credit while they are trying to break free of him. They are terrified that conceding a historical bond would cause Apollo to yell victory and tighten his grip. A scary voice inside their heads says, "We are indebted to this guy." They do feel grateful, but that does not mean that they want to stay and worship him. Fear drives Kirk and the others to hide any feelings of attachment and stoke their anger and rage. Their plan is desperate, but Kirk says that he sees no other way. They will do anything to loosen Apollo's stranglehold. They enflame Apollo with the message, "You mean nothing to us. This place stinks so bad that we'd rather die than stay here."

Similarly, teenagers cannot always show affection or express gratitude towards their moms and dads when they are trying to take charge of their lives and leave home. They fear that the attachment will undermine their efforts toward independence and lead to protracted childhood. In extreme cases, adolescents can repudiate any bond with their parents and disparage everything about them. Appreciating the forces at play can help caretakers get through these moments and stay calm. Teenagers are in the midst of a desperate struggle to differentiate, claim authority over their own lives, and move out. Adults should remember that their child's underlying longing for independence is healthy. Naturally, they want to think for themselves. Healthy kids want to control their destiny. Good parents understand that their protection and supervision are only temporary.

Apollo is stuck in the past. Perhaps the ancient Greeks worshiped him, but that was then, this is now. He wants to preserve something that is fleeting by its nature. Maybe he thinks that gods should be able to stop time; everything would then be as it always had been. Apollo has not mourned life's transience. He wants to freeze the moment. He chastises the clock for marking time. As sun god, why not just stop the celestial furnace in its tracks?

Apollo's rigidity spotlights a truth about parenting. As children grow, caretakers need to change in response. Toddlers are dramatically different than teenagers. We do not put sixteen-year-old students in playpens, nor do we give preschoolers the keys to the car. The parent/child relationship is in perpetual flux. Older children do not need their moms and dads the same way that they did when they were younger. The changing role of adults is not better or worse; it is just different. Teenagers need to break free, and sometimes they push hard. Parents should be wary of trying to hold on too tight.

There are rewards for parents who accept their child's autonomy. Youngsters become fellow adults. There is less opportunity for conflict after children have moved out. The empty nest has other pleasures as well. Young adults develop wisdom of their own, which can be delightful for parents who are open to it.

Imagine how differently things would have turned out if Apollo said to Kirk and the others, "Wow. You have really made something of yourselves! I was thinking of helping you out, but you obviously don't need it. Hey, maybe we gods can learn something from you as well! We could exchange diplomats and open a dialogue. What do you say?"

> Lieutenant Palamas falls in love with Apollo, but Captain Kirk tells her to shun him. With difficulty, she follows her orders and her conscience. She realizes that Apollo gets his way by bullying people. An enraged Apollo creates a fierce thunderstorm.

> Spock "punches some holes" in the energy field surrounding the *Enterprise*, which makes it possible to fire the phasers. On Kirk's order, the *Enterprise* destroys Apollo's temple, the source of his power.

> Questioning himself for the first time, Apollo wonders if he asked for all that much. Kind but direct, Kirk replies that they have outgrown Apollo. The once-deity demanded something that humanity can no longer give. Apollo speaks to the departed spirits of other Greek Olympians. He says that they were right, his time had passed long ago. The broken god fades away, to where the other Eternals are.

Kirk, Palamas, Spock, and the others do what is necessary. Once out of danger, Dr. McCoy says that he wished they could have found a way out without hurting Apollo. Indeed, it is hard to watch people suffer even when they bring it on themselves. Similarly, most teenagers have no desire to distress their parents; they just want to claim ownership of their lives. They sometimes make this point by saying to Mom and Dad, "I'm not doing this to hurt you." Adolescents are in the right to push back when adults hold on too tight. Children are not responsible for protecting their caretakers from feelings of loss. People should not sacrifice their growth just to make somebody else happy, just as Kirk and the others were right not to capitulate to Apollo even though it made him angry.

What do we make of Apollo's fate?

Viewed from the perspective of Apollo as a possessive father, the ending is troubling. Life is not over for adults when their children leave home, not even close. A whole new world can open up once in-home parenting comes to an end. The fifth decade and beyond can be rich, full, and rewarding. People often find a degree of self-acceptance that eluded them when they were younger.

Apollo misses out on the golden years because he cannot or will not mourn the loss of his children's dependency. The term "grief" refers to the emotional pain we feel when somebody or something we love gets taken away. "Mourning" refers to the process of working through the crisis, eventually reorganizing one's life. Afterward, people still feel sad, but the memories do not interfere with their day as much as before. Apparently, gods do not mourn. If he were a person, we might say to Apollo, "You will get through this. It's hard right now, but you will not feel this way forever. Take one day at a time." Apollo's response would be, "Nope; it's over for me."

Star Trek's allegory usually supports emotional growth, so the ending is a little puzzling. Kirk and the *Enterprise* will be okay, but what about Apollo?

Shelley's elegy "Adonais" suggests another way to understand the metaphor. From this point of view, Apollo is akin to the beautiful and talented youths, Adonis and Adonais. Whereas death claimed the mortal men, Apollo is taken to the beyond by irrelevance. His time has passed. He is no longer needed. What he offers has no value.

But wait. Consider. Starfleet lives on because Apollo was there when humanity was young. No man lives who was not once a boy, and no boy fathers himself. Apollo's "white radiance of Eternity" shines through his work. Look how his children have prospered. He is immortal, indeed. His task complete, he calls and is taken to the "abode where the Eternal are. The One, that is light, beauty, and love, now shines on him."

Chapter 13: Kolinahr

Star Trek's viewership during its first season was so-so. Networks watched the ratings closely because their revenue depended on the number of people tuning in. In year two, NBC gave *Star Trek* a less attractive time slot for its target audience, and its ratings declined further. In an age of video streaming, it is odd to remember that people had to watch an episode when it broadcast, or they missed it. The public also had to choose between competing shows, and the networks often pitted their best offerings against each other. Thus, a quality program could flame out if the airtime was unfortunate or the competition was formidable. *Star Trek* fans rescued it from cancellation during year two by mounting a letter-writing campaign, which prompted NBC to renew the series.

In its third season, *Star Trek* aired at 10:00 PM Friday night; this time slot was an even bigger challenge than that in year two. NBC also cut the show's budget. For a variety of reasons, the writing quality declined. The first episode that fall was "Spock's Brain," arguably the worst installment of the entire three-year run. The final chapter aired on June 3, 1969. "Turnabout Intruder" is another contender for last place; its misogyny is embarrassing, even for the 1960s.

In syndication, *Star Trek* became a cult classic. Paramount responded with the release of *Star Trek: The Motion Picture* in 1979. The transition from television series to feature film brought some benefits, but it also gave up a lot.

Full-length movies are more elaborate than a weekly TV show and have a grander scope. Hour-long television episodes have to be scripted to fit in with the commercial breaks. In contrast, motion picture writers and directors have more latitude to tell their story. Movie special effects are more extravagant and impressive. Most soundtracks are original, composed to enhance the scenes on a second -by -second basis. Plots can be more intricate, sometimes showing emotional growth not possible in TV serials. Characters in an ongoing series cannot change too much without risking the interest of their viewers.

Star Trek's shift to feature film also gave up advantages that television has over movies. The fifty-minute episode forced writers to use time economically. Modern special effects are impressive, but there is arguably something appealing about the simpler visuals of the original series. The weekly narrative is also less likely to be drowned out by glitz. Also lost in transition is the pleasure of a new adventure every week and the flexibility to take a risk. A twenty-six installment season allowed for a wide variety of subjects and an occasional dud without chasing viewers away. With a two year gap between movie releases, it is not possible to tell as many stories. Films are a special treat rather than a regular part of our routine. When a movie flops, it puts any future projects at risk.

The *Star Trek* feature films repeat many of the themes that made the original series successful, but they also move in new directions. The first two films challenge aspects of Captain Kirk and Mr. Spock that made them so appealing in a weekly show, as we shall see. At the same time, enough of the familiar *Star Trek* action and excitement remains to captivate fans.

There are six *Star Trek* movies with the original cast. This book discusses the first and second in detail, then brushes lightly over the rest. Note that *Star Trek Generations* appeared three years after *Star Trek VI*. It featured Captain Kirk, Scotty, and Chekov along with Captain Picard and others from *Star Trek: The Next Generation*. The actors who played Mr. Spock and Dr. McCoy opted out of that project; we will follow their lead and exit our analysis at the end of *Star Trek VI*.

Star Trek: The Motion Picture is an important film with some serious flaws. The scenes with special effects are prolonged and tedious, prompting the nickname *Star Trek: The "Slow Motion" Picture*. The quality of the visuals is superb for the 1970s, but they end up distracting viewers from the story. There are countless mind-numbing close-ups of Kirk and the others looking on in wonder. The dialogue is often stilted. Some viewers were put off by the impersonal nature of the adversary and the lack of action scenes.

Despite the artistic problems, the message of the story is touching, inspiring, and hopeful. Science fiction can sometimes be about silly monsters, but it can also address psychological and deeply spiritual issues.

Star Trek: The Motion Picture

> An unknown weapon destroys three Klingon warships as they investigate an enormous interstellar cloud. The anomaly is heading directly for Earth.

The menace is on its way to Earth, suggesting that humanity or the human mind is the source of its power and danger. Without knowing more, we suspect that it represents a part of the psyche that has been split off from other aspects of our mental life and flung into space. As discussed in Chapter 2, we cannot escape our dark side by projecting it outside ourselves, in this case by catapulting it light years away. The cloud is returning, and the *Enterprise* crew must deal with it whether they want to or not. The predicament is similar to that in "The Changeling" and "The Doomsday Machine." The Federation faces an adversary of immense size and terrifying destructive potential, which metaphorically portrays a scary part of ourselves.

The cloud's expansive, hazy, and impersonal boundaries suggest that it represents feelings from early infancy. During the first months of life, we did not have a clear sense of our emotional and physical margins. Newborns feel like they encompass the entire universe, as the misty phenomenon stretches out over several parsecs. Infants also cannot contain or modulate their feelings, which is dramatized by the sudden, inexplicable, and severe way that the entity reacts to the Klingon ships. The impersonal way it disintegrates the Birds of Prey suggests that it does not understand what it is doing, that it does not grasp the reality in which it finds itself.

> On Vulcan, Spock prepares for the rite of Kolinahr—the complete purging of all emotion. Spock stops the ceremony when a mysterious consciousness calls him from space. His Vulcan elder says that the enigmatic energy touches his human half. His answer lies elsewhere.

Mr. Spock is at a crisis point in his life. For decades, he has repressed and denied his feelings and attachments. He uses logic in an attempt to hide from vulnerable parts of himself. Kolinahr takes this coping style to new heights; it signifies the complete repudiation of all emotion. His sentiments would still exist, but they would never again force themselves into his conscious awareness.

The call from space is a metaphor for the part of Spock's psyche that resists Kolinahr. A voice from within him is demanding to speak. Cut off from his emotions, Spock believes that his resistance to the Vulcan ceremony comes from somewhere outside himself. In truth, it arises from the inner needs, wishes, affections, and passions that he has banished from his wakeful awareness.

Spock is at a watershed moment because competing forces are pulling him in different directions. He has repudiated his emotional life for years, yet a sudden tug inside his head calls everything into doubt. In an instant, his house of cards built on logic comes crashing down. If Kolinahr is not Spock's answer, what is? How does a menacing interstellar fog fit into the equation?

Star Trek: The Motion Picture is a daring film because it tampers with a vital aspect of the original series' success. Spock's repression of feelings and his fanatical devotion to logic is what made his character so appealing. He was cherished by viewers who struggled like Spock to figure out and master their emotions. It would have been easy for the producers to have left Spock's character unchanged. Had they done this, it would have assured a warm reception from devoted viewers, who were expecting the Vulcan to be the same as always.

Spock's rejection of Kolinahr is a statement that he cannot go on as he has in the past. It is a crisis for him because he will need to change. The turning point also challenged *Star Trek* fans. After waiting a decade for *Trek* to return, devotees may have expected to see the familiar characters and situations they had come to know over years of reruns as if no time had passed and everything was as it had been before.

Unhappy in an administrative position, Admiral James T. Kirk uses the approaching danger to regain command of the *Enterprise*. The current captain, Willard Decker, is furious and reminds Kirk that the starship has been refitted. Kirk does not know the vessel as well as he does, Decker warns.

Kirk has Dr. McCoy conscripted and beamed aboard. Heading out to confront the cloud, Kirk forces the ship into warp even though Scotty insists the systems are not ready. McCoy says to Kirk, "Jim, you're pushing. Your people know their jobs." Kirk proceeds anyway.

An imbalance in the engines sends the *Enterprise* into a deadly wormhole. Kirk orders Sulu to fire the phasers at an approaching asteroid, but Decker countermands and directs the attack with a photon torpedo, which returns the ship to standard space.

Once alone with Kirk and McCoy, Decker explains that the new design of the ship's systems would have made the phasers ineffective. He adds his opinion that Kirk's unfamiliarity with the refitted *Enterprise* jeopardizes their mission. Kirk demands that Decker quit competing with him. In private, McCoy tells the admiral that he is the one who is competing.

Not only are the producers meddling with Spock's persona, but they are also re-examining Captain Kirk. As discussed in Chapter 4, Kirk is appealing because of his drive to control and solve every problem. He defeats any and all adversaries and never makes a bad decision. The invincibility resonates with fantasies of omnipotence in viewers, which date from our first months of life. When Kirk bests his opponents, viewers enjoy his triumph and feel enhanced mastery over the parallel struggles in their lives.

Kirk is more than flawed here; he is a narcissistic ass. It is all about his ego, not what is best for anybody else or what might be the most strategic way to neutralize the looming threat. He drafts McCoy out of retirement, practically kidnapping him. He shows no concern about what his friend might think about it. To Kirk, it's all about me, me, me. Then he forces himself on Starfleet to wrestle command from another captain who is more prepared in some critical ways. Next, Kirk demands more out of the crew and the ship than they can give; this conduct served him well in the television series, but this time it almost gets them all killed.

The message is blunt: Kirk can make wrong-headed, self-serving decisions, and his actions can trample on the rights and feelings of others, if not worse. The infallible ship's commander from the original series is gone.

Calling out Captain Kirk and Mr. Spock is a bold move for *Star Trek: The Motion Picture*; it was a risk worth taking. In successful movies, the main characters have shown some progress by the end compared to the opening scenes. They have learned something along the way or become better people after facing adversity. (Tragic drama is different; the central person follows an immoral course until it destroys him or her.) Like real people, Kirk and Spock will stick with their rigid coping patterns until they don't work anymore, or until the cost is too high. Self-reflection and change are hard, but they lead to growth.

Arriving on the *Enterprise* via a long-range shuttle, Mr. Spock seems more emotionless than ever. With his telepathic abilities, Spock learns that the cloud is a consciousness of almost perfect thought and logic.

A probe of energy scans the ship and disintegrates Lieutenant Ilia, a beautiful Delton woman who had a past romance with Commander Decker. After their breakup, she took an oath of celibacy.

Spock senses curiosity as the anomaly pulls the *Enterprise* toward its center with a tractor beam. Constructed by the enigma, an android in the form of Lieutenant Ilia boards the ship. It intends to learn about the *Enterprise* and the carbon-based units infesting it. The entity calls itself V'ger. It is traveling to Earth to find its creator, with whom it will become one.

The fact that V'ger is traveling to Earth to find its creator confirms that it signifies a part of the human psyche. Its desire to become one with its designer harkens back to the stage of infantile omnipotence when newborns feel a blissful merger with their parents and the world after they are fed and happy. A secure sense of symbiosis at that time lays a foundation for later feelings of importance, meaning, and self-esteem.

The creation of the Ilia android is consistent with the idea that V'ger portrays an infant. A fundamental way children begin to relate to the world is through imitation. Babies mimic the people and things around them from very early in their lives. The anomaly sent a replica of a real person. Its appearance is exactly like the original Ilia, yet it knows practically nothing. It is curious more than menacing.

V'ger feels stuck; in psychoanalytic language, it is fixated. It wants to understand and grow, but cannot seem to do so until it unites with its maker. Similarly, children must first bond with their caretakers if they are to develop a sense of identity and meaning. Only then can they separate from their parents and build their own lives. V'ger must become one with its creator. The merger will provide significance, insight, and understanding. The emotional logjam will break; V'ger will grow. Afterward, it can leave its designer and define its own purpose.

Decker shows the Ilia probe around the ship, hoping that his past relationship with her will arouse some emotion.

Making an unauthorized journey into V'ger, Spock learns that it comes from a world of living machines. He is shocked unconscious when he attempts a mind-meld with V'ger.

Rescued by Kirk, Spock wakes up in sick bay. He explains that V'ger is a self-aware mechanism which has knowledge that spans the universe. With all that, it is also cold and barren, lacking beauty and purpose. It is asking, "Is this all that I am? Is there nothing more?"

Spock compares himself to V'ger. Like the machine, his life has been sterile and devoid of meaning. For the first time, he realizes the importance of friendship and he embraces emotion. Spock laughs at the simplicity of his discovery.

Spock's awakening is the most touching and significant scene in this film. When he encounters V'ger's empty existence, he sees his own melancholy for the first time. This enlightenment is so sudden and startling that it knocks him out. Figuratively and literally, Spock wakes up in sick bay a new man. In a flash, he grasps that he has been running from the very things that make life worthwhile. Companionship, belonging, relationships with others and the feelings that go with them all give life meaning and purpose. Logic cannot replace love and friendship.

By acknowledging the pleasures of real life, Spock leaves his childhood longings behind. Kolinahr is just more of the same logic-worship. It is a false promise, tricking him into thinking that yet one more step will erase all the wounds that he carries inside. Spock believed that he hurt inside because he was not perfect. Once cleansed of all emotion in the waters of Kolinahr he could go to Sarek and ask, "Do you approve of me now, Daddy?"

All of us need to know in our heads that we are lovable just as we are. We also need to feel that truth in our hearts. If people do not get this message from caretakers when they are young, they are at risk as adults of brushing off the very affection that they crave. Mr. Spock can see now how he dismissed the warmth and regard of his friends and how he pretended that he did not appreciate them in return; he laughs because it was all staring him in the face.

Spock discovers that what matters most is that he approve of himself. He can stop trying to please his dad, his mom, or anybody else. His life is his own; he can be the person he wants to be. Kolinahr was nothing more than mist and air, emptiness masquerading as perfection. Spock steps from a world of abstract purities into the here and now.

> V'ger reaches earth and sends out a radio signal. When it does not receive the reply it expects, it concludes that the carbon-based units on the surface are preventing its creator from responding. V'ger places several probes in orbit, intending to wipe out all the carbon-based life forms.

> Spock tells Kirk that V'ger is a child and suggests he treat it as such.

Mr. Spock's emotional awakening has cleared his vision. Embracing his human side for the first time has enabled him to grasp a truth about V'ger that the others miss. Having discovered that he is much more than logic, he recognizes that V'ger is more than just a threat. Allowing his inner self a chance to speak opens Spock's ears to what V'ger is trying to say. Mr. Spock encapsulates his intuition by saying that V'ger is a child. The insight allows Kirk to shift his approach.

Kirk tells the Ilia android that he knows why the creator has not answered but will only reveal this to V'ger in person. Ilia leads Kirk, McCoy, Spock, and Decker to the enigma's nucleus. At the center is Voyager VI, launched from Earth three hundred years in the past. It fell into a black hole and emerged near the machine planet, which recognized the unpiloted explorer as one of its kind. Voyager's mission was to transmit information back to its designers on Earth, so the machine consciousness created the cloud surrounding Voyager and has come expecting to merge with its maker. In the union, V'ger will find the answers it seeks.

Mr. Spock concludes that V'ger must evolve. Its knowledge has reached the limits of the universe, so it must move on to another dimension. It needs a human quality to take that step.

Commander Decker volunteers to become one with V'ger. After entering a transmission code into Voyager, he and Ilia unite sensually in a whirlwind of light and wind. V'ger disappears into a higher dimension, leaving the Earth and the *Enterprise* unharmed. With satisfaction, Kirk says that they gave V'ger the ability to create its own purpose.

Mr. Spock announces that he will not return to Vulcan. His mission there is complete.

At the enigma's core is Voyager VI, an unpiloted explorer conceived, designed, built, programmed, and launched by human beings. The terrestrial origin of the threat confirms the interpretation that V'ger represents a part of us. We split off a side of ourselves that we shunned and flung it into space expecting never to see it again. Inevitably, our true nature returns and buzzes around our head like a pesky fly, impossible to ignore.

At first, it seemed that V'ger embodied the all-consuming frustration and rage of our primitive selves, that it was humanity's aggression coming back to bite us. Understandably, Starfleet's objective was to neutralize it at all costs. Spock recognizes that V'ger is not angry, enraged, vindictive, bloodthirsty, or anything like that. It was threatening Earth, but it did not understand what it was doing and was just reacting to its calling. V'ger was not a projection of human anger. The potential loss of life was incidental, from its point of view.

V'ger *yearns.* That is why it has returned to Earth. It represents all the longings we feel inside, but often hide from the world and ourselves. We sometimes disavow and project our anger; perhaps we disown our concealed aching even more. V'ger is especially hungry for symbiosis. Just as infants need to attach to their parents early in life, V'ger longs to unite with its creator. The initial fusion lays the groundwork so children can differentiate from their family later on and establish their own identity and purpose. Similarly, V'ger must combine with its maker before it can progress and evolve. As infants need the warmth, care, and love of flesh and blood people, V'ger can only discover itself through unity with a real human person.

We now understand what V'ger wants, but the story is not over. A union involves two parties. To combine with an actual somebody one needs a genuine breathing specimen.

Enter Willard Decker. He not only volunteers but also grabs the chance with relish. Why? He is not altruistically sacrificing himself to save everybody else; at least he does not talk that way. Maybe he wants to explore the unknown or bond with the entity that assimilated his former girlfriend. Are there other issues?

To answer this question, we need to return to "The Doomsday Machine," which featured Commodore Matthew Decker, Willard's father, as captain of the Federation starship USS *Constellation*. Chapter 2 discusses the episode in depth. The senior Decker's fate will throw light on his son's actions in *Star Trek: The Motion Picture*.

To recap, Commodore Matthew Decker meets a powerful device that destroys entire solar systems. After the Doomsday Machine damages the *Constellation* in a confrontation, Decker beams his crew to a nearby world for safety. He then watches in horror as the weapon pulverizes the planet and digests its remains. Riddled with guilt, Decker assumes command of the *Enterprise* and launches a hopeless attack. Spock forces him to withdraw, so Decker steals a shuttlecraft and flies it into the mouth of the enemy mechanism. Decker's self-sacrifice inspires Kirk to do the same thing on a larger scale with the crippled *Constellation*. The plan works; the Doomsday Machine is dead.

The marauding robot weapon represents a projection of Matthew Decker's violent instincts and humanity's hostility in general. Decker sought to conquer his demons by destroying the external threat. When he could not defeat the Doomsday Machine, he absolved himself by becoming a martyr.

Matthew Decker died a distraught man. Psychoanalytically, he regressed and became stuck at the earliest stage of emotional life, that which we discussed in Chapter 2. In his eyes, the universe had become nothing but danger. He could not separate his sins from those of the Doomsday Machine. The future had no meaning. Recovery was impossible. Consumed with paranoia, the commodore felt driven to destroy the weapon or perish in the attempt. Matthew Decker left a legacy of arrested development. Will the son do better than the father?

Willard Decker not only alleviates his father torment but also transforms the family legacy to one of transcendence and hope. His union with Ilia/V'ger makes everybody whole and opens new doors. Planet Earth is safe. The *Enterprise* has done the impossible, once again. The son rescues his father metaphorically by merging with a machine in a very different way. Willard intertwines with Ilia, whom he never stopped loving. V'ger has found its soul in the eyes of its maker and has been transformed.

Kirk, Spock, and McCoy wonder if they witnessed the birth of a new life form. It might be more apt to say that they just saw a youngster take that first step. We celebrate the growth of our children and each other. It nourishes us just to be present.

CHAPTER 14: KHAN

Star Trek II: The Wrath of Khan is a very different motion picture than its predecessor. It contains more action than the first movie, and the story is less philosophical. The original series episode *Space Seed* introduces Khan as an adversary.

Space Seed

The *Enterprise* discovers a sleeper ship from Earth's early days of interstellar travel, named the *Botany Bay*. Since journeys between solar systems took many years in that era, the crew is in suspended animation. The presence of the landing party triggers the revival of the ship's leader, Khan. The survivor's physical perfection captivates historian Marla McGivers. She has long been fascinated by great warriors and leaders of the past, such as Alexander the Great.

Khan recovers his strength at a remarkable pace. Arrogant and abrasive, he thinks of everything in military terms. He is vague and evasive about his ship and its mission. Except for Spock, Kirk and the other men find Khan intriguing.

Spock learns that their guest is Khan Noonian Singh, once absolute ruler of one-quarter of the Earth. Singh was the most powerful of some genetically engineered supermen and superwomen who brutally seized power. Their subjects eventually rose up and overthrew the tyrants, but their fate had been a mystery.

Lieutenant McGivers becomes more infatuated with Khan, even though he is brutal and harsh with her. In his cabin, Khan crushes her hand; the pain forces her to her knees. Khan throws her to the floor and orders her to leave him unless she does exactly what he wants; he intends to take control of the *Enterprise* and demands her help. She begs him to let her stay, "I promise. I'll do anything you ask."

Khan's grandiosity and McGivers' submission are the most curious features of this episode. How do we understand these two characters? Why do they act the way they do?

Khan considers himself a superman. In his eyes, he is brilliant, powerful, infallible, and invincible. His superiority is not an attitude; it is a fact. His destiny is to rule, and others are meant to serve. He believes this inequality is as natural as air. He embodies the worst aspects of a self-absorbed toddler fixated at the stage of infantile omnipotence. In Khan's mind, his thoughts and wishes define reality rather than the other way around. He is another case of arrested development.

It truth, Khan is a self-absorbed bully. He is rigid, arrogant, offensive, and quick to anger. His social skills are atrocious. His self-serving words and actions demonstrate no empathy for others. Khan not only has flaws but he is also an overgrown brat.

Why does Khan's insufferable narcissism appeal to the *Enterprise* crew?

Khan's self-admiration captivates others. He projects an image without weakness or vulnerability, and many find this magnetic. People like Khan touch on remnants of infantile omnipotence still present in the minds of their minions. Admirers relate to the illusion of infallibility; maybe it is achievable after all, they wonder. If Khan is without flaws, devotees can triumph over their own hurts by identifying with him. By extension, followers have the right to do as they chose and mold the world to their liking. Disciples not only dismiss their idol's shortcomings but also consider them strengths. Thus, Khan's arrogance becomes confidence; his bullying gets recast as leadership.

Spock sees through Khan's conceit, and Kirk will recognize it soon. Sometimes we are initially drawn to a blowhard, but quickly spot the bragging and hot air.

In contrast, Lieutenant McGivers does not pull away; she goes all in. Her attraction to Khan takes over her life as if she were swept away in the current of a rushing river. She even lets him humiliate and abuse her. To avoid rejection, she will agree to almost anything.

The key to understanding McGivers' struggle is her fascination with history's Caesars. Her instant love-sick adoration shows that her interest in

Khan is much more than academic. She is responding to something personal from inside herself.

McGiver's professional interest in warrior kings is a thinly disguised reference to her father, a powerful man from her past who had much influence over her at one time. She both loses herself and finds herself in the study of these influential figures, and now one of them is sitting in the same room with her. Khan's self-importance resonates with Lieutenant McGivers' childlike view of a father as brilliant and invincible. She responds to Khan as a little girl desperate to keep her dad from abandoning her.

Like most sadists, Khan is aware of the power he has over McGivers. Without hesitation, he demands total submission or he will dispose of her like garbage. He exploits her fear for his own purposes.

Why does Khan want to take over the ship, anyway? He just woke up from centuries of artificial sleep, and the first thing he wants to do is hijack the vessel that rescued him. That is madness. Khan's glib explanation is that he wants to control the *Enterprise* so he can find, "A world to win. An empire to build." Maybe that is what he tells himself.

Khan wants to capture the *Enterprise* to ward off feelings of exposure and weakness, which he finds intolerable. He is hell-bent to maintain the delusion that he is a superior, almighty, super being who takes what he wants. Feelings of hurt, loss, and helplessness terrify him. In his eyes, he relies on nobody. His faculties will never decline. He will always prevail. Commandeering the ship will bolster the self-deception that he has command over everything including his vulnerability.

> Captain Kirk confines Khan to his quarters and places a security team on guard outside his door. Khan escapes and revives the other fugitives aboard the *Botany Bay*.

Now home to Australia's capital city Sydney, *Botany Bay* is where the HMS *Endeavor* landed in 1770, marking Britain's first step towards future colonization of the continent. For years, England exported convicts to Australia and other faraway places to rid itself of undesirables.

The name of Khan's ship, *Botany Bay*, was likely meant to highlight that the travelers were criminals no longer welcome at home and on a journey to a distant land. Another interpretation is that the *Enterprise* is like the calm waters of Botany Bay. Kirk and the others rescue and welcome the spacefaring outcasts only to have them turn on their hosts and attempt to usurp the much larger property. From this perspective, the *Enterprise*'s crew members are stand-ins for the aboriginal peoples of Australia.

Khan and his thugs capture the *Enterprise* and threaten to kill Kirk and anyone else who does not agree to help them.

Alarmed by the extent of Khan's violence, McGivers rescues the captain at the last minute. Kirk floods the conference room with knock-out gas, but Khan escapes and places the *Enterprise* on self-destruct. Captain Kirk finally defeats him in a brutal fist fight.

Kirk gives Khan the option of prison or exile on Ceti Alpha V, a wild, untamed planet. Khan chooses the latter, referring to John Milton's *Paradise Lost*: it is "Better to reign in Hell than serve in Heaven." Kirk grasps the outlaw's meaning; he can relate to it.

Spock contemplates, "It would be interesting, Captain, to return to that world in a hundred years, and learn what crop had sprung from the seed you planted today."

Khan's banishment continues to evoke parallels with the Briton outlaws forcibly relocated to Australia. The metaphor is troubling, however, in the way it suggests that Khan's place of exile is uninhabited and it would be just fine if he decided to "reign" there—like a European monarch, maybe?

The final segment also shows the lengths to which Khan will go to avoid feeling dependent or weak. First, he is willing to destroy himself and the ship rather than lose the upper hand. Then, he chooses to beam down to a barren world with little hope of survival rather than face the humiliation of being held to account for his actions by fellow men and women. Khan's fear of feeling weak dominates his life.

Despite their differences, Captain Kirk and Khan have much in common. They share a driving need to stay in control of situations. Like Khan, Kirk is uneasy with any feelings of helplessness or vulnerability. To master these emotions, both men strive to be the one in charge. If they are in command of external events, they get the sense that their internal emotional life is also tightly regimented. The similarity explains why Kirk intuitively understands Khan at the end while the others are puzzled. The adversaries' names highlight the close resemblance; both begin with the letter K and have just four letters.

Spock's final musings explain the meaning of the title, "Space Seed." His words were also prescient; intentional or not, they foreshadow Khan's return.

Khan's aversion to feelings of powerlessness made him an excellent choice for the antagonist in the next *Star Trek* film. *The Wrath of Khan* continues the trend started in *Star Trek: The Motion Picture* of focusing on Captain Kirk's liabilities. Both movies show that Captain Kirk does make mistakes. His limitations stand out in a way foreign to the original series. Khan's vanity provides a stark contrast to Kirk's growing ability to recognize and tolerate missteps.

Star Trek II: The Wrath of Khan

The *Enterprise* receives a distress call from the *Kobayashi Maru*, a Federation freighter within the neutral zone. Saavik, a young Vulcan woman in command of the ship, attempts a rescue even though entering the neutral zone violates the treaty with the warlike Romulans.

Romulan warships surround the Federation starship and attack. Within seconds, the *Enterprise* is crippled and helpless. Saavik stands alone as the controls erupt in fire and smoke, and the other officers lie unconscious on the deck. Suddenly, the front of the bridge opens, revealing the scene to be a simulation. Admiral Kirk enters and scrutinizes the young captain's performance.

Saavik complains that the Kobayashi Maru scenario is not a fair test because there is no way to win. Kirk responds that coping with death is as important as dealing with life. Saavik asks Kirk how he handled the simulation, but he evades the question.

Admiral Kirk says the Kobayashi Maru simulation is meant to test an officer's ability to command, but that explanation is a red herring. The ethical choice in the scenario is to attempt a rescue. As a people, we do not stand by when others are dying if there is something we can do. Saavik does the right thing, and within seconds she is helpless, vulnerable, and at the mercy of a heartless enemy.

The Kobayashi Maru scenario states some facts then asks a question. The truths include: a moral choice does not guarantee a good outcome; sometimes every path encounters pain; our decisions can hurt people without our intending to; one person can only do so much; and our faculties and resources can be stripped from us in an instant. The granddaddy of all certainties is that we will die, sooner or later.

How did Kirk deal with the Kobayashi Maru? Can he tolerate feeling exposed and susceptible? Has Kirk made peace with his human limitations and the march of time? Finally, it asks, "Have you faced your mortality, James T. Kirk?" Like Saavik, we must wait for the answer.

In his quarters, Kirk takes out reading glasses to review a report when McCoy arrives to celebrate his birthday. The doctor advises Kirk to get back his starship command before he really does grow old.

The reading glasses symbolize all human frailties, aging, and ultimately death. Kirk feels the sting. The indestructible, infallible captain is gone; maybe he was an illusion all along. Dr. McCoy pulls the admiral out of his funk. Kirk is no longer young, but he still has some good years left in him.

The USS *Reliant* is looking for a lifeless planet on which to test the Genesis device, a mechanism that can create a whole ecosystem out of inorganic matter. When Captain Terrell and First Officer Chekov beam down to Ceti Alpha V, Khan and his followers capture them.

Ceti Alpha V was green and fertile when Khan first arrived, but a neighboring world exploded six months later. The shock wave changed the orbit of Khan's planet and killed almost all life. The only creature to survive was the Ceti eel, an aggressive parasite that enters the brain cavity through the ear. Its victims become extremely susceptible to suggestion. Khan infects Terrell and Chekov with the vermin; they become his servants.

Kirk's failures propel the story forward. Regardless of Khan's megalomania, Kirk had a moral obligation to keep an eye on the situation. He should have arranged for some assistance or at least a periodic visit from Starfleet to see how Khan and his followers were doing. Civil societies are responsible for their prisoners' basic needs. Kirk is guilty of dereliction of duty.

Kirk does not want to tell us how he dealt with the Kobayashi Maru. That is his right; after all, it was only a simulation. Ceti Alpha V, in contrast, shows that Kirk's inaction had real consequences.

Khan is still his arrogant, overbearing self. He does not evoke a lot of sympathies, but he makes for a delicious bad guy. We have seen how far he will go to gain and keep the upper hand. Khan will destroy himself before he lets somebody else win. He feels even more aggrieved after he was stranded and forgotten.

With Chekov and Terrell's help, Khan captures the USS *Reliant* and intends to avenge himself on Admiral Kirk. Joachim, speaking for all Khan's followers, encourages their leader to give up the chase, noting, "We are free. We have a ship, and the means to go where we will."

Of Kirk, Khan responds, "He tasks me. He tasks me, and I shall have him!"

A copy of Herman Melville's *Moby-Dick* sits on a shelf in the relic of the *Botany Bay* on Ceti Alpha V. Khan answers his people's plea with Captain Ahab's words, modified for outer space.

"I'll chase him round the *moons of Nibia* and round the *Antares maelstrom* and round perdition's flames before I give him up!"

Both Captain Ahab and Khan hunt their prey against the advice of their crew. They will sacrifice everything to take down their nemesis or die in the attempt.

A project code-named "Genesis" is under construction on Regula I, a space station headed by Dr. Carol Marcus and her son Dr. David Marcus. Kirk and Carol Marcus were once lovers; Kirk is David's father. The *Enterprise* receives a frantic and confusing message from Regula I, so it goes to investigate.

En route to the space station, the *Enterprise* encounters the *Reliant*, secretly commanded by Khan. Since the sister ship does not respond to the *Enterprise's* message, Commander Saavik reminds Kirk of the regulation to raise their shields. Kirk hesitates and the *Reliant* attacks, killing some crew members and crippling the *Enterprise*.

Admiral Kirk is getting pummeled. First, we learn that he gave up a relationship with an intelligent, capable, and appealing woman. Then we find out that the couple had a son, with whom Kirk has had no contact. Kirk abandoned David the same way he stranded Khan. The shine has rubbed off the admiral's veneer.

As if his private missteps were not enough, Kirk commits a fatal error by waiting to raise the shields. His reluctance is even more inexcusable because he ignored the strong recommendation of a junior officer. Kirk's mistake has cost lives and left the *Enterprise* exposed.

Kirk is facing his own Kobayashi Maru situation, but this time it is real. Within seconds, his people are dead; the ship is in flames. He will soon learn who attacked the *Enterprise*. The assailant not only has no heart but also holds a personal grudge. Now the entire crew will suffer for Kirk's delinquencies.

Khan demands that Kirk turn over any information they have on project Genesis. While stalling for time, Kirk uses a security code to order the *Reliant* to lower its shields. The *Enterprise* fires on the *Reliant*. The two damaged ships temporarily part company.

The encounter with the *Reliant* is one of the most dramatic and compelling sequences in all science fiction. The entire movie up to this point is a prelude to this one critical moment. The *Enterprise* does not know who is commanding the *Reliant*. The tension is at a peak. Khan's menacing, percussive brass leitmotif plays in the orchestra. He gloats, "Ah, Kirk, my old friend. Do you know the Klingon proverb that tells us revenge is a dish that is best served cold? It is very cold—*in space*."

Saavik reminds Kirk of General Order Twelve, to raise shields when communication has not been established. Kirk hesitates. The softer music of the score belies the looming threat.

On the *Reliant* bridge, Joachim smiles, "They still haven't raised their shields."

Khan replies, "Raise ours." A graphic on Joachim's screen show's a protective barrier encircling their ship.

"Their shields are going up." Spock advises, watching in his scanner on the *Enterprise* bridge.

At the ready, Khan commands, "Lock phasers on target."

"Locking phasers on target," Joachim says, looking back on his idol with admiration. An ironically beautiful orange and blue graphic on a second screen zeroes in on the *Enterprise*.

"They're locking phasers," Spock says, looking up.

The camera pans to Kirk in the command chair, "Raise shields."

Khan, "FIRE!"

The attack scenes strike the perfect balance: Joachim pressing the button; the *Enterprise* taking phaser and photon torpedo fire; the engineering bulkheads closing; Khan looking on; the bridge erupting in flames; officers thrown to the deck; sounds of the orchestra drowned out by explosions and chaos; and Kirk and the others lit by foreboding red emergency lighting. Then, Uhura says that the commander of the *Reliant* is signaling. "He wishes to discuss terms of our *surrender*."

That one word shocks everybody on the bridge and in the audience. Kirk's entire ethos is shaken to its foundation. As Khan and Kirk joust over the viewscreen, they are calm and do not yell or thump their chests, yet the stakes are astronomical and every second is critical. Just before the *Enterprise* counter-attacks, Kirk's soft-spoken dialogue, "Here it comes," is close to movie perfection.

> The *Enterprise* arrives at Regula I only to find that Khan has looted the station and killed everybody except Terrell and Chekov. The space station transporter was left on, set for a location deep within a nearby planetoid. Kirk assumes that some of the group escaped, so the landing party follows them down.

> David Marcus believes that Kirk and the military establishment have come to steal Genesis and use it as a weapon. When the group

materializes underground, David attempts to stab his father. His mother eventually calms him down.

Why is David so angry with Kirk? Is it just because he is afraid that the *Enterprise* intends to confiscate Genesis?

David cannot say so directly, but he is furious that Kirk abandoned him. Who would not be angry with a father who has had no involvement with his son? Kirk just walked away. It is easier for David to express outrage over Genesis than to voice his grief over how Kirk deserted him. It is too excruciating to admit how hurt he feels.

Also, David is afraid that Kirk will threaten his relationship with his mother. He has had her all to himself for his entire life, and suddenly this man comes waltzing back into the picture. Even in the best of circumstances, when a family member returns from a long absence there are always shifts that follow. David has a complicated set of thoughts and feelings. At the moment, however, it is easier to focus on anger because of how frightened and wounded he feels.

> Kirk finally tells Saavik how he handled the Kobayashi Maru simulation; he reprogrammed the computer so he could resolve the situation successfully. Kirk adds that he does not believe in a no-win scenario.

The younger Kirk of the original television series was amazingly adept at avoiding no-win scenarios. He defeated aliens, talked sinister computers into killing themselves, and saved the human race several times over.

In contrast, Admiral Kirk faces advancing age, the sacrifices he has made for his career, the people he has hurt and neglected, and a costly lapse in judgment while in command of the *Enterprise*. Kirk confronts his human limitations and the things he has lost. Is Kirk a has-been, or was Dr. McCoy right that he still has what it takes? Can he pick himself up again?

> Khan has been listening to the landing party over a communicator and orders Terrell and Chekov to kill Admiral Kirk. Unable to follow Khan's command, Terrell fires on himself instead; Chekov collapses in pain. The Ceti eel crawls out of Chekov's ear, ending his obedience to Khan.

> Khan beams up the Genesis capsule, thinking that he is marooning Kirk for all eternity.

"KHAAAN!" bellows Kirk, one alpha male to another. The scene zooms out to show the lifeless, cratered planetoid with Kirk's shriek echoing into space.

This I-Khanic scene is affectionately known as the "Khan Scream." It has been lovingly parodied by many shows, including the CBS television series *The Big Bang Theory*. Sheldon Cooper screams, "WHEEEATON!" because he blames actor and nemesis Wil Wheaton for his role as Wesley Crusher in *Star Trek: The Next Generation*.

> Kirk and the others were not stranded, after all. Spock reestablishes contact with the landing party at a prearranged time and beams them up.

> The *Enterprise* lures the *Reliant* into the Mutara Nebula, where neither vessel will have an advantage. Kirk outmaneuvers Khan and damages the *Reliant* beyond hope.

> With his starship in flames, a bloodied Khan activates the Genesis capsule. Life on both starships will end when the device detonates; the *Enterprise* cannot escape because its warp engines are still disabled.

Khan's final words are those of Captain Ahab verbatim. He is no longer just similar to Ahab; the two have become one. Khan's people are dead. (Note that there is one survivor in *Moby-Dick*, the narrator Ishmael.) The *Reliant* is in flames. All that remains is venom.

"...To the last, I grapple with thee; from hell's heart, I stab at thee; for hate's sake, I spit my last breath at thee."

> Mr. Spock saves the ship by fixing the warp engines, allowing them to flee before Genesis detonates. He exposes himself to deadly radiation in the process. As he dies, he tells Kirk that the needs of the many outweigh the needs of the few—or the one.

> During a tender moment with David, Kirk admits that he has always tricked death and then patted himself on the back for his ingenuity. David tells Kirk that he is proud to be his son. They embrace.

> Meanwhile, the Genesis capsule has created a lush new world out of the nearby planetoid. As his final resting place, will it affect Mr. Spock's body?

Kirk defeated Khan, but the cost was high. The *Reliant* is gone. The *Enterprise* suffered extensive damage. The *Regula* space station was ransacked; all but two of its scientists were murdered. The Genesis device was stolen and detonated without safeguards, leading to who knows what. The *Enterprise* took many casualties, first among them Mr. Spock. Kirk faces the most significant loss of his career. He squeaked out a win, but Kirk is no longer infallible. He can be hurt, he can disappoint, and he can make mistakes. In this film and the last, Kirk has gone from a larger-than-life hero to a real man with strengths and blind spots. He has faced his no-win scenario.

Mr. Spock's self-sacrifice shows his emotional growth. His concern for his friends and colleagues motivates him to rescue the ship. Love compels him to act, not logic. As he dies, he does not claim that he only did what was logical. The "needs of the many" prompted his martyrdom. The "many" he refers to are humans. They are *his* people. Spock belongs. He cares. His people are lovable and have value whether it is logical or not. Their welfare matters. Further, when Spock compares the needs of the many "to the one," he is speaking of himself. Would a younger Spock acknowledge so openly that he has needs like everybody else? Spock has learned to love himself and can finally say to the others, "You matter to me."

"There is no greater love than this—that a Vulcan should lay down his life for his human friends." (John 15: 12-15; SFRV, Starfleet Revised Version)

CHAPTER 15: ALL GROWN UP

Star Trek III: The Search for Spock picks up right at the point that *The Wrath of Khan* ends. The *Enterprise* is en route to Earth after the costly battle with Khan and his people aboard the *Reliant*. Kirk reflects on the events, especially the death of his dear friend Spock. He shoulders the burden of his missteps without making excuses or blaming others. Pain like this can lead to new growth. Indeed, events have brought Kirk and his son together for the first time. A new dawn, perhaps?

Wrong. From a psychoanalytic perspective, *Star Trek III* is a step backward. It retreats from the hard work of mourning and the characters revert to their personas from the original television series. The third installment undoes the hard-won wisdom of the first two movies. Before we discuss these points, however, we need to zoom out and look at the film as a total package.

Star Trek III is a successful film. Motion pictures prompt scrutiny from a variety of standpoints, and *The Search for Spock* does well on most of these measures. The acting was solid, as were the special effects and music. Box office receipts were respectable. The reviews were mostly positive. Co-star Leonard Nimoy (Mr. Spock) directed the film to wide acclaim. There were concerns about the plot, but they were not severe enough to sink an otherwise creative and fun story. Most importantly, the movie was enjoyable. It was intended to be a feel-good experience, and it worked.

Now that we have given *Star Trek III* well-deserved credit for what it accomplished, we will discuss how and why it diverges from the first two films.

Star Trek III: The Search for Spock

Dr. McCoy is detained for bizarre behavior on return to Earth. Before Spock died, he transferred his "katra," his living spirit, into McCoy. Kirk learns that Spock's body and katra must be reunited and laid to rest on Vulcan or McCoy will die. Kirk breaks in and rescues McCoy from lockdown, and conspires with Scotty, Sulu, and others from the original series to disable the USS *Excelsior* and hijack the *Enterprise* from spacedock.

Spock's coffin had landed on the planetoid "Genesis," terraformed by the Genesis device, at the end of *Wrath of Khan*. Kirk's son David and Lieutenant Saavik are exploring the new life on Genesis and find that the organic scripting also resurrected Spock as a child. David confesses that Genesis contained unapproved "protomatter," which means Spock will age by years for every few minutes and the planetoid has but hours before it breaks apart.

The Klingons are interested in the Genesis technology as a weapon. They clash with the *Enterprise* when it arrives to recover Spock's body. The adversaries jockey back and forth. During a standoff, the Klingons kill David Marcus, whom they took hostage along with Saavik and a teenaged Spock.

In a ruse, Captain Kirk agrees to surrender the disabled *Enterprise*. Instead, he sets it to self-destruct, then he and his officers escape to the planetoid's surface. Several Klingons beam aboard; they discover at the last second that the ship is about to explode. Now in flames, the *Enterprise* vaporizes as it streaks across the sky with Kirk and the others watching.

Promising the secret to Genesis, Kirk persuades the Klingon commander Kruge to beam up McCoy, Scotty, Sulu, and Chekov. Kruge then beams down to the surface to confront Kirk. As the planetoid disintegrates, Kirk and Kruge engage in a fistfight until Kirk kicks the Klingon off a cliff into a lava flow. Kirk is beamed up at the last minute. He and the other Federation officers take control of the Klingon Bird of Prey and head to Vulcan.

On Vulcan, Spock's body and katra are reunited, and McCoy regains sole ownership of his mind. While still feeling foggy, Spock recognizes Kirk and remembers that he calls him, "Jim." All gather round in celebration.

We can all relate to the wish that somebody we lost can come back. We know that it is impossible, but so what? Anything can happen in the movies. Also, the way *Search for Spock* brings him back to life is quite clever. Many people go to the movies to be entertained, not challenged. It feels good for a few hours; that is worth something. There is a place for light entertainment.

With Spock restored, however, there is no need to mourn his death. The movie turns away from dealing with that challenge in a meaningful way. Without Spock, does Kirk get depressed? Will he try to replace Spock with somebody and how will that turn out? Can he integrate what he admired about Spock into his own person? These questions could have energized new storylines, but they were scuttled. The original series usually favored painful realities over comforting fictions, so the message of avoiding loss is a little out of place.

The Search for Spock also kills off David Marcus, just as Captain Kirk has barely begun to reckon with his past. *The Wrath of Khan* posed some questions. How will Kirk deal with an adult son whom he abandoned as a boy? Will Kirk rethink his relationship to Starfleet? What legacy does Kirk want to leave? Wait, forget it. David is dead. Good grief. Of course, fictional characters meet their end all the time; in itself, the son's demise is not a problem. In this case, however, it is another plot element that takes Kirk off the hook. It removes the pressure for self-reflection and change.

The entire battle sequence with the Klingon Bird of Prey is a poor imitation of Kirk's first encounter with the *Reliant* in *The Wrath of Khan*. In the previous film, every scene before the battle flowed naturally and inevitably to that singular decisive moment. In *The Search for Spock*, the *Enterprise* arrives at planetoid Genesis and—oops—the Klingons are there too. Why not just blow each other up? They hold their fire for a few minutes anyway so the Klingons can stab Kirk's son. The death is also used to explain Kirk's hatred for the Klingons in *Star Trek VI*. The audience is expected to believe that the loss of a man whom Kirk spent barely a few hours with would change him to the core. It is cheap sentiment. We do not buy it.

The most ludicrous detail of the film is that Scotty, Sulu, Chekov, and Uhura all join in Kirk's scheme without hesitation. They are like an adolescent group of superfriends who think their mutual admiration transcends all human history. Imagine what would happen if a few people disabled a modern-day aircraft carrier and seized another one for personal use. Once arrested, they defended themselves by saying, "You just don't understand. We're best friends forever!" I am not against movies that depict the critical bonds that teenagers form with each other; those attachments play a vital role in healthy development. The message, however, is out of place in *Star*

Trek. By the way, Scotty single-handedly hot wires the *Enterprise* so that three people can pilot a vessel that previously needed over four hundred. Geesh.

One plot element that does connect is when the *Enterprise* self-destructs, and Kirk, McCoy, Scotty, Sulu, and Chekov watch the fireball streak through the sky. It is a loss for all of them, as well as for *Star Trek* fans. The actors are getting older. A chapter is ending.

Star Trek IV: The Voyage Home picks up soon after the events in *Search for Spock*.

Star Trek IV: The Voyage Home

Willing to face trial, Kirk and the other former *Enterprise* officers depart for Earth in the captured Klingon Bird of Prey. En route, they learn that an enormous unmanned space probe has entered Earth orbit and is transmitting an indecipherable signal which is wreaking havoc on the terrestrial power grid, the weather, and other things. The alien device is attempting to contact an intelligent species other than *Homo sapiens*. Their signal is a call for a response from the ocean's humpback whales, but by the year 2286, they are extinct.

The *Enterprise* travels back in time to 1986 San Francisco, captures a mating pair of humpbacks, and returns to the future. Once the whales respond to the space probe, it reverses the effects on Earth and departs. Starfleet drops all charges against the *Enterprise* officers except one count of insubordination. Kirk is demoted from admiral to captain; he assumes command of newly-commissioned *Enterprise* NCC-1701-A.

Critical response to *The Voyage Home* was mostly positive. Like *Search for Spock*, it is light entertainment. Unlike the previous film, it does not pretend to be anything but. The scenes set in 1986 are amusing. They follow a long tradition of fish-out-of-water comedy such as that in the *Beverly Hillbillies*, 3rd *Rock from the Sun*, and the original *Star Trek* series episode "A Piece of the Action." Spock is back to his emotionally clueless self, which is used to effect.

The film's message was refreshing, notably because it was an unexpected departure from the previous three movies. We are, indeed, not the only intelligent species on Earth. We have a moral obligation towards all life, sentient creatures above all. Perhaps the advocacy of *Star Trek IV* played a role in protecting the humpbacks. They were once near extinction, but current estimates put their numbers at around 80,000.

The Voyage Home also serves as Kirk's get-out-of-jail-free card. He escapes real accountability for his actions in *The Search for Spock* by saving humanity from annihilation—again.

Star Trek V: The Final Frontier is considered a critical and commercial failure. There is a perverse pleasure in tearing apart movie flops. They become the butt of endless jokes and witty put-downs. I enjoy such banter as much as anybody. We will set the sarcastic impulse aside for now, and discuss why the film fails to connect on an emotional level.

Star Trek V: The Final Frontier

The banished Vulcan Sybok teaches that emotion is the key to self-knowledge. He misuses the Vulcan mind-meld to heal others' "secret pain," which also subverts their free will and compels them to join his quest. He seeks Sha Ka Ree, a mythical planet that will reveal the ultimate truth, what all people have sought since time began.

Attempting to secure a starship for his quest, Sybok and his followers take human, Klingon, and Romulan hostages on Nimbus III, the Planet of Galactic Peace. The *Enterprise* travels from Earth to rescue the captives. A meddlesome Klingon, Captain Klaa, pursues them, intending to make trouble.

Kirk and the others mount a raid. Spock has the chance to kill Sybok but holds his fire because they are half-brothers. The *Enterprise* crew joins Sybok one by one as he heals their pain.

Spock witnesses his birth during Sybok's attempt to convert him. A young Sarek, Spock's father, looks down with disgust at his half-human son. Spock is not troubled by the scene. He tells his brother that he is not the outcast boy Sybok left behind on Vulcan. Spock adds that he has found himself and his place.

Kirk refuses to cooperate with Sybok. He protests that loss and guilt don't magically disappear. Our past choices and mistakes make us who we are, Kirk says. "I need my pain!" he declares. Sybok grudgingly makes peace with Kirk, because the captain is needed to navigate the ship through the energy barrier surrounding Sha Ka Ree.

The *Enterprise* traverses the energy field intact. Sybok, Kirk, Spock, and McCoy beam down to the surface. A vision appears, initially sounding like God. When His prime interest turns out to be using the *Enterprise* to breach the energy barrier, Kirk says, "Excuse me, what does God need with a starship?"

Two lightning bolts fire from the false god's eyes and hit Kirk in the chest. Sybok sacrifices himself to help the others escape and to atone for his arrogance and vanity. The Klingons complicate Kirk's retreat but also help by killing the imposter god. It so happens that the Klingon ambassador is aboard the *Enterprise* and orders Captain Klaa to stand down.

On first glance, it might seem that this film should work. The message is more personal and philosophical than *The Voyage Home*. Kirk embraces his past mistakes as well as his successes, and Spock says he has found his place. Sybok learns that he has been chasing a wild goose and accepts responsibility for his folly. These are strong themes, consistent with many of *Star Trek*'s original episodes.

There are two problems, however, regarding Kirk and Spock. First off, there is a maxim in screenwriting to *show, don't tell*. For instance, if the message is that Mr. Spock no longer feels tormented by his father's disapproval— show it. Let Spock's actions, expressions, and decisions speak for themselves. Let viewers draw their own conclusions; don't hit them over the head with what they should think. Reveal the character's struggle through details the audience can see on the screen; use dialogue sparingly. Similarly, if Captain Kirk respects his mistakes as much as his successes—show it somehow. It is corny to have him say, "I need my pain."

The second problem is related to the first. Kirk and Spock reached their emotional home long before they met Sybok. They do not change, grow, or learn anything new as a result of the events in the movie. Both men were at peace with themselves at the beginning and remained so at the end. This lack of change is why Spock had to use dialogue to say he had found his place, because that happened before the film even started. Sybok contrasts with his fellow Vulcan and half-brother, but Spock did not overcome his wounded inner child through Sybok; he had already figured this out on his own. Similarly, Captain Kirk did not need Sybok to learn that his mistakes were painful but made him a better man.

On a societal level, it also seems that the movie might have something to say. The subject matter could hardly be more weighty. We have seen the horror of false prophets in David Koresh of the Branch Davidians and Jim Jones of the Peoples Temple, for example. The phrase "drink the Kool-Aid" entered the public dialogue in the United States in allusion to the mass suicide in Jonestown. Demagogues also create a cult of personality, even though their devotees do not live separately from the rest of our communities. Exploring the evil of cults seems like a compelling subject for a feature film.

The reason that *The Final Frontier* does not succeed as an examination of religious fanatics is that Sybok resembles cult leaders only superficially. He is not cruel by nature. There is no self-glorification and no lust for power as an end in itself. He is a lost little boy searching for a mommy and daddy to love him. His followers in the story are merely props, to show what Sybok is hungry for himself. The only characters that matter in the story are the two Vulcans and Kirk. The Klingons show up just to fill some time and artificially inflate the drama.

The Final Frontier has one redeeming feature—the scene when Kirk asks, "What does God need with a starship?" The clip is available on YouTube for those who do not want to sit through the entire film. The most effective dialogue in the scene is spoken by God when he starts a line with, "This starship, . . ." Those two words with the voice actor's intonation tell the audience everything they need to know about the creature and its intentions.

Star Trek VI: The Undiscovered Country is the final voyage of the USS *Enterprise* with its original crew. It explores adult themes, as opposed to reworking childhood issues in metaphor. The title alludes to Shakespeare's *Hamlet* (Act III, Scene I), in which the undiscovered country is death. In *Star Trek VI*, the reference is to peace between former enemies. The movie was written and produced as the Soviet Union was coming apart. The film released on December 6, 1991; Soviet President Mikhail Gorbachev resigned December 25 the same year. The following day the former Soviet republics were granted independence. During that time, there were also tenuous moves toward peace in the Middle East. The first Oslo accord was signed in 1993.

The Klingons quote Shakespeare repeatedly in the film. Possibly this was to give Shakespearean actor Christopher Plummer a chance to shine as Kirk's Klingon nemesis General Chang. Maybe it was done to say that the Klingons are not all that different from us. It could also be a way to capture the verbal one-upmanship that went back and forth during the Cold War. At one point, the Klingon Chancellor Gorkon goads Kirk with, "You have not experienced Shakespeare until you have read him in the original Klingon." Perhaps *Star Trek* just wanted to sound erudite as the careers of the original series' officers came to a close.

Mr. Spock struggles with managing his expectations of others, another adult theme. Now that he can admit that he really does care about a lot of stuff, Spock struggles to figure out what he can and cannot change and what he can expect from others.

Star Trek VI: The Undiscovered Country

The Klingon moon Praxis explodes, destroying their home planet's ozone layer. Life there will become impossible within fifty years. They cease all hostilities with the Federation and want to talk.

Spock volunteers Captain Kirk and the *Enterprise* to escort Klingon Chancellor Gorkon's battlecruiser *Kronos One* to negotiations on Earth. Spock wants Kirk to embrace peace with the Klingons, yet Kirk objects. He calls the Klingons animals and tells Spock that the Federation should "let them die." Kirk has not forgiven the Klingons for killing his son David.

Alone in his quarters, Kirk asks himself how history will get past people like him.

Kirk's hatred is out of character. He does not sound like the starship captain who rescued the *Enterprise* by controlling his hostility towards the Klingons in "Day of the Dove." Indeed, it has been reported that *Star Trek* creator Gene Roddenberry objected strongly to portraying Kirk as a bigot. Using David's death to ramp up Kirk's resentment feels like a cheesy manipulation by the writers. With that said, the idea is to contrast Kirk at the beginning of the film to where he is by the finale. He spans a greater distance if he starts at a lower point. A friend of mine who generously proofread this manuscript pointed out that perhaps Kirk's anger is misdirected guilt he feels in regards to David. It is a good point, but I just don't feel like giving the writers a "pass" on this issue.

Spock has only recently discovered his emotions, hopes, and dreams. He is eager and enthusiastic, like many young adults. Since he is committed to reconciliation, he makes the mistake of thinking others will share his vision. He volunteers Kirk for the diplomatic mission, trying to force an agenda on his friend. As most adults learn, attempts to change other people's feelings and values are rarely successful and can exacerbate problems or cause new ones. Spock may be right that nonviolence is ethically superior to harboring resentment, but he can't shove it down Kirk's throat. Spock wants the world to be what he thinks it should be rather than what it is.

In a highly unusual move, the movie portrays the two main characters at odds. It addresses adult themes, so Kirk and Spock are depicted as separate people, not as like-minded best buddies with different strengths. An early scene shows the *Enterprise* officers at a classified briefing. The large conference room sequence with many bigwigs is unlike any other passage in the franchise's history; it reinforces the focus on grown-up issues. After everybody else leaves, Kirk and Spock argue from opposite ends of the long conference table, emphasizing the rift that has opened up between them.

Spock is in his quarters with Lieutenant Valeris, a captivating young female Vulcan officer who graduated from the Academy at the top of her class. Valeris asks Spock why he has a picture of the expulsion from paradise in his quarters. To remind him that all things end, responds the senior Vulcan.

Valeris says that the Federation has reached a turning point. Her meaning is unclear, yet Spock does not ask her to elaborate. This mission will be his last, he says, and he hopes she will replace him aboard the *Enterprise*. Valeris answers that she can only succeed him, not replace him.

After rendezvous with the Klingon ship *Kronos One*, the Chancellor and his officers beam aboard the *Enterprise* for a formal diplomatic dinner. Kirk does little to conceal his dislike for his guests, while Spock rephrases Kirk's opinions to make them sound warm and conciliatory.

The chancellor seems genuinely interested in peace, calling it "the undiscovered country." The other Klingons are provocative, especially Chief of Staff General Chang.

After dinner, Spock is frustrated that Kirk and the other *Enterprise* officers openly express their distaste for the Klingons.

Spock continues trying to force his agenda on Kirk and the others. The hostility at the dinner table is palpable, yet Spock wants to dismiss it. He reinterprets the words, so they mean what he wants them to. One might say that Spock is just being tactful, but true diplomats know and accept how their side feels behind closed doors. In contrast, Spock has blinders on. At best, the others are highly ambivalent about reconciliation with the Klingons. The picture of paradise in his quarters may be more than a reminder that everything is temporary. He may be longing for the simpler days when all that concerned him was logic.

Spock is also trying to force an agenda on Lieutenant Valeris. He wants her to follow in his footsteps, to be a disciple carrying his values and mission. She pushes back respectfully, by saying she can succeed him but not replace him. Spock could have learned more about Valeris if he had asked what she meant that the Federation was at a turning point, but he preferred to see her as the Vulcan he wanted her to be.

The *Enterprise* appears to fire on the Klingon ship; then two assassins beam over and mortally wound the chancellor. The Klingons prepare to attack, but Kirk surrenders to avoid all-out war. He and McCoy beam over to *Kronos One* to emphasize that the *Enterprise* does not understand what has happened and to try to save the chancellor's life; he dies anyway. Gorkon whispers his last words to Kirk: "Don't let it end this way, Captain."

Kirk and McCoy are arrested, convicted, and sentenced to the Rura Penthe penal asteroid. The Federation does not attempt a rescue because it would jeopardize the chance for peace.

Kirk confesses to Dr. McCoy that he had been terrified of the future. He was so accustomed to hating Klingons that he could not imagine a galaxy without the Neutral Zone. They must escape because the forces trying to sabotage the peace effort will strike again.

With some help, Kirk and McCoy make it outside the energy field on Rura Penthe where Spock can beam them up.

Kirk's surrender shows his better nature. The assassination could have escalated in a flash to total war. When it counts, Kirk puts his grievances aside to advance higher ideals. The underground penal colony is a frightening vision of the ugly parts of our mind, filled with dangerous, grotesque monsters. Kirk's change of heart allows him to escape from the hellish prison, a metaphor representing his fears and prejudices.

Spock deduces that a cloaked Romulan Bird of Prey underneath the *Enterprise* attacked the chancellor's ship. Kirk and Spock discover that Valeris arranged the chancellor's homicide and then murdered the assassins.

Using the Vulcan mind meld on Valeris, Spock learns who else is involved in the conspiracy; first among them is General Chang. Captain Sulu of the USS *Excelsior* signals Kirk that the peace conference is at Camp Khitomer, and the two vessels head there at maximum warp. Spock admits that it was arrogant presumption to volunteer Kirk for the mission. He also realizes that Valeris' Vulcan accomplishments biased his view of her; he did not see her for who she really was.

Kirk accepts Spock's amends by saying that peace was worth a few personal risks. He adds that he and Spock are both extremists— perhaps the best road lies somewhere in between them.

It is Spock's turn for fearless self-reflection. He discovers that his principles can blind him to the feelings and beliefs of those around him. Spock placed his priorities above everybody else. He forced the others on a mission they detested. His enthusiasm for negotiations almost got his two closest friends killed or worse. In his arrogance, he thought that the noble nature of his vision meant that others would fall in line. As a person, he matters, but no more than everybody else.

Spock made a similar mistake with Lieutenant Valeris. His hopes and dreams clouded his vision. He presumed that she shared his values because she was Vulcan, talented, and ambitious. Like a controlling father, he wanted her to continue his legacy without considering that she might have plans of her own. Spock misses cues that might have helped him uncover Valeris' treachery sooner. Like all humans, his preconceived notions can distort his view.

General Chang, in command of a Bird of Prey, attacks the *Enterprise* and the *Excelsior* as they arrive at Khitomer. Chang can fire his weapon without uncloaking his ship, so the Federation vessels take heavy damage. Spock and McCoy rig a scientific probe to pinpoint and fly up the Klingon's exhaust pipe. The maneuver locates the assailant, and the *Enterprise* and *Excelsior* destroy it.

Beaming down to Khitomer, Captain Kirk and the others prevent the Federation President's assassination. Kirk pledges his support for the late-Chancellor Gorkon's undiscovered country.

Back on the bridge, Kirk congratulates himself and the others for saving civilization once again. The *Enterprise* receives orders to return to spacedock to be decommissioned. Spock says that if he were human, he would tell them, "Go to hell." Chekov asks, "Course heading, Captain?"

Kirk smiles. "Second star to the right, and straight on till morning."

℘ The End ℭ

Index

Printed in the United States
By Bookmasters